"Be careful, Zach, I don't want to see you in Emergency again."

Zach let go of Abby's hand and placed his palm on his chest. "I promise." He turned to go, then spun around.

"Oh, hell," he muttered and grabbed her around the waist. Pulling her against him, he kissed her, inhaling the sweet honeysuckle scent. The rich taste of her swam in his brain as she willingly opened her mouth under his. An erotic fantasy of white sheets and sunshine swirled through his head. He wanted her, not here, but somewhere private, where they could lock out the world, where he could forget the terror that haunted him. His body tightened, and he pulled away, dropping his arms to his sides.

For a long breathless moment, they stared at each other.

"Now you'd *really* better not show up as a patient again. That was most unethical...."

ABOUT THE AUTHOR

Tina Vasilos has written romantic suspense for many years. She has traveled widely around the world, and she uses her trips to research her novels. Tina and her husband live with their son in Clearbrook, British Columbia.

Books by Tina Vasilos

Don't miss any of our special offers. Write to us at the following address for information on our newest releases.

Harlequin Reader Service
U.S.: 3010 Walden Ave., P.O. Box 1325, Buffalo, NY 14269Canadian: P.O. Box 609, Fort Erie, Ont. L2A 5X3

In Her Lover's Eyes
Tina Vasilos

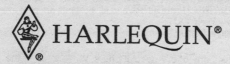

HARLEQUIN®

TORONTO • NEW YORK • LONDON
AMSTERDAM • PARIS • SYDNEY • HAMBURG
STOCKHOLM • ATHENS • TOKYO • MILAN • MADRID
PRAGUE • WARSAW • BUDAPEST • AUCKLAND

ISBN 0-373-22532-6

IN HER LOVER'S EYES

Copyright © 1999 by Freda Vasilopoulos

Printed in U.S.A.

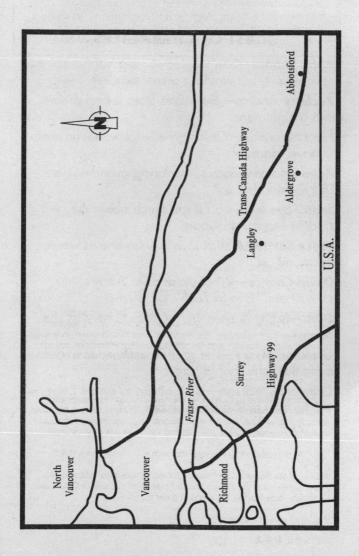

CAST OF CHARACTERS

Abby Chance—She wanted to help her handsome new patient, but would it prove deadly?

Zachary Andros—He wakes from a bad dream into a nightmare.

Eleni Mavrakis—Zach's greedy ex-wife who seems to have vanished.

Katie Andros—Zach's interfering grandmother. Did she do Eleni in?

Jane—She knows a bit too much about the Andros-Mavrakis dispute.

Lance Stuart—A slick lawyer who knows where the money is.

David Chance—What stake does Abby's ex-husband have in Zach's problems?

Dora—Is Eleni's eccentric aunt as fluttery as she seems?

Gretchen Myers—The grim housekeeper who saw more than she should have.

Constable Jackson—Is he about to arrest Zach, or will he wait until a body shows up?

Chapter One

"It was a freak accident," Abby's friend Jane confided as they filled their coffee mugs in the hospital cafeteria. "But it seems fishy to me. Forklifts just don't run away like that."

Abby's eyes widened. "You mean—"

Jane glanced around, lowering her voice as they moved down the line to the cash register. "I'm sure Eleni's behind it. His ex-wife. She's a witch with a capital *B,* if you know what I mean. They say she's been dragging him through the courts for almost three years. 'Hell hath no fury,' and all that."

"Are you together?" the cashier cut in.

"I'll get it," Abby said quickly, digging into her purse.

"Three dollars and forty-six cents," the cashier intoned.

"Don't ask me what he ever saw in her," Jane continued as they sat down at a table. "Unless it was the money, as everyone said."

"But he's rich, isn't he?" Abby let her gaze wander around the cavernous room, largely deserted in midafternoon. A couple of other nurses sat at a table near the windows, and in the far corner she recognized a family whose child had been a recurring patient in pediatrics from the time she'd worked in that department. She wondered if the little girl was doing better now. Probably not, worse luck, if they were here.

"He's rich now," Jane stated. "But he was only starting out when they got married. Interest rates were still high, so the first years must have been a struggle. Her money would have come in handy."

Hearing the slightly spiteful note in Jane's voice, Abby brought her attention back to her friend. "You don't know that."

Jane shrugged. "No, I don't. And it seems the tables are turned now. Eleni wants a big cut of his business enterprises."

Abby's mouth curved in amusement. "Where did you hear all this?"

"Jack's cousin used to go to school with Eleni. They're still friends. And Jack and the cousin's husband play racquetball together every week. You know how men like to gossip."

"Do they?" Abby sipped her coffee and took a bite of her brownie. "I guess I'll take your word for it."

"Believe it," Jane said. She rolled her eyes in a parody of ecstasy. "But isn't he a hunk, with that gorgeous black hair—I wish I had that natural curl. And I could just swoon at those brooding dark looks, even if his eyes are blue and not brown or black as you'd expect with his coloring. He could park his shoes under my bed at any time."

Abby burst out laughing, hoping the blush that warmed her cheeks didn't reveal her similar thoughts. Thoughts she had no business entertaining about a patient. "Jane, I'm shocked. You've got Jack. And women haven't swooned since Victorian days."

"Maybe they should revive it. I'm married, kid, not dead. I can look." Jane's brown eyes narrowed. "How about you? He's your patient for the next two days. You get to fetch his bedpans, bathe him—"

"Uh-uh," Abby cut in, shaking her head. "I heard him complaining to Dr. Scott already, and he told him he could get up as long as someone was in the room, and walk as far as the bathroom."

Jane wrinkled her nose. "Too bad. But it doesn't change the fact that he's your patient and it's not that busy up there right now. You can get to know each other. And when he gets out, he'll ask you to dinner, and who knows where it'll go from there."

"Yeah, right," Abby said flatly. "He's going to want to see his nurse once he's out. He's already made his feelings clear enough. I'm his jailer. He wanted to go home right out of the emergency room, with his head full of stitches and barely able to stand upright."

"Shows he's got grit. Good quality in a man." Jane drained her mug and got up. "Well, back to the fray."

Waving to a couple of their colleagues who'd just started their break, they left the cafeteria. Against her will, thoughts of Zachary Andros, her new patient, and the hunk in question, taunted Abby as she ran up the stairs to the second floor. Jane was right; he was gorgeous. And any woman with red blood in her veins would notice. It was a wonder that Jane hadn't noticed that she wasn't exactly immune to Zach's dark good looks, in spite of his complaints.

Nurses weren't supposed to get involved with their patients, especially one who'd be gone tomorrow, or the next day at the latest.

She nodded to Cynthia, the head nurse, who was sitting at the nursing station. "How's our new patient?" she asked as she picked up his chart and scanned it.

"He's got a couple of visitors. I think one of them is his ex-wife."

His ex-wife. A chill ran through Abby's body. She chided herself. Probably she was overreacting to Jane's words, which might only be gossip, exaggerated a hundred times in the telling. Eleni must have heard of his accident and decided to see how he was. She wouldn't be bothering him with business at a time like this.

Still trying to reassure herself, Abby hurried down the hall. The door to his private room was closed. That in itself wasn't ominous, since he could call the nursing station with the bed buzzer. But it was certainly irregular; she had left the door open, and according to the chart no one else had been in there in the half hour since she'd been gone.

She paused, the painted wooden door cool under her hand.

"Well, I guess I'll see you in court, then." The woman's voice rose to a shrill, almost hysterical pitch. "We'll see if you get away with this."

Abby clenched her fist as his deep voice washed over her. "Go ahead. I can't stop you. But I will stop you from taking my business."

"*Your* business?" The woman gave a nasty laugh. "The business you started with *my* money."

"Which I've repaid several times. Now, will you get out of here and let me sleep?"

Abby gave a perfunctory knock and pushed the door open without waiting for anyone to answer. Zachary Andros was supposed to have quiet and calm for the next twenty-four hours. The woman in the room was certainly not complying with Dr. Scott's orders.

"Excuse me," Abby said in her best assertive manner. "I'm afraid you'll have to leave."

The woman looked her up and down as if Abby were something repulsive she'd found on the bottom of her shoe. Her narrow nostrils flared. "And who are you to tell me to leave?" she asked in a tone that could have frozen water in July.

Abby lifted her chin, setting her jaw. She wasn't about

to let this woman in a suit that cost more than Abby's entire wardrobe intimidate her. "I'm his nurse, and he needs rest. You'll have to leave."

The other occupant of the room, a muscular man Abby had barely noticed, moved out of the corner and took the woman's arm in a firm grip. "Come on, Eleni. We'll come back another time."

Eleni shook off his hand and moved closer to the bed. Zach lay against the pillow, his face pale. "Just get out of here," he said wearily, his voice barely above a whisper.

"I'll get out when I'm damned good and ready, Zachary Andros," the woman snapped. "Not before. And I'm sick to death of you telling me what to do."

Her face wore an angry flush beneath her flawless makeup. At first glance, Abby would have guessed her to be around thirty. But now that her rage had hardened her features and emphasized the tiny lines around her cold green eyes, she looked every year of her age, which Jane had mentioned was thirty-seven, two years older than her former husband. Eleni's gaze swept over Abby again, her eyes showing about as much emotion as bottle shards.

Abby shivered and stepped forward. The woman's heavy, musky perfume enveloped her in an almost tangible cloud. Abby dipped her head, wrinkling her nose to suppress a sneeze. "Look, Mrs. Andros—"

"Ms. Mavrakis, if you don't mind. I don't want any reminders of our dismal marriage, or anything else from this man."

Except his money, Abby thought uncharitably. "Ms. Mavrakis, you'll have to leave or I'll be forced to call security."

She lifted Zachary's wrist and checked his pulse. A little fast, but not bad considering the provocation. She gently turned his head, her fingers feeling the rasp of his beard stubble. The wound behind his ear looked raw and red but the stitches held the broken skin firmly together. Only one looked a little loose, but it was right at the end and not critical. "You have to lie still. Don't thrash your head around."

"I knew those construction sites were dangerous," Eleni said, standing close to the side of the bed.

"We take every precaution," Zach muttered, the words slurring.

Abby whirled around, nearly treading on Eleni's cream leather pumps. "Goodbye," she said pointedly, her thumb on the call button. Cynthia, the head nurse, with her formidable bulk would rout the visitors more effectively than the elderly security guard who was probably dozing in one of the lounges.

"We're leaving," the man with Eleni said with an embarrassed smile. "Come along, Eleni." A lawyer, Abby guessed, noting the custom-tailored suit and the monogrammed leather attaché case. Younger than Eleni, probably around thirty. An eager, ambitious lawyer but one who retained a modicum of feeling.

This time Eleni allowed her cohort to move her toward the door. But she couldn't resist a final shot over her shoulder. "I'll be back, Zach. You can count on it. And I know where to find you. No more of this nonsense about being out of the office and out of range of your cell phone."

The door swung closed after them. Abby waited until the faint click of Eleni's heels faded into silence before turning back to her patient.

"See why I didn't want to stay here," he muttered, shifting painfully. "I'm a sitting duck."

The door abruptly swung open and a man, also carrying a briefcase but wearing a tank top and tennis shorts, burst in. He strode across the room to the bed. Her head suddenly as light as a balloon, Abby clutched the end of the bed.

First Eleni Mavrakis, and now this. She shouldn't have bothered to get up this morning.

No, that wasn't fair, to put David in the same category as the odious Eleni. David had been her friend. It was her fault that that hadn't been enough.

He skidded to a halt, his sneakers squeaking on the polished tiles, his eyes on the man in the bed. "What happened, Zach? I came as soon as I heard."

"This morning, or a couple of minutes ago?" Zach said sardonically. "Give me a car accident over Eleni any day."

Abby pulled herself together. Her divorce from David had been by mutual consent, not at all acrimonious, but she hadn't seen him since it had been finalized. She thought of him occasionally with a kind of fond, pleasant nostalgia.

"I hope this won't take long. Mr. Andros needs to rest. Hello, David," she said, proud of the evenness of her voice.

Zach's eyes widened. "You two know each other?"

David Chance smiled at Abby. "You might say that. We used to be married. In the Jurassic period. You're looking good, Abby."

"So are you," she said, the strangeness dissolving. After all, they'd been friends long before they'd become lovers and marriage partners. They should have left well enough alone.

"Yeah, Abby Chance," Zach drawled. "If I'd been thinking straight, I would have guessed."

Abby's heart gave a disconcerting little flutter in her chest. He'd noticed her, at least long enough to read her name tag. She arranged her face into a stern, professional expression, chiding her adolescent reaction to the man. She was crazy to even think of him personally. He carried enough emotional and legal baggage that she'd be stupid to want anything to do with him once he was out of here.

"Well, I suppose you have business to discuss," she said briskly. "I'll leave you alone but only for five minutes. Mr.

Andros has had more than enough excitement for one day, and he needs to rest.''

David raised his hand in a Boy Scout salute. "I promise, Abby.''

Aware of both men's eyes on her, she walked out. In the hall, she leaned against the wall, letting her breath out in a long rush. Her face felt as if it were burning, and her heart hammered against her ribs.

So David must be Zach's lawyer. Surprising that Jane hadn't conveyed that little gem of information.

"HAVE YOU KNOWN David long?" Abby asked casually when she brought in Zach's supper tray later. Not much of a supper, actually, only juice and Jell-O.

"Just a month or so," Zach said. His color was better, the lines around his eyes and mouth fainter after a two-hour nap. The bruises on his face were turning from blue to green, although most of them were camouflaged by the growing stubble on his jaw.

He moved gingerly, his injured ribs obviously painful. He was lucky they weren't broken. Even so, he faced several weeks of discomfort. "My previous attorney got fed up with Eleni's shenanigans and quit. David has a reputation for unraveling the knottiest problems, so I hired him. How long ago were you married?"

Abby set the tray on the bed table and moved to the end of the bed to crank it up. "Like David said, in the Jurassic Age. We were both children, barely eighteen. We eloped on our grad night, fourteen years ago. It lasted seven years."

"He married again, didn't he?"

She fussed with the bed crank, finally getting it to retract, telling herself she wasn't hiding. She was acutely conscious of those deep blue eyes on her, eyes the color of a mountain lake at midnight. Disconcerting and startlingly beautiful with his olive skin and strong features. "Yes. He's got two little girls."

"Does that bother you?" Zach asked.

She glanced at him, surprised at the question and trying to see why he would ask something that personal. His expression remained neutral, although his eyes gleamed. But that might have been because of the slight fever he was running. "No, it doesn't bother me," she said evenly. "I'm glad he's happy."

She arranged the table to the correct height and swung it over the bed. "Is there anything else I can get you?"

He glanced at the meager meal. "How about a hamburger with fries?"

She smiled. "Maybe tomorrow, if you behave yourself and take it easy. No more fireworks."

"How about you, Abby?" he asked. "I take it you didn't remarry, since you still have David's name."

"Never met anyone who wanted to put up with my working hours," she said flippantly, uncomfortable under his scrutiny. Pointedly, she pushed his tray a little closer. "Enjoy your dinner."

He looked down at it, his mouth curling. "Yeah, sure," he muttered, picking up his spoon. "Thanks a bunch."

"HE WAS IN AGAIN, yesterday morning," Jane said when Abby walked into the hospital on a Friday evening ten days later.

"Again? Who?" As if she didn't know, her heartbeat accelerating.

"Zachary Andros. Another bump on the head."

Ice hollowed Abby's stomach. "Where is he?"

"Gone," Jane said briefly.

"Gone? Wouldn't he stay overnight if he had another head injury?"

"It wasn't that serious, only a goose egg. His vital signs

were normal...." Jane frowned. "There was something about his coordination—I'm not sure. His speech seemed a little slurred."

Abby frowned. "Alcohol or drugs?" He hadn't struck her as the type to overindulge in any mind-altering substance, legal or otherwise.

"Negative, for alcohol, anyway. Any tests for drugs aren't back yet." Jane shrugged. "I probably imagined it. Dr. Scott wanted him to stay, but he insisted he was okay. The police were here, questioning him while he waited for the doctor. I don't know what it was about." She frowned. "Something's going on. I heard them asking about Eleni."

"Has she been bothering him again?"

"Not around here. He didn't stay long enough. I suppose you've come for the key."

Jane reached into her pocket and handed Abby a set of keys. "Here you go—the key to our palatial summer cottage. Enjoy the weekend. I'll call you if I hear anything."

"It doesn't matter." The last thing Abby needed was thoughts of Zachary Andros cluttering up her time off.

"Well, okay. You know where to find everything? How to hook up the power?"

Abby threw her friend a smile she didn't feel. "How hard can it be? I'll figure it out."

"Call me when you get there." Jane gave her a quick hug. "I don't like the look of that sky. I hope it doesn't storm again."

ABBY RECALLED those unfortunately prophetic words hours later. She'd had to pack her car and tidy up her place. When she'd gone to leave her key with a neighbor who would water her small garden if the weather turned hot, she'd found he was out. Abby had been forced to wait several hours for him to come back. By the time she left town, dusk had fallen, a glowering, unnatural dusk formed of green-tinged, pregnant clouds. They had started dumping their burden an hour ago, just when she'd hit the curvy mountain road.

Rain lashed the windshield, defying the wipers to whisk it away. The wind, an invisible predator on a rampage, hammered at the little car. For the tenth time in as many minutes, Abby found herself hunched forward, as if putting her nose closer to the windshield would allow her to see the road through the blinding sheets of rain. She leaned back, a muscle clenching in her neck. She risked freeing one hand from the steering wheel to massage the ache. Not that it helped much.

She turned on the heater, swearing mildly when it failed to clear the mist gathering on the inside of the glass. In fact, the film became thicker. Using the edge of her hand, she wiped a spot clean. If only the air conditioner hadn't died in May. It would have demisted the glass in no time.

Trees, ominous shapes against the black night, swayed over the road, spattering the car with drops the size of walnuts. Abby flexed her hands on the wheel, debating whether she should pull over until the worst of the storm had passed. She chewed on her bottom lip. No, better to press on. If one of the trees came down in the rising wind and blocked the road, she would be stuck in the car until a road crew cleared it. That might be several days on a secondary road like this.

If only she hadn't agreed to Jane's suggestion that she spend the weekend at the cottage. If only the weather wasn't more reminiscent of February than July. If only her car was newer and better equipped. Muttering imprecations, she sucked in her breath as the tires skidded in a puddle. She let the car slide, steering toward the middle of the road, hands loose on the wheel. The rubber found traction and gripped. She braked lightly, pumping the pedal, and edged toward the side of the road. She would just stop for a moment and find a rag to wipe the fogged windows.

That was when she saw it. A dark figure stumbling along the grassy verge. Startled, she jammed her foot on the brake. Mistake. Her stomach lurched sickeningly as the car slid toward the edge of the road. She eased off the brake, squeezing the steering wheel gently to the left. Too late. One wheel bumped off the pavement, sinking into the mud. She braked again, sending up a silent prayer of thanks when the car abruptly stopped.

The rain slanted in silver ribbons before the headlights. The figure turned. She saw a man, head bent against the driving wind and rain, wet clothes plastered to his body. He took a step toward the car.

Then, suddenly he disappeared from her view. She pushed the car door open, leaving the engine running. In the wet weather, she wasn't going to take the chance that some electrical connection would short out, leaving her stranded in the middle of the forest.

The rain peppered her face with a thousand stinging needles. Wind roared in the trees, combing the wet branches. She crossed in front of the car, stepping cautiously. Where had the man gone? Was there a ditch beside the road, invisible in the darkness?

Or had she imagined seeing him?

She found him lying facedown in the soaked grass, barely lit by the headlight beams. The long, lean body appeared lifeless. She crouched down, hesitating before touching him. The faint rising and falling of his back under her hand told her he breathed. She groped for his wrist, set her fingers against his pulse. It was a bit rapid, but strong and steady.

She decided he wasn't going to die anytime soon. Exhaustion, and the cold seeping into his body through the wet clothes had likely brought about the collapse.

Grunting with the effort, she turned him over. She gasped, feeling as if she'd been punched in the stomach. What was Zachary Andros doing out here at the edge of nowhere? Had he been in another accident? She hadn't seen a car on the road, or beside it, but in the thick darkness she could have missed seeing a derailed freight train.

The rain pelted his face and even in his semiconscious state, he winced, turning his head. A cold rivulet snaked down the back of Abby's neck. She jerked back to full alert, chiding herself for woolgathering when she should be helping him.

If he lay there much longer, he was in real danger of hypothermia, but she didn't want to move him without first checking for injuries. She ran her hands efficiently over his body. After a moment, she sat back, satisfied. There were no broken bones, although she had felt the faintly rough line of the recently healed scar behind his ear, the injury that had kept him in hospital the first time. The new growth of trimmed hair around it prickled her fingers. She shivered, goose bumps rising on her skin, partly from the cold, partly from nerves.

She had to get him out of the rain.

The wind whipped her hair into her eyes as she got up and walked around the car. She pushed the wet strands impatiently back, dragging the stray locks together and re-fastening the clip at her nape. When she pulled open the car door, heat greeted her, stealing her breath.

Leaning over the driver's seat, she unlocked the passenger door. Water dripped from her nose and eyebrows, forming dark splotches on the gray upholstery. She wiped her hand over her face and dried it on her jeans. She was only going to get wetter.

Outside, the rain had increased, if that was possible, pouring over her in torrents. And the wind roared in the trees. Somewhere far away, thunder muttered. Or maybe it was Mount Baker, stirring out of dormancy. That would be all she needed, a volcanic eruption on top of the storm.

Abby opened the passenger door. Fortunately, the wind blew from the opposite direction, not directly into the car. Slipping and sliding, she went back to the still figure on the ground. He lay where she'd left him, one arm slung over his face, giving scant protection from the rain.

Abby caught her breath. Had he recovered consciousness? She knelt beside him, knees squelching in the muddy grass. "Hey, wake up. This is not a good place to sleep."

She shook his shoulder. He groaned softly, his arm falling to the ground. "Mr. Andros, Zach, wake up," she called more urgently. "I can't lift you unless you help."

He blinked, groaning again. Abby tucked her hands under his arms and pulled.

"Hey, take it easy." The sound of his voice startled her. She let go of him. His head thumped against her knee.

"Thanks," he said clearly, his tone wry.

"I'm sorry." She wrapped her arm around his shoulders. "Do you think you can get up if I help you?"

"Head hurts like a bitch." He didn't open his eyes. "In fact, everything hurts like a bitch."

"I don't doubt it," she murmured sympathetically. "What are you doing wandering outside in the rain, anyway?"

"Not enough sense to come in. That's what my mother always said." He struggled to sit up, his hands slipping on the wet grass as he tried to brace himself. Abby heaved his shoulders up, propping his torso against her thighs. Now all she had to do was get him the rest of the way up and into the car.

To her surprise, he rolled away from her, onto his side, gathered his legs under him, and managed to scramble to his knees. "If you can't walk," she suggested, "maybe you can just crawl. You have to get into the car, out of the rain."

He stretched out one hand. She took it. Using her as a prop, he struggled to his feet. Unsteady, but upright. "Just point me in the right direction."

His fingers bit into her shoulder as she took a step forward. Despite his apparent confidence, she knew he would have fallen without her support. Wrapping one arm around his waist, she took another step, acutely conscious of how thin he was. His ribs felt like barrel slats.

By the time they had taken the few steps needed to reach the car, her breath rasped in her throat. Sweat mingled with the rain dripping from her face. Despite his wasted condition, he weighed a ton, and thirteen years of shifting patients in hospital beds hadn't prepared her for toting a tall man out in the field.

"Let's just get you turned and you can slide onto the car seat," she panted.

He twisted in her grasp, his knees buckling. "Oh, no, you don't," she muttered. "I can't lift you off the ground again."

He managed to remain upright. He swayed against her, his breathing rough and labored. Pain burned through Abby's shoulders as she took his full weight. She sensed he was about to pass out again. "One more step back," she ordered, making sure the firm words penetrated deep into his consciousness.

He moved back, more of a stumble than a step, and collapsed onto the car seat. Letting out a breath in relief, Abby tugged him straight so that he wouldn't fall across the other seat. Grimacing at the mud caking his shoes and pant legs, she lifted first the left and then the right leg into the car. She pushed her own wet hair out of her eyes, realizing she'd lost the clip. "Fingers clear?" she said. He wiggled the hand that lay on his thigh. She smiled faintly and slammed the door.

The heater, churning out warm air, had cleared the windows, although she knew they would fog up again, especially with two bodies in the car generating humidity. She got in, shut the driver's door, and flipped on the interior light.

Zach sat with his head against the headrest, eyes closed. Was he unconscious again? She couldn't tell; he might be sleeping. His drenched sweater clung to his chest, steaming lightly in the heat. Reaching across for the seat belt, she breathed in the scent of rain, wet wool, and the faint, tantalizing ghost of a musky cologne. Shaking her head, she clipped the buckle securely into place. He didn't move.

His black hair lay plastered to a well-shaped head. The ends were drying already, curling against his forehead and around his ears. She checked the clipped area behind his ear. She was pleased to note that the cut had healed completely, stitches removed days ago.

A frown etched a groove between his thick black brows. Pain compressed his lips into a thin line. She wondered how his mouth would look smiling. Funny, during the two days he'd been her patient, she'd never seen him come closer to a smile than a wry or sardonic twist of his lips. She pushed away the thought. She had no time for this. She had to get him to a hospital or a clinic, and herself to the cabin.

"Hi, Abby." His voice, low and rough, made her jump.

"Hi, Mr. Andros," she said, heartbeat speeding up.

"Zach, please," he said. "You had no trouble with it before."

"So you knew who I was."

"Your perfume."

"I don't wear perfume."

He shrugged, wincing again. "Soap, shampoo, whatever."

His eyes fell closed once more, as if the dim light hurt them. He shivered convulsively.

"Why did you leave the hospital?" she muttered, her gaze on his pale face. "They should have tied you to the bed."

He smiled faintly. "You weren't there, Abby."

"I do get a day off once in a while." Turning off the interior light, she shot him a glare he didn't see, and shifted the car into gear, feeding it gas. The tires spun ineffectually for a moment, then found traction. Steering gently, she eased the car out of the mud and onto the pavement. Checking the road in both directions, she made a U-turn, heading back the way she'd come. She could call an ambulance from the gas station.

The small car shuddered as a gust of wind whipped over it. The wipers beat a pattern that barely disturbed the sheets of rain pouring down the windshield. And, as she'd expected, the insides of the windows fogged up once more, reducing visibility to a hazy mist.

Zach still sat with his eyes closed, seemingly oblivious to where they were going although he must realize they weren't going in the direction he'd been walking. Maybe he didn't care.

She used a cloth she found in the side door pocket to wipe the glass in front of her, at the same time setting the wipers on high. A dark mass loomed before her. She slammed on the brakes. The car skidded sideways, coming to a stop next to the fallen tree that blocked the road. Wind-driven green leaves scattered over the hood, and glued themselves to the windshield.

Abby pounded her hand on the steering wheel. "Well, that does it."

Zach opened his eyes, shivering so hard she could hear

his teeth chattering. He cleared his throat, the faint sound becoming a harsh, muscle-racking cough. Turning pale, he wrapped his arms around his ribs until the spasm passed. "Where are we?" he asked groggily, breath rasping.

"Next to a tree. We can't go back, and you need a doctor."

"No, I don't." His voice sounded stronger. "I've had enough of doctors. All I need is some rest. Just get me up to Sunset Cove and I'll be okay."

"I'm not going that far," Abby said. "That's the far end of the lake. What's up there?"

"A summer cabin. I haven't been to it in years but I figured it would be a good place to recuperate."

And Eleni probably wouldn't think to look for him there, Abby thought. Aloud, she said, "I doubt if we can make it up there tonight. That road isn't paved. It's going to be slippery as—never mind. This car won't be able to make it."

He dragged in a ragged breath. "Okay, just drop me any place. Back at the gas station. I'll get a ride back to town. Maybe this wasn't such a good idea after all."

"Unfortunately, the gas station is on the far side of this tree." She put the car back into gear. "I guess I'll just have to take you with me. But don't blame me for the consequences. I think you need a doctor."

"I'll trust you to take care of me," he said.

Exasperated, she ignored that. She carefully turned the car on the road and headed back up the mountain.

"I promise not to sue," he added.

"That's comforting," she muttered, again leaning forward and squinting through the wind-lashed rain. She drove past the spot where she'd picked him up, keeping a sharp eye out for more downed trees. "How did you get this far?" she asked. "I didn't see a car."

"My car's still in the body shop after the forklift accident. I've been taking taxis.'' He sounded a little more alert although he had again closed his eyes. ''This afternoon I walked to a truck stop and got a ride in a logging truck. The driver dropped me at the gas station. I figured I could walk to the cabin.''

Abby risked taking her eyes off the road to gape at him. ''But it's nearly ten kilometers up to Sunset Cove!''

''It wasn't raining when I started. I stopped to rest under a big hemlock. I guess I fell asleep because the next thing I knew it was dark and raining like hell.''

Abby frowned as she concentrated on the road. She couldn't put her finger on it, but some parts of his story sounded a bit suspicious, as if he were only telling part of it. Jane's comment about slurred speech came back to her. What did she really know about Zachary Andros?

Well, the bedrooms at Jane's place had sturdy locks. She'd be safe enough.

Chapter Two

Abby saw a sign ahead, a pale ghost in the rain. Good thing she hadn't missed it. She thought she remembered the way from previous visits, but the narrow forest roads looked different in the dark.

Gravel crunched under the wheels as she turned right. Fir twigs and several sizable branches littered the road ahead of the car, evidence of the wind's ferocity. Zach said nothing, except for a stifled moan when the wheels jolted through a pothole.

The road curved, and the headlights strafed across a substantial cedar house. Abby swallowed a laugh. Jane always referred to it as a cottage when it actually contained five bedrooms, three baths, and a greater square footage than the average city house. Abby was familiar with the layout, having spent weekends there with Jane and a group of their friends. This was her first time there alone.

Only she wasn't alone, was she?

She drove as close to the door as possible. Although a wide verandah lay across the front of the house, it was only two easy steps from the ground. If necessary she could drag Zach up them. Braking, she killed the engine and the lights.

"Just sit here for a moment. I'll open the house and start the generator."

Without waiting for a reply, she got out of the car and

ran up onto the verandah. Behind the house, the wind roared like heavy surf in the giant fir trees. The scents of ozone and resin filled the air.

Abby fumbled in her purse for the house key, wishing she'd had the foresight to attach it to the car key ring earlier. She found it, pulled it out, and turned it in the lock. The door swung silently open. Abby groped for the flashlight she knew would be on the hall table. The rubber-coated cylinder felt reassuringly heavy in her hand, and the strong beam of light flashed around the hall, illuminating pale walls and a golden, quarry-tiled floor.

Hurrying to the back porch, she unlocked the little shed at one end. The generator ran on propane supplied by a huge tank set at the edge of the forest behind the house. Following the instructions Jane had shown her several weeks ago, she turned it on. She checked that the water heater next to the generator had started. Also fed by propane, it would heat enough water for a shower by the time she unpacked the car. *Correction, two showers.*

Back in the house, she turned on lights, and raised the thermostat. She would run the furnace long enough to drive away the chill and the musty smell of the closed house. Later she could start a fire in the fireplace; Jane always kept plenty of wood around.

She returned to the front hall, reaching for the light switch. A hand came down on her shoulder. She gasped and whirled around, heart hammering against her ribs. Zach's blue gaze met hers. She let out her breath in a gust. "Oh, you scared me. How'd you get in here?"

The corner of his mouth lifted slightly. "I managed to drag myself. You left the door open."

She shrugged. "So? There's no one else around. Not in this storm." She gestured toward the living room. "Why don't you sit down and I'll bring in my stuff. It'll warm up shortly."

"And this is July. Feels more like winter." He rolled his eyes although his face remained deathly pale. He stood, shivering, his shoulder braced against the wall.

Frowning, she ran a hand over his forehead. Cool, but the lines at the corners of his mouth deepened. "Are you sure you can make it there?"

"Actually, no. But if I can't walk, I can always let myself slide down the wall. I won't fall."

"Never mind," Abby said briskly. "I'll give you a hand."

"More than a hand, I'm afraid."

"All right, a shoulder. Just wrap your arm around me."

He mumbled something that sounded like "a pleasure," but she couldn't be sure. The glance she sneaked at his face told her nothing except that he was in considerable pain. His clothes were clammy and wet, as cold as if he'd been in a walk-in cooler.

Together they struggled into the living room, where she let him sink onto the cushy leather sofa. She crouched down and untied the muddy sneakers and slipped them off his feet. "There, now you'll be okay. Just rest for a moment and then we'll see about some dry clothes."

She draped an afghan over him, again inhaling the scent of masculine cologne, wind, and rain. Straightening, she turned back toward the hall. "Thanks," he said behind her, his voice faint.

"You're welcome." She hurried out to the car. This was crazy. He was practically a stranger. She had to stop reacting to him every time they got close. Surely she could think of him as a patient instead of a man. But as before, this man, wounded or not, made her far too aware that she was a woman. And that she hadn't had a date in months or met anyone who genuinely interested her in years.

Cold rain dripped off the trunk lid and trickled down the side of her face when she leaned in to take out her suitcase.

A dose of reality, she thought, shivering as thunder again rolled across the sky.

She carried her suitcase and jacket up onto the verandah, and returned to bring in bags of groceries and lock the car. Not that anyone would steal it out here, but you couldn't be too careful. After all, she'd sensed a certain untruthfulness in Zach's words, perhaps because he'd seemed reluctant to look at her when he told his story. He might view her car as transportation to his own cabin, once the rain stopped and the road dried out.

Warm air greeted her along with the dry, cooked-dust smell of a furnace that hadn't run for a while. In the living room, Zach lay flat on his back on the sofa, his arm slung over his face. His feet were propped on the arm of the sofa. One of his white socks had a hole in the toe, a flaw she found oddly endearing, especially since he was probably rich enough to throw his socks away after one wearing.

She carried her things up to the second floor, picking a bedroom near the stairs. Unzipping the case, she rummaged through her clothes. She dragged out an old pair of sweatpants she wore for lounging. Lean-hipped as he was, they should fit him. Too short, probably, although he was only about three inches taller than her own five-eight.

She held up the matching shirt, shaking her head. He'd never fit in that. His shoulders were too broad, despite his apparent weight loss.

Carrying the pants, she went downstairs and out to the mudroom off the kitchen. She gave a little sound of triumph as she unearthed an old sweatshirt belonging to Jane's college-age son. It was dotted with dried paint stains, but would keep her guest warm until his own clothes dried.

She returned to the living room, clothes dangling from her hand. She ran a hand through her hair, aware of her own clothes sticking clammily to her body. She needed to change as well.

"Hello?" She shook his shoulder. "Can you get up and make it to the bathroom? The water will be hot by now. After that, I'll fix us a snack."

He opened his eyes, blinking thick black lashes. "What? Is it morning?" he asked, the words slurred.

"Not yet, but you have to get out of your wet clothes or you'll have pneumonia. There's a shower down here, just off the kitchen. It'll save you climbing the stairs."

Grimacing in pain, he sat up. He staggered to his feet, frowning as if he couldn't remember how to walk. He clutched his left side and she recalled his agony when he had coughed in the car. Injured ribs, even if they weren't broken, could cause excruciating pain.

What had happened to him this time? She wished she'd asked Jane for more details, but she'd been too busy trying to hide how much the news of Zach's second accident—or whatever—had shocked her.

Her heart contracting in sympathy, she again draped his arm over her shoulders and guided him to the bathroom door. "Do you think you can manage alone now? Sorry it isn't a bathtub. A hot soak would do you good, help those ribs. They're still painful, aren't they?"

"Only if I cough or laugh. Not that I've had much to laugh about lately. And I think I bumped them again night before last." His voice was a little stronger than before.

She frowned. "Did the doctor check them?"

"Yeah, they're okay, only bruised."

"So you don't have any bandages to worry about getting wet. Do you need help to get undressed?"

A ghost of a smile crossed his features. "Under other circumstances, I'd love it. But I wouldn't want to waste the opportunity. No, I can manage on my own, thanks."

"Okay." She wasn't sure whether she felt relieved or disappointed. "Just leave the door unlocked and yell if you have problems."

Abby headed upstairs, shedding her clothes as soon as she entered the bathroom there. She glanced in the mirror and grimaced. Her cheeks were too flushed and her eyes too bright, and a streak of brown mud adorned her forehead. Sticking out her tongue at her reflection, she turned away and stepped into the shower. A short time later, comfortable in dry clothes, she bundled up her wet, mud-stained jeans and sweater to take down to the laundry room.

In the kitchen she found her guest looking marginally more alert. He sat at the table, his chin propped in his palm. A little color had returned to his face. In the harsh kitchen light she saw a swelling under one eye. Also acquired in his latest mishap?

Her gaze wandered lower. The old sweatshirt fit him well, but the elastic on the bottom of the pant legs gripped him at midcalf. His feet were bare, toes curled against the cool tiles. She would have to hunt through the drawers in the bedroom for some socks.

"Where are your wet clothes?" she asked.

"Still in the bathroom. I'm sorry. It hurts to bend."

"Never mind. I'll get them."

She stuffed all the muddy garments into the washing machine, then added soap and started it. She just hoped both pairs of jeans had been washed often enough not to turn everything else blue.

"Do you want something to eat?" she asked, returning to the kitchen. "Or maybe some hot chocolate?"

"Hot chocolate sounds good."

Abby poured milk and chocolate mix into two cups and put them in the microwave. Closing the door, she punched in the time. "I don't know if I should light the fireplace. It's almost eleven. Do you want it?"

"Don't bother for me." As if to belie his words, a shiver rippled through his body.

The microwave pinged. She took out the mugs, stirred

both, and set one before him. He grasped it between his palms as if he needed to suck the heat into his soul. "Are you all right?" Abby asked. "I turned down the furnace, but I can crank it back up if you want."

"I feel like I've been used for a punching bag. But it's nothing a good night's sleep won't fix."

She fiddled awkwardly with her mug, turning it this way and that, blowing gently on the steaming liquid. Finally she looked up, meeting his dark blue gaze. "Having second thoughts?" he said, with unmistakable amusement. "Don't worry. I'm harmless."

"I never thought anything else," she said steadily. "It's not as if we're total strangers."

"But you don't know me," he said, his eyes somber. The little frown lines reappeared between his brows.

She groped in the second grocery bag, which she hadn't unpacked, pulling out the newspaper. This morning's paper, stale news by now. She opened it on the table.

The headlines screamed at her. Prominent Vancouver Businesswoman Missing. The color photo showed a smiling Eleni Mavrakis hanging onto the arm of the man Abby had seen in Zach's hospital room. The caption identified him as her lawyer.

The earth tilted, an uncomfortable sensation that echoed in her stomach. She tipped the newspaper up so that Zach couldn't see what she was reading, and turned to page two. Moving her gaze quickly down the page, she scanned the story.

Eleni Mavrakis, formerly Andros, is missing. In a brief interview, Gretchen Myers, Mavrakis's housekeeper, informed this reporter that Zachary Andros, the missing woman's ex-husband was at her house the evening she vanished. "They had a big fight," Myers said. "Right after that, the power went off. The police have asked me not to talk about what I saw. But I have every reason to believe he killed her and disposed of the body.'' The police would not comment on Ms. Myers's allegations.

The animosity between Mavrakis and Andros, especially during their acrimonious divorce proceedings, is well-known in Lower Mainland social circles. Zachary Andros has been questioned by the police. A call to Mr. Andros produced only the terse comment that he had been in the house, but that Ms. Mavrakis was alive and well when he left. A police spokesman would only say that the matter is under investigation, and is being treated as a simple missing persons case at the moment.

Heat washed through her, followed by icy cold. Panic, an emotion she thought she'd conquered after years working in a hospital. She stared at the paper, blind and stunned, not daring to look up at the man opposite her, the man who had looked so normal until a moment ago.

The police had questioned him. That didn't indicate imminent arrest, but—

She jumped when Zach reached out his hand and covered hers, his palm warm from the mug, hard and smooth. ''Listen to me, Abby.''

Abby jerked her hand back, almost tipping her chair over. Her knees began to shake. The paper slid from her nerveless fingers, falling closed.

A thin smile curved his lips, all humor gone, as he took in the headlines. ''I see the papers didn't waste any time. I wonder who leaked the story. The police said they wouldn't talk to the press. But don't worry, Abby, you're in no danger. The police haven't even laid charges.''

The police. They'd been at the hospital. She knew she should have questioned Jane more thoroughly about Zach's

latest visit to Emergency. "That's reassuring," she managed to mumble through stiff lips. She eyed him warily, as
if he'd turned into a stick of dynamite with a very short
fuse.

"They came into the hospital to talk to me, right behind
the ambulance," Zach said. "The emergency-room staff
couldn't stop them."

"And?" Abby prompted when he paused.

"And nothing. They found me at her house but since I
was unconscious—" he touched his head "—when the police came I couldn't tell them anything about what happened. They were satisfied that I had nothing to do with
Eleni's disappearance." He made a sound of derision.
"Disappearance. She probably went off on a business trip
and didn't tell anyone. Wouldn't be the first time."

Abby stared down at the paper. Today's date, Friday.
The paper came out in the morning. "It says she's been
missing since Wednesday night. Two days."

He shook his head, his mouth tightening. "It was Thurs-
day morning by the time the police were notified. It didn't
make yesterday's paper, luckily."

"But Jane said—"

"Your friend, in Emergency? I was brought in yesterday
morning and I left as soon as they checked me over. I
stayed in a hotel until this afternoon when I decided the
summer cabin might be a better place to recuperate than
my house, where there were probably a dozen reporters
waiting for me to come home."

That made sense, Abby realized. And she'd been on
night shift and, what with sleeping all day and errands to
run afterwards, hadn't bothered to listen to the news. And
Jane had been off, too, so she hadn't filled her in.

Until this afternoon, with only the vaguest conjectures.
Abby stifled a moan. Why hadn't she asked for more details

instead of letting her mind go off on a flight of fancy with dreams of Zach?

Call when you get there. Jane's parting words echoed in her mind. She slid her chair back and reached for the phone on the wall behind her.

Instantly Zach was beside her, his hand covering hers. "I don't want anyone to know where I am."

"Why?" She yanked her hand away. She couldn't think straight when he was that close. Fear and some sort of crazy obsession twisted together to muddle her brain. "Are the police after you now?"

"Not as far as I know." He shoved his hands into the sweatpants pockets, clenching them into fists. "But I don't know if someone else might be after me. That's the other reason I stayed in a hotel last night. I didn't want to go home unless I knew it was safe. I wouldn't be much good in a fight with these ribs."

Was he paranoid? Abby fought down her renewed apprehension. "No, I guess you wouldn't." She pasted a reassuring smile on her face. "Look, I won't give you away. But I need to call Jane, to tell her I made it. She's going to worry, with the storm."

He sat heavily down. "Fine. Just don't tell her I'm here."

If she was smart, she would also call the police and find out whether his story was true. Maybe later, she promised herself.

The house shuddered under a violent gust of wind. Thank God the generator ran on propane, not at the whims of flimsy power lines that could come down in the wind at any time. She didn't know what she'd do in the dark with a man she wasn't sure she could trust. A man who might have harmed his wife.

Harmed. She almost laughed. *Murdered*—wasn't that

what she really thought? Which was crazy. Zach Andros wasn't a murderer.

Lifting the receiver, she punched in Jane's number. She brought it to her ear. Nothing. She poked the disconnect button and listened. No dial tone.

"Line's probably down," Zach said.

"I could have guessed that," she said testily.

"So I guess it's just us two against the world."

She got up and carried her mug to the sink, emptying the cold dregs of her chocolate down the drain. "You can take any bedroom down here. Don't forget to turn out the lights. Good night."

By the time she reached the top of the stairs and found her room, she was shaking so hard she had to sit down on the bed. She lowered her head and dug the heels of her hands into her aching eyes. Talk about being attracted to the wrong man. This time she'd really done it, picked someone not only rich and arrogant but with a vindictive ex-wife who had disappeared. And he'd been questioned by the police, which must mean he was suspected of having something to do with the disappearance.

The newspaper. She'd only skimmed the article. What did it say exactly? Stupidly, she'd left it downstairs.

Dragging herself up from the bed, she tiptoed across the room, slipping the lock and cracking the door open. No lights on. He must have gone to bed, although she hadn't heard anything.

She crept down the stairs, her sock-covered feet silent on the wooden steps. She'd forgotten to look for socks for him. His feet must be so cold.

Ruthlessly, she turned off the thought. Why should she be concerned about a man who might be a murderer?

The luminous kitchen clock showed that forty minutes had passed since she'd fled upstairs. Had she really sat that long ruminating?

The storm appeared to be passing. Rain no longer lashed the windows. The porch light outside spilled a dim glow across the large living room and through the kitchen doorway. The newspaper was a pale blur on the table. She grabbed it, and turned, smashing her nose against a hard chin.

Tears flooded her eyes. She blinked them away, the pain receding under the onslaught of other sensations. Hot skin stretched over solid muscle, the soft hair on his chest tickling her bare arm. His clean musky scent filled her nostrils. She wanted to close her eyes and drink in the essence of him. "Must you keep doing that?" she snapped instead, burying her foolishness under anger.

He flicked the light switch at his side. She recoiled from the sudden glare, closing her eyes briefly. "I came for a glass of water," he said. "I didn't know you were here until you moved. Why didn't you turn on the light? Never mind, don't tell me. You didn't want me to know you'd come back down, in case I do you in like I did Eleni."

"Did you do her in?" Abby asked, possessed by a weird fatalism.

"No!" He practically yelled the word, making her jump. The paper, crushed between them, rustled. Abby took a quick step back, her tongue coming out to slide nervously across her lips.

For an instant she saw heat leap into his eyes, then they narrowed. "Abby, I swear I didn't touch Eleni. She was alive when I left her house. I was feeling dizzy, ill. I must have fallen, because the next thing I knew I was lying on the step outside and her housekeeper was screaming blue murder. I must have blacked out again because I woke up when the police and an ambulance arrived. I found out later that Gretchen had to go to the store down the road to call them because the power and phone lines were down. Eleni was gone, along with her car."

"Do the police suspect foul play?"

He raked a hand through his hair, smoothing the glossy curls. "They suspect me."

"Without any evidence?"

"Well, Gretchen said she heard me arguing with Eleni, which was true. I didn't deny it. She said I must have killed her and bundled her out in the living room rug, which is missing. That doesn't mean much. Eleni could have sent it out for cleaning the day before, which was Gretchen's day off. I think Gretchen imagined the whole thing, although I'd never suspected her of having any imagination before."

"Where is Eleni's house?"

"In the woods, south of Langley. Lots of trees. One fell on the lines but the utilities crew were out first thing in the morning." His mouth twisted. "Can't have the power off to any of the rich people's houses. They might not be able to fax their broker."

"You're one of those rich people, Mr. Andros."

"Yeah? I won't be when Eleni gets through with me. And you had no trouble calling me Zach before." His hands lifted, as if he would touch her. He dropped them before he made contact. "Abby, I didn't kill her. I'm innocent of everything—except stupidity that I didn't see her for what she was when I met her."

"We all make mistakes," Abby said, not without sympathy. She'd been there too, but it was her own mistake, not David's.

"But the police seem to think she might have been murdered. There were stains on the floor. They're analyzing them to see if it's blood. I guess they believe Gretchen, even if there's no body."

"They convicted some guy in Alberta for murdering his children without finding their bodies. I heard they just found them recently, quite by chance."

He eyed her intently. "You're taking this very calmly. You haven't booted me out into the storm."

Calmly? If he only knew how erratically her heart fluttered inside her chest. Jane had filled her in on the former Mrs. Andros after Zach was discharged after his car accident. The bitter divorce had been final for a year, but the lawyers were still arguing over the property settlement. If Zach had killed her and disposed of the body, there were those who would have cheered his actions.

"The storm's over, in case you haven't noticed." Abby took a long, fortifying breath. "Like you said, there's no body. And no evidence of violence."

"Thank God for that," he said fervently. "Do you mind if I go to bed? My head aches so much I can hardly see straight."

"Sure, go ahead. Do you want some aspirin or something? I'm sure there's some kind of painkiller in the medicine cabinet."

He made a dismissing gesture. "If I need it, I'll get it." He walked gingerly down the hall and a moment later she heard the bedroom door close.

She shook herself, fingers clenching around the newspaper. Zach wasn't a killer. Besides, everyone was innocent until proven guilty.

In her room, behind a door whose lock suddenly appeared disconcertingly flimsy, she opened the paper to the story.

Upon rereading it, she realized the report contained lots of lurid speculation but little substance. It went so far as to imply that Zachary Andros must have killed his ex-wife, since he apparently had both motive and opportunity. But it vas only an implication, with the veiled criticism that by their silence the police might be endangering the public. There was no mention of a missing rug, only that faint stains from the hardwood floor were being analyzed.

She finally went to bed, her mind buzzing. Where was Eleni? And what had the housekeeper seen that led her to believe Zach had killed his wife?

ZACH JOLTED AWAKE, his heart pounding. He sat up in the bed, his gaze swinging wildly around the unfamiliar room. This wasn't the hotel where he'd slept yesterday. Nor was it his house. Too well furnished. His own house was under construction and he'd been sleeping on a cot in one room with sawhorses forming the major decor.

That dream again. He'd had it last night. He shook his head. What if it wasn't a dream? What if it was a memory? A body lying on the rug. Blood pooling under the dark head.

It would mean Gretchen was right. He'd killed Eleni.

Chapter Three

Zach woke to sunlight streaming through the window and the scent of bacon drifting on the air. He stretched lazily, his mind blissfully empty. A quilt lay like a cloud over him. He pushed it aside, leaving only the sheet covering his body. After waking once, with the disturbing dream humming in his brain, he'd fallen back into a deep sleep mercifully devoid of nightmares.

The room was stuffy. He should get up and open the window, but for the first time in forty-eight hours he felt rested. His stomach growled, reminding him he couldn't remember the last time he'd eaten. Despite the tantalizing scents coming from the kitchen, food would have to wait. He needed to get his brain in gear and assess the situation.

Where was Eleni? What was she up to? The panicky certainty that she was behind everything that had happened to him lately returned. He'd managed to keep it at bay while he'd escaped from the hospital and holed up in the anonymous hotel room. But last night, waking in the dark woods had brought it rushing back.

When he'd seen the car lights, he'd debated ducking into the soggy underbrush, hiding until he was safely alone again. But the aftereffects of his latest injuries had caught up to him. One moment he'd been walking, the next he'd been eating grass and mud.

He couldn't believe it when his angel of mercy turned out to be Abby Chance. Abby of the soft voice and softer hands who had looked after him in the hospital when he'd been battered and bruised from the accident with the fork-lift.

Had Eleni arranged the accident? He couldn't picture her talking with some burly construction worker, or worse, some gun for hire, perhaps in a seedy bar, but how well did he know her? They'd been married for six years, although during the last four he'd seen little of her.

For a while they had occupied opposite ends of the huge house she'd insisted upon having built shortly after the wedding. When she'd finally agreed that a divorce wouldn't give her father a heart attack and cause her mother to go into a decline, he'd moved out.

That had been almost three years ago. The austere, featureless apartment he'd rented couldn't have been more of a contrast to the house he'd left. And for the past six months he'd lived in the old house he'd bought near Abbotsford, occupying one room while he renovated the rest.

Eleni had come out there once. He saw the way her nose turned up at the sight of the plain cot, and his clothes hanging on a bar fixed in the corner of the room and covered with a plastic drop cloth to protect them from the dust. "How can you live in such squalor?" she asked disdainfully, her high heels clicking on the hardwood floors he was refinishing.

"How can you live in that glass-and-marble mausoleum?" he'd countered, long past caring about preserving even a semblance of civility between them.

"You built it," she reminded him.

"My company built it, to your specifications. I was away when much of it was done, remember?"

"Yes, you were always away in those days."

Realizing scant months after the wedding what a mistake

he'd made, he'd insured that his presence was necessary on every out-of-town project his construction and development company took on. And her comment had rated no reply.

Now, despite the closed window, he could hear a robin chirping outside. Nearby he heard the light bang of cupboard doors and the gentle rise and fall of Abby's voice as she hummed some song or other.

He flexed his body under the sheet. A few aches and pains, but bearable. Somewhere in the back of his head, his brain still felt fuzzy, and his mouth had a dry, hungover taste to it. He knew he should get up, but he wasn't ready to face Abby just yet.

Last night, in the kitchen, when she'd licked her lips, he'd almost leaned over and kissed her. What if he had? Would she have bopped him one with the newspaper? Or, tantalizing thought, would she have opened her mouth and welcomed him inside?

A certain part of his body stirred, showing signs of interest for the first time in longer than he wanted to contemplate. Abby. Even her name conveyed gentleness, kindness, nurture, and caring. Relief, like a cool glass of water on a searing summer day.

Not that she was dull. No, he'd seen the flashes of fire in her eyes and the determination and assurance with which she'd sent Eleni from his hospital room ten days ago.

She wasn't like the women who usually caught his attention. She had somewhat angular features that would look distinguished even when she was old, and dark brown hair. Last night he'd seen that hair loose, and the wild curls around her face gave her a piquant beauty that wasn't evident when she wore it pulled back for work. But her eyes made her truly beautiful. Those deep brown, exotically slanted eyes had looked at him as if she understood everything and could make the pain go away with only her touch.

The double blows to his head must have addled his brain

but good. Zach shook himself, and swung his feet to the floor, groaning faintly as he stretched the muscles over his ribs. One leg had stiffened up as well, a reminder that fork lifts didn't mix well with Jaguars.

He limped over to the window and pushed it open. Another perfect summer day. The scent of wildflowers rushed in. Sunlight sparkled on the dew-misted grass. At the edge of the trees, near the propane tank, a deer stood, antlers in the air, its black nose twitching. As he watched, barely breathing, it shook its head, turned, and paced majestically into the forest.

Zach let out his breath, a sense of peace filling him. Yes, his instincts had been right. Here, away from the city, he could heal his battered spirit and gird his loins for his next battle with Eleni.

He pulled on the sweatpants Abby had lent him and opened the door. On the floor outside he found his own clothes, clean and neatly folded. Picking them up, he closed the door. After putting them on, he bundled the borrowed garments together for the washing machine.

In the bathroom he grimaced at his reflection. He looked as seedy as a street bum, with three days' growth of beard, the faint discoloration of old bruises and lopsided hair that hadn't quite filled in the shaved spot behind his ear. Only his eyes had improved. They looked back at him, clear, no longer bloodshot.

He washed his face, deciding to forget the shave for now. He'd have plenty of time once he made it to his own cabin. Another favor he'd have to ask of Abby Chance. Another debt he wouldn't be able to repay.

He found her in the kitchen, breaking eggs into a cast-iron frying pan. Bacon, crisp and brown, just the way he liked it, lay draining on a paper towel.

"Oh, good morning," she said, turning her head. "I was about to call you. Breakfast is almost ready."

She stepped briskly to the toaster as bread popped up. "Here, let me do that," he said, taking the knife from her and dipping it into the butter dish.

"Okay." She dropped another two slices into the toaster and pushed down the lever before returning her attention to the eggs. "How do you feel this morning?"

"Stiff." He flexed his shoulders. "Not bad, all things considered."

She reached past him to take plates from the cupboard. He stifled an urge to lean toward her, inhaling her fragrance. Honeysuckle, this morning. She must have cologne or bath powder in a variety of flower scents, light and delicate, only discernible at close range. It made him want to be closer still.

He must be losing his mind. Loneliness and disillusionment didn't excuse him. Abby wasn't the sort of woman for a casual affair. She was a forever woman, who would be supportive and loyal. Not like Eleni, who'd used and discarded him.

The thought of Eleni served its dampening purpose. He remembered his vow to let a lot of time go by before he involved himself with another woman. Especially one like Abby, who deserved better than his wounded psyche and cynical soul.

The next batch of toast popped up and he buttered the slices. "More?" he asked.

"Two are plenty for me, but if you want more…"

"No, that should be enough." He set the plate on the table, which was decorated with a vase of bright pink roses. Queen Elizabeth, he recalled. His mother had had one of the tall bushes in front of their first house. He wondered how his parents were doing on an extended holiday in their native Greece. Although they'd both been born in Canada, they still kept up ties to their ancestral country.

Abby came to the table with two plates loaded with eggs

and bacon. His mouth watered. "This is a feast. I would have thought a nurse would be concerned about cholesterol, and serve only dry toast and skim milk."

"Once in a while doesn't hurt." She smiled. "When did you last eat?"

"I don't remember. Probably the hamburger I picked up before I checked into the hotel yesterday. And I don't think I ate much of it. I felt too sick."

"You should have stayed in the hospital. You might have had another concussion."

"Dr. Scott said not. Just a bump."

"How did that happen?"

He shrugged. Truth was, he couldn't remember much about that evening at all. "Must have fallen and hit the steps. Or somebody hit me."

Her eyes widened and she laid her fork on the edge of her plate. "Is that possible?"

"Anything is possible."

"You mean you don't remember?"

"Not really. It's all a blur. Dr. Scott said it would come back to me."

She tore the corner off a slice of toast and thoughtfully chewed it. He could see the questions she wanted to ask, but she didn't voice any of them. Afraid of the answers, perhaps? After all, she didn't know him at all.

He applied himself to his food, noticing she ate her bacon and finished the slice of toast but pushed leftover bits of egg around her plate, as if she'd suddenly lost her appetite. Hungry, and not knowing what he would find at the cabin, he ate all of his and three slices of toast.

"Are you finished?" he asked when he was done.

"I guess so." She got up and refilled their coffee cups, stirring milk and sugar into her own.

Zach sipped a little of his, black with only sugar added. Pushing his chair back, he carried their plates to the sink, scraping hers over the garbage can. He ran hot water over them and the frying pan, adding detergent he found under the sink. Abby set her mug on the counter and threw the dishcloth into the soapy water. "You don't have to do that. You should be resting."

"I've rested enough. Besides, I haven't even thanked you. Don't the Chinese have a saying that if you save someone's life, they belong to you? Washing the dishes is a small thing."

"I didn't save your life." She picked up her mug and moved away from him.

He turned to face her, bracing his palms on the edge of the counter on either side of his hips. "You never know. I could have died out there. I could have gotten pneumonia, or have been crushed by a falling tree that had been struck by lightning."

She pursed her lips, not quite covering a smile. "Well, you'll be relieved to know that I'm releasing you from any obligation. It's my job to help people."

"Not on your days off. And not a recurring patient who can't stay out of trouble."

She shifted the mug from one hand to the other, keeping her gaze fixed on the floor in front of her. "How much trouble are you in?" she asked soberly.

"More than you want to know."

She looked up and he read sympathy in her eyes. For some reason it irritated him that she still saw him as her patient, not as a man. *Get real, Andros,* he told himself. *Just because you're lusting after her doesn't mean she's feeling the same thing. You're just two people thrown together by circumstance, and in an hour or two you'll be leaving and you'll never see each other again.* Somehow the thought depressed him.

The sound of a vehicle crunching on the gravel outside sent them both to the window. "Phone company," Abby said, noting the telephone logo on the side of the white van.

She opened the front door. Heat and the scent of pine on the fresh breeze greeted her as she stepped out into the sunshine.

"Morning, ma'am." The telephone lineman touched the bill of his cap. "A tree hit the line down the road."

"I know," she said. "I nearly drove into it last night, trying to get back to the gas station."

He frowned, puzzled. "Back?"

"I thought I'd need an ambulance."

His eyes sharpened. "That was a bad storm last night. Not fit to be out in. Was somebody hurt?"

Zach pushed himself away from the door frame and stepped onto the porch. "She was worried about me. But I'm okay," he said. "You wouldn't know how the road is up toward Sunset Cove, would you?"

"You won't be going up there anytime soon, I'm afraid. There's a major washout. It'll be several days before it's repaired. Lucky thing there's only a couple of cabins beyond it, and both were empty. Nobody stranded."

Except me, Zach thought. He was stranded here, unless he hiked through the woods, not a promising prospect. Dense rain forest, little visible trail, and a deep ravine stood between him and the solitude he sought. He was stuck. He should have been feeling frustrated but instead he found himself looking forward to getting to know Abby better. Solitude suddenly held less appeal than her company.

"Anyway," the lineman continued, "your phone should be working again. We reconnected the lines. I'll just test it." He punched out numbers on the handset on his belt. At once the phone began to ring inside the house. "All set, then." He swung back into the van, waving as he turned it and drove away.

Abby remained on the steps, arms crossed over her chest,

her hands cupped around her elbows, and watched until he was out of sight. "Well," she said, not meeting Zach's eyes, "I guess I'd better phone Jane. She'll be worried."

"Yes, do that." Was it her imagination or did amusement sparkle in his deep blue eyes? And how did she feel about spending more time in his disturbing company? She decided not to answer that, either.

Jane, having just returned home from night shift, answered the phone on the first ring. "Abby, I'm so glad you're all right. Any problems?"

She glanced around. Zach hadn't followed her inside. The door still stood open, letting in sunshine and birdsong. "Problems?" she repeated. Zach's warning not to tell anyone he was here echoed in her head. She ignored it. Even though he hadn't murdered her in the night, she still didn't know if she could trust him. Better if someone knew he was with her. And Jane wouldn't repeat it.

"Just one. About five eleven, too dark, too good looking, too haunted."

"What?" Jane yelped, so loudly that Abby had to jerk the phone away from her ear. "Not Zach Andros!"

"The same, big as life." She briefly filled Jane in on how she'd found him beside the road. "And now he can't get up to his place because the road is washed out. So I'm stuck with him unless I drive him back to town."

Jane laughed, so long and hard that Abby was tempted to lay the phone on the counter and abandon it. "Lucky you," Jane said when she finally could talk. "You can get to know each other over Scrabble or Monopoly or strip poker. There's lots of games in the hall closet. Although I could think of some better games to play with a man like him."

Abby looked around again. No Zach. "They think he killed his wife," she whispered into the phone.

"Ex, dear," Jane reminded her. "If he did, the world is well rid of her."

"Yes, but what if he really did?"

"Not a chance. Not Zach. There's not a violent bone in his body."

"Isn't there? You didn't see the way he glared at Eleni that day in the hospital. If looks could kill…"

"What does he say?" Jane asked.

"He says he didn't do it. But I don't know whether to believe him."

"Believe him, Abby. And enjoy him while you've got him. But don't count on it being permanent. Well, I'm off to bed. Got another shift this afternoon. 'Bye."

"'Bye, Jane."

"Wait," Jane called just as she was about to hang up. "One thing. Don't do anything dumb like falling for him. He has too much excess baggage."

"My thoughts exactly," Abby said, vowing to write the words in black marker and post them on the fridge door. Don't fall for a man who's just been through a messy divorce and is now in the middle of an even messier property settlement. "I'll remember. 'Bye, Jane. Oh, don't—" She broke off, realizing she was talking to a dead line. Jane had hung up before she could ask her not to tell anyone Zach was here.

That thought disappeared as Jane's warning echoed in her mind. *Don't fall for him.* The words might be kindly meant, but Abby had a sinking feeling that they had come too late. Hadn't she already started to tumble down the dangerous slopes toward…

Toward what? Lust? Maybe. Caring? Certainly. Trust. Not likely. Could it be love, illogical as that might seem?

Hardly, she told herself, knowing she was lying. Maybe she wasn't in love with him yet, but she was more than halfway there. She'd waited long enough, reaching the ripe old age of thirty-two without experiencing a love that touched her soul. She'd fooled herself briefly into thinking she'd been in love with David, whom she'd known forever. She hadn't understood the difference between love and friendship then. She did now, and had been careful. Not that she'd had much of an urge to fall in love.

Until now. And with a man who could hurt her. Who couldn't possibly return any of her barely awakened feelings. A man who was mired in the pain of the past, who would never trust another woman. She could tell herself this until she was blue in the face but knew she was only denying the inevitable. Love didn't listen to logic; it just happened.

And she was deathly afraid it was happening to her right now.

She moved over to the sink and dried the dishes, taking refuge in the practical. Then she squirted more soap onto a cloth and washed the coffee mugs and the pot, drying them as well, and putting them away. She finished by wiping the counter and the sink until they were spotless.

Zach hadn't returned.

She was out in the yard straightening plants battered by the storm and deadheading roses when the phone rang. Jane? Not likely. She'd be sleeping. Who else knew she was up here?

She wiped her hands on her already muddy shorts and ran into the house, snatching up the receiver. "Hello?"

"Abby, hi," David said. "Is Zach with you?"

She stifled a gulp of surprise. "Zach? Why would he be here?"

"Come on, Abby. This is me, your ex-husband and old buddy, who knew you through braces and first bras. I know he's there."

She gave up trying to think of convincing lies. "Okay,"

she admitted. "He's around somewhere. I think he went for a walk. How did you know he's here?"

"He called yesterday and told me he was going up to his cabin, with the stipulation I tell no one, even under torture." More or less what he'd told Abby, she thought in dismay. "They told me at the hospital that you were staying at your friend Jane's summer place, and I knew Zach's cabin is farther up the road. So I called Jane and after she got over the grumps from me waking her, she told me he was with you. How'd that happen? I thought I'd have to send you up there to give him a message."

"He tried to walk to the cabin last night."

"In that storm? Is he crazy?"

"Maybe," she said, amused. "You know him better than I do."

"Yeah, I guess. Another of your rescues, Abby?"

She stiffened, recalling his complaints about how much time she spent at the hospital during their marriage, often staying to comfort some sick child after hours. "What makes you say that?"

"Oh, Jane told me all about it." She heard him draw in a breath. "Don't hurt him, Abby," he said softly. "He's really vulnerable right now. Eleni—well, I guess I can't tell you. Client confidentiality, and so forth. Can you find him? I really need to talk to him."

"I'll go out and see. Hold on."

She walked around the house, checking his room in case he'd come in while she was in the garden. The bed was neatly made, but there was no sign of Zach.

Back in the hall, she opened the front door. Zach was just coming up the drive from the road, his face drawn and weary. He'd probably tried to go too far but she could see the walk had done him good. His movements were freer, less stiff than in the morning.

"You shouldn't overdo," she scolded mildly. "Exercise is good but not too much at a time."

"Yes, Mother," he said, grinning.

She ignored that although her heart jumped at little at the sight of that smile. Even unshaven and exhausted, he looked like every woman's dream. In fact, the tumbled curls sticking damply to his forehead and the dark stubble on his jaw gave him the sexy look of a man who'd just gotten out of bed. "David is on the phone for you."

The grin slipped, became a frown. "How'd he know where I was?" he said coldly. "You told Jane, I suppose."

Abby met his eyes without flinching. "Sorry. I forgot," she fibbed. She gestured toward the house. "Better get it. He's holding on. I'll be in the back garden."

He started to bound up the steps, but winced and slowed down, setting each foot carefully on the wooden planks. The ribs, she guessed. At the top, he turned to glare at her. She shrugged. So he was mad at her; he'd get over it.

OUT OF ABBY'S SIGHT, Zach hugged his arm to his side. He'd overdone it, walked too far, and then had no choice but to walk back. He'd rested for a while, but it hadn't helped much. The damn weakness. He couldn't understand it. His injuries weren't that serious.

Anger, directed at Abby, drove out the exhaustion. Blast her anyway. He'd asked her not to tell anyone, but she'd obviously told Jane the first chance she got.

Damn it, wasn't there any woman he could trust?

He picked up the phone, carefully tamping down the anger. "David, what's new? A guy can't get away from you, even out here."

"I take it you're in good hands."

An odd note in David's voice sent a frisson down his spine. "Is that a problem with you? That it's Abby?"

David gave a laugh that sounded forced. "Abby? No, not at all. I'd be happy for her if she found someone new."

Zach stifled the irritation that remark awoke in him. Was David implying that Zach couldn't be that someone? And hadn't he made up his own mind that Abby was off-limits? Why did it bother him that David thought the same? He might as well face reality. Abby didn't trust him either, or she wouldn't have talked to Jane about him. "I have to settle with Eleni first," he said obliquely. "You know that."

"Yeah, well, it's gotten more complicated. The cops want to talk to you again."

"I thought they decided I wasn't guilty."

"Just to talk," David assured him. He paused. For dramatic effect, Zach suspected; he'd seen him use the tactic in the courtroom. "Your blood and urine tests came back."

"Yeah? Must have been pretty boring." Was he joking to put off hearing what he was beginning to suspect? Suddenly he was scared, a chill tightening his stomach.

"What did you have to drink or eat when you went to see Eleni?"

"Just a ginger ale. Eleni went to the kitchen to get it. I heard her open the can. Why?"

"She slipped you a mickey, my friend. Some drug that causes you to forget what happens while you're under its influence. Sometimes known as the date-rape pill."

Chapter Four

Zach laughed; he couldn't help it. "Well, she didn't have her way with me. I'd know if she had."

"Yeah, I guess you would." The humor faded from David's voice. "But what else have you forgotten? Apparently this drug can make you do things you wouldn't ordinarily consider."

Goose bumps broke out on Zach's skin. He was glad David couldn't see him. "I left the house," he said tonelessly. "I woke up on the steps with a lump on my head. That's it."

"And that's what you told the police?"

"Yeah, what else would I tell them? It's the truth."

David sucked in an audible breath. "All of the truth?"

"What do you mean by that? It's all I remember. Eleni was alive when I left. In fact, she was yelling at me." His mouth turned down, and depression drizzled through him. "As usual."

"Okay," David said. "I believe you."

"What do the police want?"

"Just to talk, to check out any gaps in your story."

Zach's head began to ache. "Truth is," he muttered, "I wouldn't know if there were any gaps."

"What was that?" David said. "I can't hear you."

"Never mind. I'll come in as soon as I can."

"It's okay. Give yourself a little time. I can hold them off for a day or two." David paused, and Zach waited for him to mention Abby again, but all he said was, "I'll be in touch."

"Yeah, fine," Zach said. "That's what I pay you for."

David laughed and hung up.

"What do the police want?"

Zach jumped as Abby spoke behind him. "I thought you were working in the garden," he said.

"I'm finished. I came in to wash my hands." She ran water into the sink and pumped the little soap dispenser. "Do you need to go back to town?"

"You'd have to drive me. I don't want to spoil your holiday."

She dried her hands on a towel. "Not much of a holiday if the phone keeps ringing and you're hiding out."

"I'm not hiding out," Zach said emphatically. "The police just want to talk to me again, see if I remember anything other than what I already told them about the night Eleni disappeared. I was pretty dazed at the time."

"So, do you want to go back?"

He sat down heavily. "I don't know. David says there's no hurry. But, I don't want to put you out. I can call a taxi to come and get me."

"Well, there's plenty of room here. You can wait until Monday if you want. I have to be back at work for the evening shift then. Jane doesn't mind if you stay here."

He gritted his teeth. "Speaking of Jane, why did you tell her I was here, after I asked you not to?"

She looked him square in the eye. "She's my best friend. I just forgot to tell her not to mention it to anyone, okay? So sue me. She only told David. It won't go any farther. And what are you scared of anyway? That Eleni's ghost will come and get you? We don't even know if she's dead."

"No, we don't. But why else do the police want to talk to me again?"

"To finish their reports. Apparently the department is very fussy about reports."

"Tell me about it. Eventually the world will drown in reports. And we thought computers were supposed to eliminate all the paper." He shifted on the chair, debating whether he should have another cup of coffee after it had been sitting on the warmer pad all morning. Better not take the chance, he decided. His stomach didn't feel all that great.

"Tell me, Abby," he said conversationally, giving her as easy a grin as he could manage, "what happened between you and David? He seems like a nice guy, good-natured, the perfect husband type, I'd guess. And I may not know you that well, but from what I've heard you're a pretty super lady. So, what gives?"

She leaned back against the counter, staring down at her sneakers as if she found the smudges of mud on them fascinating. Finally, when he had almost given up on an answer, she raised her gaze to his. "We were friends who should have never become lovers."

The statement jolted through him. "And I guess you could say that Eleni and I were lovers who never became friends," Zach said with a candor that surprised him. He scowled, the memories of his stupidity still rankling. "No, I don't think it was ever love. More like lust gone mad. Anyway, whatever it was quickly deteriorated until we became bitter adversaries. Seems to me friendship is a good basis for marriage."

Abby shrugged. "It can be, I suppose, but there was no fire between us." Pink color ran up her cheeks, and her long, dark lashes swept down. "Maybe I'm just not meant to feel the passion books and movies talk about."

"Everybody should, once in their lives." Zach thought

of the early days with Eleni, when he had been so blind. Blind to her faults, seeing only the woman who could run a major corporation on her own, had done it since her father's illness forced his retirement. Blind to her two previous marriages, readily accepting her excuses of being too young the first time, and on the rebound the second. Six months after their wedding, the scales had fallen from his eyes—but that was another story, one he didn't intend to share.

"Have you?" Abby asked.

He scrambled to organize his thoughts. What had they been talking about? Oh, yes. Passion. Love. "No, no I haven't. And I'm not likely to, now."

"Neither am I."

Was it his imagination or did her voice sound bleak and sad? "You're still young, Abby," he said, aware he was mouthing platitudes. "You'll have your chance."

She pushed away from the counter, briskly turning to pour another mug of the black sludge that had been coffee earlier. "Not much younger than you. I'm thirty-two. And I've given up waiting for a knight in shining armor to ride up on a white steed." She spooned sugar into the coffee, and poked her head into the fridge for the cream. She poured in a goodly dollop and slammed the fridge door.

"You're not going to drink that, are you?" Zach asked in horror, his stomach clenching.

She stirred and drank, not even a grimace marring her face. "No worse than what we get at the hospital when I work Emergency."

"I thought you were supposed to heal the sick and injured, not add to their ranks."

The saucy grin that spread across her face made her look like a naughty girl. "Industrial-strength coffee keeps us tough."

"What made you go into nursing?"

She cradled the mug between her palms, hoisting her hips up on the counter, feet swinging gently. "Oh, I don't know. It was the only thing I ever did that my parents approved of. I should have become an auto mechanic if I'd really wanted to irritate them."

"Unhappy childhood?"

"Not really. Just rigid. My parents were in their forties when they had me. Big surprise. I think they were bewildered by a baby who grew up and became a big-mouthed, sassy kid who lived in a dreamworld half the time."

This was a surprise. Zach wouldn't have thought she was anything but practical. He filed away the information—not that he had any idea what he could do with it. He had to settle this thing about Eleni before he went on with the rest of his life. "Are your parents still alive?"

A faint shadow crossed her face. "No, they died when I was in nursing school."

"I'm sorry. Was it an accident?"

"No, not an accident. My dad died of cancer and several weeks later my mother had a stroke. It was as if they needed to be together. The odd thing is," Abby said, staring down at the dregs of her coffee, "they never showed it. They had separate bedrooms, and I never saw them kiss or hug each other. But it seems one couldn't live without the other."

Zach thought of his parents, always hugging each other and their two children. As a teenager, their easy affection had embarrassed him, especially when he'd walk into the kitchen or living room and find them kissing passionately, his father's hands on his mother's hips, holding her close. Now he understood it for what it was, the richness of their love, something he'd never experienced. And at thirty-five, long beyond hopeful youth, he was unlikely to. "Sometimes it's like that," he murmured.

Abby set down her mug with a businesslike click. "Okay,

let's get back to the original question. Do you want to go back to town today or stay until Monday?''

Elbows on the table, he sank his chin into his palms. Did he want to face the police and the probably ravenous media while he still felt as if his head was as fragile as an eggshell? On the other hand, wasn't staying here with Abby, alone, just as dangerous to his peace of mind?

Eleni had vanished. Maybe he should go back and start looking for her. At least talk to Lance, her sleazebag lawyer. He'd always had the feeling Lance was smarter than the unimaginative doorknob he appeared to be. If anyone knew where Eleni had gone, it would be Lance.

If that failed, maybe David could hire a private detective. And speaking of David—

He fixed his eyes on Abby. "You never answered my question. What happened with you and David?"

"Long story, pretty boring. I spent too much time at my job, and not enough time on my marriage. That's the short version. You don't want to know the details."

He couldn't detect any emotion behind the words or in her face. Which made him wonder whether she was genuinely indifferent, or hiding what she felt. He cast his mind back to that afternoon in the hospital. Even doped up with painkillers, he had been aware of her surprise at seeing David. He hadn't detected any disturbing undercurrents. Maybe she didn't harbor any ghosts from her marriage that would haunt a new relationship.

As if it mattered to him.

"I don't want to put you out by staying," he said.

Abby waved away his concern and shrugged. "It's okay with me. It's up to you."

"I guess I'll stay for the weekend, then," he said abruptly. "Do you want me to make lunch?"

She glanced at the clock on the wall. "It's early yet. And

a sandwich will do for me. I'm going for a walk first. Want to come?''

He schooled his face not to show that he was tempted. "No, I think I'll take a nap. I'm still a little wiped."

"That's natural." She eyed him and he sensed her shifting into nurse's mode. "You're pale, and there are lines around your mouth. Do you need a painkiller?"

He fingered the lump above his temple, wincing at the tenderness under the skin. "No, I'll live." Pushing back the chair, he got up. "See you later."

EXCHANGING HER MUDDY sneakers for leather hiking boots, Abby set off down the slope toward the lake. At the shore, she picked up a flat stone and skipped it across the tranquil water. Five bounces before it sank. Not bad for someone who hadn't skipped stones in years.

She sighed. What was she going to do with Zach all weekend? Why had she impulsively told him he could stay? She'd come to the country for no other reason than to find a few days of solitude, recharge her emotional batteries, and here she was getting involved with a man whose problems were more complex than she wanted to think about.

Where was Eleni?

Zach showed no signs of incipient or overt madness. She refused to believe that he could have been instrumental in Eleni's disappearance. On the other hand, hadn't Ted Bundy, the serial killer, looked as innocent as a schoolboy?

Still, Jane had vouched for Zach's nonviolent character. Abby latched onto that thought. Maybe someone was trying to frame Zach. He was a rich man; he must have enemies.

Abby left the lake behind. She tromped through the woods, her boots crunching on a blanket of last year's dead leaves. A gray squirrel scampered down the path ahead of her, hopping onto the low branch of a cedar and scolding shrilly. "Yes, I'll leave," she told it, with a wry smile. "I know I don't belong in your territory."

The squirrel cocked its head to one side, then turned, flicking its bushy tail, and scrambled up the scaly trunk. A moment later, she heard another join it, both of them screeching at each other, or maybe at her.

She edged past the cedar, climbing higher up the bluff above the lake. When she reached the top, she stood, feet braced. The wind, cool and fresh after last night's storm, belled out her shirt, drying the sweat on her face.

Far below, the lake lay like a mirror, reflecting the surrounding hills, green trees and white, rocky outcroppings. A trout leaped out of the water, snatched a passing fly, and sank below the surface. A widening circle of ripples sparkled like sapphires scattered across silk.

Unbidden, Abby's thoughts turned back to Zach. The walk and the stiff climb had eased her misgivings. It would be churlish to kick him out. The house was big enough. They could share it without getting in each other's way.

No matter what had happened with him and Eleni, Abby needn't fear him. She wasn't Eleni, and he wasn't a deranged killer who attacked at random. Abby was safe enough, especially behind her locked bedroom door.

Her mind less troubled, she headed down the hill toward the house. The sound of an engine droned through the trees. Squinting against the sun, she stared at the lake. A motorboat? They weren't prohibited, but most boaters stayed at the far end, where the marina and a village of cottages clustered around a little bay.

She saw nothing moving on the placid water. A heron sailed over her head and landed in a stand of bulrushes. Balanced on one stick-thin leg, it scanned the shallows for unsuspecting frogs.

Abby hurried down the path, sending stones bouncing ahead of her. Spotting the road below, she veered from the path and down an embankment, hanging on to weeds and saplings as she slipped and slid her way to the bottom. It was easier to walk on the hard dirt surface than to push her way through shrubs and blackberry vines on the overgrown path.

A car was definitely coming up the road, still out of sight, but nearing the last curve. Abby reached the house and waited on the porch. She glanced at the front door. Still closed. No sign of Zach. The blinds in his room were drawn, presenting an opaque face to the outside. Likely he was still sleeping, exhausted from the morning's exertions.

The sun glinted on chrome, dazzling her eyes. A car, engine purring, rounded the curve and neared the house, its suspension barely jolting on the ridged ruts. A black Mercedes, antique but lovingly kept, Abby noted. Hardly a speck of dust marred its glossy ebony paint—a miracle, given the condition of the road. Her gaze moving down to the tires, Abby almost laughed. Mud packed the treads, grounding it in reality.

The car stopped, the engine dying without so much as a hiccup. The driver's door opened and a woman got out. She wore a wrinkled khaki suit with a long skirt and multi-pocketed jacket. Wisps of her white hair escaped from the bun at her nape and clung to her soft cheeks.

"I must get air-conditioning in that car," she declared before ducking back inside to retrieve a purse the size of a small suitcase. Slinging the strap over her shoulder, she slammed the car door. She strode across the yard, her pace energetic and graceful, belying her age, which Abby guessed to be at least seventy.

Her body appeared thin and fit in the baggy clothes. Her eyes were a bright, inquisitive blue as she looked Abby up and down. She came up the porch steps, boots clumping on the wooden planks. Abby glanced down, and stifled a laugh. Under the long skirt, she wore red-trimmed, gray wool work socks.

The woman followed her gaze, lifting the edge of the skirt. Her strong, wiry legs were bare and lightly tanned. "Practical and comfortable," the woman said. "I've always made that my policy. Fashion be damned." She stuck out her hand. "You must be Abby. Is Zachary around?"

Abby flinched as the bony fingers crushed her hand. "Yes, I think he's inside."

"I'm here, Grandma," Zach said behind her, his voice full of dry emphasis. "How did you find me?"

He pulled her into a tight embrace, his hands coming up to cup her face as he planted noisy kisses on both her cheeks. He had to stoop to kiss her; the top of her head barely reached the middle of his chest. Turning with his arm around her waist, he said, "Abby, this is Katie Andros, my grandmother, the bane of my childhood. Also, the love of my life."

"And you've been a naughty boy, I hear," Katie said, frowning in mock severity. Her blue eyes twinkled and suddenly Abby knew why they'd looked familiar. Zach's were the same shape, although darker in color. "It's all over the newspapers. Just between us, what have you done with Eleni? Dropped her down a well someplace?"

Zach paled. "Grandma, you know me better than that." To Abby's ears, his protest sounded a bit lame. Did he have something to hide after all, just when she'd decided he was innocent?

Katie reached up and pinched his cheek. "Of course I do. But Eleni is enough to tax anyone's sanity, even a person of your unflappable composure." She winked at Abby, who offered a smile that felt distinctly forced. What was going on here?

"Well, children," Katie went on, linking her arm

through Zach's elbow, "I wouldn't say no to a nice cup of tea and maybe a sandwich. It was a tiring journey."

"How did you know where to find me?" Zach asked in an ominous tone. "Only David knows where I am."

"He's a man, isn't he?" Katie asked archly.

Zach groaned. "You got it out of him and he didn't even know he was giving you the information."

"That's right. At first he looked stubborn, denied hearing from you, but he let it slip that he'd talked to Abby. From there on, it was easy."

"How do you know David?" Abby asked. "I understand he's only worked for Zach for a short time."

"Oh, I had him do some work for me, several months ago. I was the one who recommended him to Zachary." Katie dropped her purse on the floor and sat down on a kitchen chair. "By the way, Abby, one reason I came up here was to thank you for saving Zachary's life."

Abby felt her face grow hot. She turned away to put the kettle on for tea. "I'm sure he would have survived. I only did what anyone would."

"Not every woman would have picked up a man she barely knew," Katie declared. "I'm very grateful you did. Head injuries can be tricky."

"Grandma, Abby's a nurse," Zach said. "She knows about head injuries."

"Of course she does. She's considered one of the best nurses on the hospital staff." She poked Zach in the shoulder. "And don't call me Grandma. Makes me feel old."

Zach draped an arm around her and hugged her close. "You'll never be old, Grandma."

Katie rolled her eyes, looking at Abby. "Young people these days. They won't listen, they give you no respect at all." She threw back her head and laughed, a bright, tinkling sound that echoed around the room. "And good for you, Zachary. Don't take any guff from anyone. Be your own man. You've always known that, except when it came to Eleni.''

''Yeah, Eleni.'' Zach sat down as if his knees had given out.

''Here you are, Mrs. Andros,'' Abby said, setting a cup of tea in front of her. ''Milk, sugar?''

''No, thank you, dear. And please call me Katie.''

Abby nodded. ''How about you, Zach? You look as if you could use a cup of tea.''

''Okay. Just plain.''

Abby turned to pour it. ''I'll make us some sandwiches. Are you planning to stay the night, Mrs., er, Katie?''

''If it wouldn't be too much trouble. I know Jane has plenty of room.''

Zach nearly choked on his tea. ''Is there anyone you don't know?''

''Well, I am on the hospital board. Naturally I know Jane. I talked to her only last week. She sang your praises, Abby, especially the way you got rid of Eleni when she came to scream at Zachary after the forklift accident. Has your car been repaired yet?''

Since the question was directed at Zach, Abby turned her attention to buttering bread. She added ham, mustard and mayonnaise, and slapped pairs of slices together, cutting them in half and stacking them on a plate.

''Next week, maybe,'' Zach said. ''They had to order some of the parts from England. Not too many Jaguars in wrecking yards that they can salvage fenders and doors from.''

''You should have gotten a Mercedes.''

''Then the parts would have had to come from Germany. Not much difference.''

Katie sipped her tea, her eyes lighting up when Abby set the plate of sandwiches on the table. ''Those look lovely. Thank you, dear. I'm absolutely ravenous.''

"You're always ravenous," Zach teased. "And you never gain an ounce."

"Exercise, dear boy. Exercise. I walk five kilometers every morning, rain or shine. I'm proud to say I'm seventy-six, and I can outwalk most people half my age."

"Well, you certainly don't look it," Abby said.

Katie tossed her a youthful grin, showing excellent teeth. "Thank you. I know you're flattering me, but it's nice to hear, just the same." She helped herself to a sandwich and took a healthy bite, chewing appreciatively.

Abby began to eat her own sandwich, more at ease than she'd been since she'd picked up Zach last night. Katie effectively provided both a character witness for Zach and a chaperone. Not that they needed one, but he'd come close to kissing her once already. She didn't want to risk the consequences if he followed up on the urge. She'd probably melt into a puddle at his feet and humiliate herself utterly and completely.

They finished eating. Zach carried the plates to the sink and poured more tea. Katie folded her hands together on the table and looked from one to the other. "So what are we going to do about Eleni?"

Abby started to push her chair back. "I'll leave you—"

Katie grabbed her hand and held her in place. "Stay. You're in this, too, whether you want to be or not. I think Eleni's up to some devious scheme of her own, just to get Zachary in trouble. And you might well get caught in the fallout."

Abby subsided in her chair, determined to keep an open mind. She didn't want to be involved, but Katie had given her no choice. No, finding Zach and picking him up had put her knee-deep in this mess. If she was brutally honest, she'd have to admit she'd gotten herself into this. So she might as well hear Katie out.

She glanced over at Zach. He sat, head bowed, his eyes

fixed on his tea, as if the dark brown liquid held the key to the chaos his life had become. As if he sensed her gaze, he lifted his dark lashes. Her heart wrenched at the pain in his eyes. And it would only get worse, she knew with eerie premonition.

"Zachary should never have married Eleni," Katie declared.

"Grandma, I've heard this a million times," Zach said wearily. "You were the only one who advised me against it. Everyone else thought it the match of the century, her established business marrying my struggling company."

"Well, you didn't struggle for long, did you?"

"Yeah, maybe I should thank Eleni for that. After the honeymoon was over, I spent so much time at work that it couldn't help but prosper."

"Eleni did the same, didn't she?" Katie asked. "Plus all those charity events she went to, and nightclubbing with her friends. No wonder you grew apart."

"I know. I should have listened to you, Katie."

Katie took a long sip of her tea. "Anyway, I saw Eleni last week at a hospital board meeting. She's on it, too, you know. She looked distinctly frazzled, not herself at all. And Lance met her outside with an urgent message. They went off together."

"Lance is a moron," Zach said flatly. "Besides, everyone knows he's Eleni's boy toy."

"Is he? I think he's smarter than he looks and that he knows exactly how to milk the goose that lays the golden eggs." Katie didn't seem to notice the mixed metaphor as she went on. "Lance is getting more and more power in Eleni's business enterprises. I wouldn't be surprised if he does a lot of deals without Eleni's knowledge."

"If she's given him that power—" Zach sounded bored.

Abby sat back, wondering where all this was going.

"I think Lance is taking advantage of her. He seems to

have an awful lot of money to throw around. He just bought one of those new BMWs, the kind in the James Bond movie.''

"Maybe she paid him a bonus.''

"Maybe. Or maybe he helped himself.'' Katie drank more of her tea, her face animated. "Have you made any progress in the property settlement with Eleni?''

"Is that what it was all about, that day at the hospital?'' Abby asked.

Katie patted her hand. "Probably. You see, the divorce was final months ago, but they're still hashing out the settlement since there is a lot of money involved on both sides, complicated by the fact that Zachary made most of his after the marriage began. He was doing okay before, but he became rich in the past five years.''

She was way out of her league, Abby thought with a weird little pang, no matter what Jane said about Zach being just a regular guy who happened to have a lot of money. At least, if Eleni didn't get her hot hands on most of it.

"The gist of it is, I don't trust Lance or Eleni, Zachary,'' Katie said. "And I think you'd be wise to watch your back.''

The phone rang, slicing through the tense silence that followed her words. Abby gestured for Zach to get it, since he sat closest.

"Zach here.'' Brief pause. "What can I do for you, David? You said there was no rush.''

Abby could hear the crackle of a voice on the other end. Zach listened, his face becoming grim. "Okay,'' he said, and hung up.

He turned to the two women. "We have to get back to town. They've found Eleni's car.''

Chapter Five

"Where?" Abby asked, swallowing hard, her throat muscles working.

"Was she in it?" Katie asked, typically ghoulish, Zach thought, amusement seeping through his numbed mind. Katie loved Stephen King's books.

"No, she wasn't in it," Zach said. "It looks as if it was stolen by joyriders. Somebody walking a dog saw it in a wooded area in Surrey, only a couple of kilometers from her house. They called the cops. David says it was in sorry shape, the usual for stolen cars, the inside trashed, fender dented, and the back bumper nearly torn off. The police have taken it in to be analyzed." Dread filled him as he considered what that would entail. If blood was found in the car, he'd be toast. He might as well turn himself in and confess.

Confess to what? Having bad dreams? Wishing Eleni would leave him alone? He hadn't done anything.

Had he?

He became aware of Katie's eyes on him, a little frown etching a line above her straight, patrician nose. The line smoothed out and she got up, lifting her purse from the floor and settling the strap on her shoulder. "If they want you in town, we'd better get started back. You know how I hate driving in the dark."

Zach pushed back his chair, getting to his feet. "You won't have to drive, Katie. I'll do it. I'm sure Abby will be glad to have her quiet weekend."

Abby smiled, although he could see tension at the edges of her mouth. "I'm afraid after this it'll seem too quiet. You're welcome to come back when you're finished in town."

"Thanks," Zach said. "But I think it's time I stopped running."

"Well, be careful of that head. You've got a bad bump there."

"Are you absolutely sure you're up to driving?" Katie asked, reaching up to run her fingers into Zach's hair, gently probing the tender area.

He forced a smile. "I'm fine, Grandma. And as you say, it's still daylight. We'll take it slow."

He had nothing to pack, nothing to keep him longer, but suddenly he was reluctant to leave. It wasn't the solitude, although that had given him a needed breather. No, it was Abby, her gentle, undemanding presence, her generous willingness to give him the benefit of the doubt when he knew the press and the police would be waiting to draw, quarter, and hang him.

Katie cleared her throat noisily, and he realized he'd been staring at Abby as if he were memorizing her. He shook his head to clear it.

Katie took Abby's hand in hers and squeezed it. "I enjoyed meeting you. We must have lunch one day. May I call you?"

"Of course. It's been a pleasure to meet you," Abby replied.

"I'll be waiting outside," Katie said.

Zach and Abby were suddenly alone. He took the hand she extended. It snuggled intimately into his palm, her fingers cool, strong, the kind of fingers a man wanted to soothe his pains. "I hope we'll meet again, under more pleasant circumstances," he said, hoping she didn't hear the catch in his throat.

To his astonishment, she leaned forward and dropped a light kiss on his cheek. "Be careful. I don't want to see you in Emergency again."

He let go of her hand, and placed his palm on his chest. "I promise." He turned to go, then spun around. "Oh, hell," he muttered, and grabbed her around the waist. Pulling her against him, he kissed her, inhaling the sweet honeysuckle scent. The rich taste of her swam in his brain as she willingly opened her mouth under his. An erotic fantasy of white sheets and sunshine swirled through his head. He wanted her, not here, with his grandmother just outside, but somewhere private, where they could lock out the world, where he could forget the terror that haunted him. His body tightened, and he pulled away, dropping his arms to his sides.

For a long breathless moment, they stared at each other. Finally Abby spoke, her voice unsteady. "Now, you'd *really* better not show up as a patient again. That was most unethical."

He burst into laughter, the last thing he would have expected. "I'll try not to." He tapped his finger against her nose. "Goodbye, Abby. Thanks for everything."

LONG AFTER the purr of the car engine faded into silence, Abby stood in the middle of the kitchen. He was gone. An honest man, he hadn't made any promises. She wondered if she would ever see him again, or if she would only read about him in the newspaper.

Moving at last, chiding herself for daydreaming about an unattainable man who was, after all, little more than a stranger, she carried the tea mugs to the sink and washed them. Afterwards she went for another walk, up the road toward his cabin, turning back only when the washout prevented her from going farther.

Back at the house, she made supper and watched the news. Zach didn't appear, although the lead story featured the discovery of Eleni's abandoned BMW. "Ms. Mavrakis is still missing," chirped the perky news anchor. A photo of Eleni in an upswept hairdo flashed on the screen. "The missing woman is thirty-seven years old, five feet, six inches tall, a hundred and twenty pounds. She has dark auburn hair and green eyes. Anyone with information on her whereabouts is asked to call city police."

Abby went to bed at eleven, taking the mystery novel she intended to finish reading. Somehow it didn't have the same impact now, compared to the real mystery in her life.

Not *her* life, she reminded herself sternly. Not anymore.

On Sunday morning she drove around to the other side of the lake and attended the small church there, afterwards lunching at the resort hotel nearby. The afternoon dragged. She found the lake still too cold for swimming; it tended not to warm up until nearly August. She hiked in the woods until she was exhausted, falling asleep as soon as she fell into bed that night.

She woke to a dull, cloudy Monday, feeling wired and edgy. So much for the relaxation she'd expected of the weekend. She took a shower, ate a bowl of cornflakes, and packed her bag. She might as well go back early; at least in town she had things to do.

Driving down the mountain, she told herself that she didn't care what happened to Zach, that it was out of her hands. But she knew she lied.

ON TUESDAY MORNING Katie phoned. "I didn't wake you, did I?"

"Hello, Katie. No, I was on evening shift last night. Home by midnight."

"Oh, good. I hope your weekend wasn't spoiled by the weather yesterday. And wouldn't you know it, it's beautiful again today." She paused to take a breath. "I know it's short notice, but can we meet for lunch? My treat."

"No problem," Abby said promptly, while a scolding little voice inside her head asked: *Why prolong the agony? He's not for you. Shut up,* Abby told it. *This is Katie,* not Zach. "I'm scheduled for the evening shift at the hospital again."

"That's fine. We can meet at noon. Shall we say at Jimmy's Place? See you then."

"I THINK ZACHARY'S in more trouble than he'll admit," Katie announced after they had ordered their food and were sipping iced tea. They sat out on the restaurant patio, shaded from the hot sun by large umbrellas. Katie wore a loose, flowered dress and flat sandals. The ubiquitous, satchel-sized purse hung from her chair.

"Why do you think that?" Abby asked, her heartbeat speeding up. "There's been nothing on the news."

"Well, he's not answering his phone, which probably means the news media have been hounding him. I finally drove down to his house this morning. Got him out of bed. He should have thanked me for it, especially since I came with doughnuts and coffee. He certainly hadn't been sleeping, judging by the way he looked. And he hasn't shaved for days." She shook her head. "That's not like Zachary at all."

"Have the police talked to him?"

"Of course they have, but there's not much they can do as long as she's missing. There's no evidence of foul play."

Katie made an indignant sound in her throat. "Same old story, nagging him to reveal what he's done with Eleni." Her voice dropped. "Or her body. They don't believe he doesn't know anything. Why would he? Eleni is an adult.

Even when they were married, she had her own life. She does what she wants. Always has, and I'm sure she's not about to change now.''

"I'm surprised that the police are so active in this case," Abby said. "Usually the person has to be gone for quite some time before they issue a missing-person report.''

"It *has* been six days," Katie pointed out. "But part of their interest is because she maintains a high profile in the community. She had engagements scheduled that she hasn't shown up for. And then there are Lance Stuart, her lawyer, and Gretchen Myers, her housekeeper. Gretchen still maintains she saw Eleni bleeding on the living-room floor. Lance is putting on the pressure, insisting that the police arrest Zachary.''

Abby's hand shook. Ice cubes clinked in the glass she clutched in her fist. "Is there any evidence?''

"Not a shred, thank God. They're still going over the car, but I'm betting they won't find anything there either. I believe they've gone back to the house and scraped at the floorboards, trying to find proof of Gretchen's story. Silly woman. Eleni was not an easy woman to work for—maybe Gretchen finally gave in and did her in herself.''

Katie looked up, smiling at the waitress who brought their food. "Never mind for now. Let's eat.''

Katie dug in as if this was the last meal she'd ever eat. Envying her ability to consign the stresses of her life to separate compartments, Abby picked at her teriyaki chicken. Maybe that composure came with maturity. Maybe Abby would have acquired it by the time she reached Katie's age.

For now, her thoughts churned like water in a washing machine.

"You know, you'd be good for Zachary," Katie announced when she'd finished her vegetable stir-fry and declined dessert. "You're levelheaded and compassionate, two things Eleni wouldn't understand if they hit her over the head." She clapped her hand over her mouth, chuckling. "Oops, shouldn't have said that. That's what Gretchen insists happened to Eleni. Says she was bleeding from a head wound. Personally, I think Gretchen's been watching too many movies and dreamed the whole thing."

To which Abby had no real answer. "Tell me about your charity work," she suggested, thinking to steer the conversation to a safer subject.

Katie gestured impatiently. "Boring stuff, unless you're involved in it. Tell me what it's like to be a nurse. That's what I should have done, but I got married instead. In those days, a woman wanting a career meant going against everyone's expectations. And I hardly spoke English, coming over from Greece as a teenage bride. But we did okay." Her eyes softened in nostalgia. "We had fifty-one good years. More than most people get."

"My marriage didn't last," Abby said. "I think it died of boredom."

"Better boredom than to beat it to death," Katie said. "Eleni and Zach never should have married. Both families wanted it—except me—but no one listened to me. Grannies are supposed to sit in the corner and knit." She laughed. "I've never knitted in my life."

She sipped at her wine, leaning back in her chair and crossing her legs. "It was a big wedding at one of the finest hotels in Vancouver, flowers, eight bridesmaids in matching dresses. They looked like pairs of bookends in fuchsia taffeta. Too much money, too ostentatious. In my day, people had weddings where you roasted lamb, danced, and had a good time. Nobody cared which designer made your clothes. I saw Zach's face at the reception. He was clearly wondering what he was doing there. The groom often seems redundant at these society affairs."

Katie closed her eyes for an instant. "I was right about

the marriage, and I've wished a thousand times that I hadn't been. Zach deserves to be happy. I hoped he would be once he was free of Eleni. But now he's more entangled in her clutches than ever. Never mind. Tell me about nursing.''

ZACH SWUNG the sledgehammer and knocked another cracked brick out of the fireplace. He'd known the house needed work when he bought it—''wants tender loving care'' was how the real estate agent had put it. *Care* wasn't the word, he'd quickly discovered. A bulldozer would have been kinder and gentler, put the thing out of its misery. A solid foundation and beautiful maple millwork had blinded him to its faults. Repairing rotten floor joists, fried wiring and leaky, outdated plumbing had occupied him and a team of skilled technicians for months.

The fireplace turned out to be hopeless, beyond saving. A severe leak around the flashing had caused water to seep into the masonry. In winter it had frozen and cracked nearly every brick.

New roofing insured that no further damage would occur. And he had the rest of the summer to make the house livable. As for restoring it to its former glory as a wealthy mining executive's country house, that would follow. Zach didn't want grandiose decor. It would be his home, where he would make his own memories.

Ruthlessly he shut out the recollection of Eleni's contempt for his relatively modest house.

He swung the hammer again, gaining satisfaction from the stretching of his muscles, the honest ache in his shoulders that came from hard work, not stress. Sweat dripped from his hairline into his eyes. He paused, leaning on the hammer, and pulled an already damp handkerchief from his pocket. He mopped his face, then ran the cloth over his bare chest, probing gingerly at the tender spot over his ribs.

Almost healed. They only bothered him when he didn't exercise.

He squinted at the sunlight pouring through the cracked, dusty windows. Hot out today. If he was smart, he'd go down and get a drink from the cooler, then rest for an hour.

Instead, he stuffed the handkerchief into his back pocket, and adjusted the dust mask over his mouth and nose. If he made himself tired enough, maybe he'd sleep tonight and not dream.

He picked up the hammer and slammed it against the brick. Clouds of dust eddied around him, painting another layer on the window glass. This had once been the master bedroom; he thought he'd use it for a den when he finished the renovations.

The sound of an engine sent him to the window. He leaned out through the open casement, craning his neck to peer around the corner of the house. A familiar white van lurched up the broken concrete driveway. The heating company, come to install the new furnace. He stripped off the mask, tossing it on the pile of broken bricks.

Keeping to the side of the room, he headed for the door. He glanced at the floor, at the water stains etching the hardwood planks. That spot was weak, one of many where the joists needed replacing. He should mark it with tape or something. If someone stepped there, they might fall through. With the high ceiling, it was ten feet down to a ceramic tile floor below.

One more thing to attend to, he told himself as he ran down the curving staircase. The house was like a vampire, sucking time, money, sweat and blood.

The electrician's van arrived behind the heating company's. Zach greeted the men, old acquaintances by now, if not friends. In fact, he'd gone out for a beer with them several times, and given them work on some of his commercial construction projects.

"I guess you know where it goes," he joked. "I'll be upstairs if you need me."

He grabbed a soda from the cooler, and popped the top, downing half the can at one gulp. He took a deep breath and finished the fizzy liquid, tossing the empty can into the blue recycling box. It clanked on top of the other cans. He'd have to empty the box soon. No garbage pickup out here.

Soon the rhythmic boom of a car stereo startled the crows who gathered on the edge of the roof. Zach swallowed a grin. The sound system in the approaching little beater cost more than the whole car. Mercifully, the booming died along with the engine. Silence reverberated in the still, hot air. Two lanky teenagers got out of the car and ambled over to the cooler, snagging a couple of cans.

"Hey, Zach, how's it going, man? Cops been around?"

"Yeah, looking for you," Zach said, deadpan.

One of the kids, Aaron, tensed, his gaze darting around the cluttered yard. "No way, man."

"Yeah, for gross insubordination," Zach said. "And if you don't know what that word means, it's a reminder to finish school."

"Oh, we're going back in September," the other boy, Chris, assured him. "After slaving here all summer, it'll seem like a holiday."

Zach set the boys to work with the power sanders, showing them how to manipulate the heavy machines so that the old finish came off the floors without creating gouges. Two sanders, a small rotary machine for the edges, and a bigger one for the larger expanse of the floor.

This was their third day on this particular job and they were getting pretty good at it. And they complained less than they had during the heavy labor of roofing.

Out in the hall, he found the electrician adding breakers to the fuse box. "Shouldn't take long, Zach," the man said. "You'll be in here, with everything done, before winter."

Winter was months away. Zach wasn't sure if the news should cheer him or depress him. "I certainly hope so. If nothing else goes wrong."

"Shouldn't. Oh, I'll have to shut off the main breaker for a few minutes later."

"No problem," Zach said.

The electrician tightened a screw. "Carpenters are coming next week to do the floor joists, aren't they?"

"Should be. They had to special-order the lumber. It's hard to find two-by-twelves that long anymore." Zach glanced at his watch, rubbing away the white dust from the crystal before he could read the time. Two o'clock already. He hadn't eaten lunch.

"Guess I'll go out for a sandwich," he said. If he went through a drive-in, he wouldn't have to wash and change. "Keep an eye on those kids for me, will you?"

"Sure thing."

A crash reverberated through the house. Zach's heart stopped, stealing his breath, then resumed at triple speed. An eerie buzzing filled his ears, and the room tilted beneath his feet.

A gnarled hand landed on his arm. "Zach, are you all right?"

Zach swallowed his heart back into his chest. "Yeah, I guess so. What was that?"

"I don't know, but you turned as white as a ghost."

"Too much stress lately." Zach tried a laugh that sounded like a croak instead. Forcing his shaky legs to move, he went into the next room. Both boys sat on the floor near the wall, laughing like idiots at the sight of the rotary sander head lazily swirling across the room on its own. The heavy unit lay on its side next to them, the source of the crash.

"Haven't I told you guys to check the retaining nut once

in a while?'' he yelled, adrenaline still pumping. "It works loose and needs to be tightened.''

Their laughter died. Scrambling to their feet, they stared at him as if he'd grown horns. "Sorry, man. Guess I forgot.'' Aaron, his eyes warily fixed on Zach's face, retrieved the round sander disk and reinstalled it, tightening the bolt with the wrench attached to the power cord.

Zach dragged in a long breath, raking his fingers through his hair. Grimacing at the dust that sifted around him, he crouched and checked the nut. "Okay,'' he said gruffly, clapping Aaron on the shoulder. "Should hold for a while. But watch it, okay?''

"Sure, man.''

Aaron started the machine and moved it slowly across the floor. Zach turned to leave the room, ducking his head as he saw Chris and Aaron exchange glances.

"What's up with him? He's sure jumpy lately.'' Chris's voice carried clearly over the sound of the sander as Zach reached the bottom of the stairs. The roar of the second machine drowned out Aaron's reply.

Just as well, Zach thought. He didn't need to hear two teenagers playing amateur psychologist. And they were right. Any little thing set him off these days, although he usually managed to keep his temper under control.

Tuesday today. Eleni had been missing for six days.

He pulled on his shirt and headed out to the car he'd rented. The Jag was still in the body shop. Turning onto the road, he debated buying road insurance on the MG stored in the garage behind the house. No, better leave it there, out of the rubble and dust. He'd worked so hard on the restoration the past two years, he didn't want to risk damage to the bright red finish. And the tiny trunk wouldn't be much use when he needed to pick up building materials.

In town, he saw a gray VW Rabbit ahead of him in the fast-food pickup lane. A car like Abby's. He'd tried not to think of her since he'd left on Saturday. But every once in a while, her quiet face would appear behind his eyelids, especially when he lay sleepless in bed at night. Or the taste of her mouth would echo through his body like a well-loved song.

If his own treacherous memories weren't enough, his grandmother reminded him. Since Saturday, she'd phoned him twice on some pretext, and somehow brought Abby's name into the conversation. Katie didn't have a subtle bone in her body.

"Well, Grandma, I'm not buying," he said aloud, earning himself a puzzled look from the fast-food cashier.

"A burger and fries. Extra onions on the burger, and a side of mayo," she said. "That'll be four seventy-five."

He paid her, drove to the edge of the lot and turned off the ignition. He wolfed down the burger and took his time with the fries, dipping them into the little paper cup of mayonnaise and savoring every fat-filled calorie.

He wondered what Abby was doing. Was she working? Or was she sleeping off a night shift? Unbidden, the thought of her lying in bed, her face flushed and peaceful, came into his mind.

He crushed the food containers and stuffed them back into the bag. Damn it, she was haunting his days.

Just as what could have happened to Eleni haunted his nights.

"WELL, HOW WAS your lunch?" Jane asked Abby as they met in the cafeteria for dinner break later that evening.

"Lunch?" Abby said innocently. "What lunch?"

"With Zach Andros's grandmother. She's a neat lady, isn't she?"

"Yes, she is," Abby agreed. "How did you know about lunch?"

"She called me for your phone number, early this morning."

"So that's how she got it. I'll be glad when the new phone book is out. At least I'll be in it."

"You shouldn't move so often," Jane said.

"I only moved once. It was just at the wrong time and missed the phone book."

"So, talk," Jane said. "Did she give you all the low-down on Princess Eleni?"

Abby hesitated. Usually she and Jane shared everything, working out problems and finding solutions. The only time she hadn't was when she and David had separated, possibly because she didn't want to be told she was wrong. Oddly, when Jane heard Abby had found her own apartment, she hadn't said anything either way, and she and her husband remained friendly with David as well as Abby.

"Not much," Abby said. "The police are still looking for her."

"Come on, Abby, I can read that in the newspaper." Jane stirred her coffee. "But then, why would you talk about Eleni when you could discuss the gorgeous Zach?"

"I think Katie has me pegged as Zach's next wife," Abby blurted. Horrified, she clamped her mouth shut and glanced nervously around at the surrounding tables. Most were fortunately unoccupied, since it was nearly eleven. No one had overheard her. "Or maybe significant other," she finished lamely.

Jane burst into laughter. "That's Katie for you. Always matchmaking. I think that you'll find Zach makes up his own mind. He loves her dearly, but he knows when to ignore her."

Abby huffed out a breath of relief. "That's the impression I got, too. Besides, why should he be interested in me?"

Jane cocked her head to one side, her eyes twinkling. "Why shouldn't he be?"

Abby mulled over her own question as she went back to work. Zach needed a new wife like he needed a dose of bubonic plague. The worst thing he could do would be to marry again before the dust had settled from his last marriage.

And Abby would be the last person he would pick. He hadn't even shown any personal interest in her. A little jolt of electricity zipped through her body. That kiss, lush, full bodied—she could still taste it. She hadn't been kissed like that since—maybe never. David had always satisfied her, but it had never been hot and mindless.

That kiss hadn't shown indifference. She had felt the reaction of his body. It must mean something.

On the other hand, men often didn't need a lot of stimulation. He might have kissed her only out of gratitude. And he'd pulled away quickly enough, and made no mention of seeing her again. He didn't care about her.

Or did he? The question dogged her.

Chapter Six

Blood. So much blood. It pooled under her head. He couldn't see her face, her dead face. Her hair, dark auburn this week, lay in tangled curls over the wound. He crept closer, the room shifting and blurring before him. He shook his head. Dizzy. He couldn't figure it out; he'd only had half a can of ginger ale.

He knelt at her side, taking her limp hand in his. No pulse. The fingers felt cold and clammy, like seaweed. He reached to push back her hair, found he couldn't. Dread of what he'd see paralyzed him.

He staggered to his feet, taking a step back. His shoe slipped. He looked down. Blood, black in the dim light from the flashlight lying on the mantel. The battery almost spent, it emitted only a ghostly glow.

Falling to his knees, he crawled to the phone. He picked it up, using the built-in light to read the numbers. He pressed them but no reassuring beeps emerged from the receiver. Dead.

As dead as the woman lying on the Aubusson rug, obliterating the soft shades of pink and green with her blood.

Scattered drops of rain hit his face. He stared up at the sky, at the clouds flitting across the face of the moon. His car stood on the driveway. He fumbled in his pocket for the keys, grunting when the pointed metal bit into his palm.

He swayed on his feet, struggling to gather his scattered thoughts.

There was the car. He had the keys. What was he supposed to do with them? He knew if he thought about it, it would come to him. Somehow, his brain seemed to have slowed down. His knees collapsing, he sat down on the shallow step. If he could sleep for a moment, the deadly fog would clear.

A scream shattered the night, slicing through his groggy senses.

He jerked up, his body coiled for attack, his arms instinctively coming up to protect his head. Biting down on the inside of his cheek, he opened one eye. The sawhorse cast a shadow across the floor. The cot creaked beneath his weight.

His own house.

The scream continued, echoing through his head, high-pitched, desperate, pulsing on and off. A faint orange light flickered through the room.

He leaped to the floor as if he'd been shot. His momentum sent the cot crashing against the wall. Bits of loose plaster drifted down like snow, adding to the litter on the floor.

Zach scrabbled in the darkness for his jeans, yanking them on and clawing the zipper up. Snatching a flashlight, he tore down the stairs, his feet hitting only every third tread. He flung himself through the hall, slowing momentarily when he bashed his hip on a crate near the back door. He fumbled with the dead bolt, the shriek of the smoke alarm piercing his eardrums.

He wrenched the door open, and froze in his tracks.

Too late. Too late. The words echoed through his brain. As if to confirm his conclusion, the screaming smoke alarm in the garage died abruptly. Angry red flames licked hungrily around the edges of the garage door.

One of the cordless phones lay near his hand. He punched in 911 and tersely gave the address. Then he stared at it in disbelief. In his dream the phone had been dead.

The acrid stench of smoke filled the night, gagging him. This wasn't a dream.

Dragging the garden hose, he ran across the wet grass to the garage. He turned on the water. The pitiful stream sizzled against the hot building, vaporizing instantly. He grabbed the door handle and swore as it burned his palm and refused to turn. Too late to get the keys. Sometimes he forgot to lock the doors, but not tonight. Groaning in despair, he let go and ran the water over his hand to take away the sting.

Dropping the hose, knowing it was useless, he went around to a window. He picked up a two-by-four and swung it against the glass. Fragments exploded inward, but the sudden wave of heat drove him back. He couldn't get in.

Running back to the house, he grabbed a heavy plaid shirt from a hook next to the door. Outside, he soaked it with the hose and draped it over his head. He managed to reach the window. Inside, the MG sat in a lake of fire. As he watched, eyes burning from smoke and heat, the shiny red paint he'd lovingly buffed, started to curl and turn black. In a moment, it was over, the car disappearing behind a wall of flame.

Zach stumbled back, scrubbing his hands over his face. The acrid odor of singed hair filled his nostrils. He swallowed as his stomach heaved. The shirt was almost dry, giving off the stench of scorched wool. He ripped it off his head, tossing it aside.

A new sound carried over the crackle of the fire, a siren wailing its warning. The firefighters were on the way, but they wouldn't be able to save the garage. He could only be grateful that there was no wind to drive the fire toward the house.

A loud whoosh and another wave of searing heat sent his gaze upward. Flames leaped through the roof, swiftly eating away the asphalt shingles he'd put up only last month.

The fire truck roared up beside him and stopped. Two yellow-clad firefighters efficiently unrolled a hose and sent a geyser of water over the flames. The fire hissed and squealed, as if fighting death. Smoke billowed, stealing breath from Zach's lungs and driving him back behind the truck.

In ten minutes it was over. The black skeleton of roof rafters rose starkly against the moonlit sky. Ignoring the firemen's warning, Zach moved close to the garage, aiming his flashlight into the open door. His MG's tires were still smoldering. Only the frame of the car remained, a tangle of black, twisted metal.

"You've got insurance, I trust," one fireman asked.

"Yes, of course," Zach said dully. The storage insurance on it would pay the value of the vehicle but it couldn't begin to compensate for the hours he'd labored to make it a work of art. It couldn't replace the memories. The MG had been more than a car; it had been a lifesaver just when his marriage was going to hell.

Now it was gone.

The other fireman joined them, carrying a roll of yellow tape. "I'm going to have to ask you to stand back while I secure the area. Someone will be by in the morning to check out the cause."

"Arson, isn't it?"

The man gave Zach a sharp look. "Why do you say that?"

"I'm not stupid. I didn't keep anything inflammable in the garage and there was no gas in the tank of the car. The wiring in the building was brand-new. Besides, if it had started in the wiring, it would have smoldered in the wall for a while. The smoke alarm would have gone off before flames took hold.''

''You had a smoke alarm in your garage? Most people don't, because of the nuisance of it going off every time you start a car.''

''I had it hooked up to the house, so I'd be able to hear it in there.'' Zach clenched his fists, wanting to scream. He coughed instead, agonizing spasms lacerating his throat. ''But it didn't work. I still didn't make it in time, damn it.''

''If there'd been wind,'' the fireman said, ''it could have saved your life. Don't touch anything, will you?''

Zach watched, his mind numb, as they furled tape around the burned-out shell. ''By the way,'' the tallest fireman said as they rolled up the hose and secured it on the truck, ''to answer your question, yes, I'd guess it was arson. Have you had a look at your garden shed over there?''

''No. Why?''

''The padlock's been removed with bolt cutters. We found a plastic gas container near the garage wall, under the broken window.''

''Broken window?'' Zach said. ''I broke the window.''

''The window on the other side's broken as well, and it doesn't look as if it's the result of the fire. I'd say someone poured your lawn-mower gas inside and tossed a match after it. In seconds, the whole garage was fully involved.''

He looked closely at Zach as he coughed again. ''Are you sure you don't want me to call an ambulance? You should have your lungs checked.''

''No, I'm okay.''

Shrugging, the fireman swung himself up into the truck and started the engine. Above the rumble, he called down to Zach. "Phone your insurance company in the morning. We'll be giving you a detailed report later."

The truck turned ponderously, rolling over the wet, trampled grass. Halfway down the driveway, the brake lights flashed as it stopped. Zach saw a white police cruiser pull up alongside the truck. The driver exchanged a few words with the fireman. The truck drove off.

Zach waited, bracing himself for another encounter with the law. At least this time they couldn't suspect him. Or could they? He choked on a bitter laugh. The way things were going lately, they'd accuse him of setting fire to his own garage for the insurance.

Well, if he had, he would have made damn sure his antique car on which he'd lavished hundreds of hours of time and sweat wasn't inside.

"I'm Constable Powers," the cop said civilly enough.

"Did someone call you?" Zach asked.

"No, I heard about the fire on the radio. Are you all right?"

Aside from his burning eyes, his raw throat, and his lungs feeling as if they'd been scoured by a blowtorch, he was just peachy. "I'm okay," he said. He coughed harshly.

The cop looked at him closely. "Are you sure? You probably inhaled some of the smoke. And your hands could use first aid."

Zach held them open. On his palm, a red welt ached dully. He noticed blood seeping sluggishly from a cut near his thumb. Must have done that when the window shattered.

He coughed again, hacking until his throat seized and he felt as if he were choking. Wheezing, he fought to get his breath. The cop took him by the arm and led him to the cruiser, opening the door so Zach could sit down. "What you need is the emergency room and a whiff of oxygen. Come on, I'll take you. Where are your keys? I'll lock up your house."

"On a hook, just inside the door." Too spent from the coughing episode to argue, Zach stayed where he was. *Arson*. The word throbbed in his ears, beating in sync with his heart. Who had done it?

The cop came back and handed him his keys. Zach tried to stand up, to get into the car. He couldn't move; his legs seemed to have no connection with his brain. Humiliated, he let the cop help him to face forward. He pulled the seat belt across his chest, fastening it with trembling hands.

"Always hits you afterwards," Powers said cheerfully, starting the car. "You're high on adrenaline and then you just flake out. It's like paralysis. I remember one time in a hostage situation, after the guy was handcuffed, the children safe, I threw up in the flower bed next to the house. Couldn't help it. I had to get someone to drive my car back to the station."

Don't talk about it, Zach begged silently, his stomach suddenly heaving. *I don't want to hear any more.*

He let his head fall back, and the short ride to the hospital passed in a blur of street lamps, headlights, and occasional brake lights. Not too many cars out at four-thirty in the morning. In the east, the sky lightened to a delicate green.

The hospital emergency sign glowed red against the gray dawn as they pulled up outside. Powers helped Zach inside, seating him on a molded plastic chair. A sleepy-eyed nurse at the desk listened to the policeman's report, tapping the information into a computer. Another nurse came up and took Zach's arm, helping him to a chair in front of the desk. "Do you have your Care card?"

Luckily his wallet was in the back pocket of his jeans. Fingers thick and clumsy, he pulled it out, extracting the proof of insurance. Powers gripped his shoulder for a moment. "You'll be all right now."

He strode out, his boots clumping on the tiled floor. The doors swished shut behind him. The question of how he

would get home flitted through Zach's mind, then was lost
as the nurse asked for his name, address, and date of birth.

He answered mechanically, his head nodding occasionally. It felt too heavy for his neck; in fact, his whole body
seemed weighted by some foreign substance that had invaded it. By the time the nurse had gathered all his partic-
ulars, he could barely speak, his total attention focused on
remaining upright on the chair.

Just when he thought he'd collapse in an ignominious
heap on the floor, a dark head poked around the corner.
"Zach, what are you doing here?"

He jerked his head up, his heart lurching at the sight of
her. "We're going to have to stop meeting like this." His
voice broke off into a coughing spasm.

"Never mind," Abby said briskly. "Don't try to talk.
Can you walk?"

"How far?"

"About ten steps. Luckily we've got an empty bed right
up front."

Wrapping an arm firmly around his waist, she helped him
to the bed. He sat on the edge of it, for the first time realizing he was shirtless and barefoot. Soot streaked his
chest and he could only imagine what his face looked like.

"Lie down," Abby said.

"I'll get the bed all dirty," he protested, a token gesture
to manhood, proving he was tough. In reality, he could
hardly resist the temptation to lie down and lose himself in
the sweet oblivion of sleep. Maybe when he woke up, this
would all turn out to be a nightmare.

"Don't worry about the bed. We've got plenty more
sheets." Abby gave him a push and he sank down. She
forestalled any further macho impulses by snapping an oxygen mask over his mouth and nose.

He lay back, letting himself go, breathing deeply and
basking in the sight of her. Near the end of an all-night

shift, her light makeup had rubbed away, leaving a shiny flush on her cheeks. Faint smudges of mascara beneath her eyes softened them, emphasizing their depth. Her hair tumbled in untidy curls around her face, although the back of it was still confined in a bun.

She must be tired, yet her step was brisk, her movements sure and competent. "Do you do this every night?" he mumbled beneath the mask, the words unintelligible.

Strapping the blood-pressure cuff to his arm, she touched his cheek, pursing her lips. "Sshh, don't talk."

Blood pressure done, she placed the stethoscope on his chest, the metal circle cool against his skin. "Take deep breaths. As deep as you can."

She listened, frowning in concentration, moving the device around until he was sure she'd memorized every lobe in his lungs. "Not bad," she murmured. "What happened? No," she added when he tried to talk, "wait until I take the mask off. Just breathe deeply for a few more minutes. I'll be right back."

He almost fell asleep, although no more than five minutes had passed when she returned. She set a basin of water on the stand next to the bed and dipped a cloth into it. He nearly groaned in pleasure as she stroked the warm cloth over his chest and arms, wiping away the soot and sweat. Little red blisters dotted his skin, stinging as the water touched them. Luckily nothing too serious.

"Can you turn on your side?" she asked.

He heaved himself over, so that she could wash his back. No pain there, only the warm, soothing sensation of her gentle strokes. She dried him with a towel. "Okay, you can lie on your back again."

He stifled a moan as overstressed muscles cramped. He let his arms flop down at his sides, thinking he might never be able to move again. Abby deftly unhooked the face mask and set it aside. "How's that?"

He swallowed. "Throat's sore."

"Give it a couple of days. Next time, stand back when there's a fire."

"I'll remember that."

"Do you want to talk about it?"

Weariness weighted his eyes and his muscles. "Maybe later," he mumbled. "Tired. You're not going to kick me out, are you?"

The words slurred and he slept.

HE WOKE to the clatter of dishes and the not-quite-silent padding of shoes as the shift changed. He opened his eyes, found himself face-to-face with Abby as she moved a stethoscope over his chest again. Lifting his hand, he saw that it was bandaged. She must have done that while he slept.

"Are you still here?" he asked, his voice rasping painfully.

"Just going off now," she said, as cheerfully as if she hadn't just worked a twelve-hour shift. "Dr. Scott says you're okay, so you've been discharged. Do you need a ride home?"

If he could get up. "I can call a cab."

"No, I'll be happy to drop you off. I often go for a drive to unwind after a night shift."

"Okay, if it's no trouble."

The room spun as he let his feet slide to the floor. He waited a moment, conscious of Abby's hand on his arm. She smelled of the astringent hospital soap. Not like herself, he mused vaguely. She usually smelled like flowers.

He stood up, swaying slightly before he gained his balance. "It's like learning to walk again."

"Stress and adrenaline do funny things to the human body."

Squaring his shoulders, he managed to walk to the waiting area that, even this early, contained a snoring drunk taking up two chairs, and a mother with a baby in her arms and a toddler huddled against her. "Have a seat for a moment," Abby said. "I just have to pick up my purse. Are you sure you don't want a wheelchair?"

"No way," he said. "I'm feeling better every minute."

ABBY STOPPED the car in front of the house. "Is this okay?"

"It's great." Zach reached for the door handle. Physically, he felt as if a truck had run over him, but the dizziness had worn off and he had no trouble walking once he'd put his legs into motion. Mentally, he wasn't so sure how he felt. Disoriented, certainly, and confused.

During the twenty-minute drive he'd thought about the fire. Was it a random arson? Several months ago, there had been a rash of suspicious fires in the area, but most of them had occurred in abandoned buildings. They had stopped after the police made an arrest. The man was still in custody, as far as he knew. A known firebug, he couldn't be trusted not to start more fires.

Of course, any community this size probably had more than one person who liked to play with matches and gasoline.

He looked across at Abby. Sunlight streamed in through the windshield, highlighting the faint lines that exhaustion had put around her eyes. Eleni's skin had been as smooth as porcelain under her exquisitely applied makeup. Not a single flaw was allowed to mar that perfection.

Abby was refreshingly lacking in vanity, not caring if people saw her real face. She hadn't even bothered to powder her nose.

Honesty—that was a quality he thought he'd never see in a woman again, other than in his grandmother.

"Well, I guess you'll want to go home."

She smiled, the corners of her mouth a little tense. "No

hurry. You still haven't told me what happened. It obviously wasn't the house.''

''It was the garage, behind the house.'' He got out of the car. The slam of the driver's door told him Abby had followed.

He walked around the house, dread crowding into his chest. The smell of smoke hung in the cool morning air. He shivered, remembering the heat and flames shooting up into the sky.

Dew lay on the grass, giving it a silver sheen. A perfect spiderweb hung in the rhododendron beside the house. He paused, staring at the droplets of moisture trapped on the filaments, each a prism caging a miniature rainbow. He could have stayed there all day, watching the miracle of nature, aware of Abby next to him, silent but somehow comforting.

He made himself move. Around the corner and into the back yard. Tire tracks crisscrossed the lawn, and a puddle on the concrete in front of the garage reflected the newly risen sun. All that remained of the building were blackened rafters poking into the sky. He stepped closer, peered inside through the gap where the main door had been. The MG looked worse by daylight, burned beyond recognition. And what hadn't burned had melted, fused into a mass of foam padding, plastic and leather.

He turned away, fists clenching at his side. His face felt tight, as if the muscles had frozen.

Who had done it? The feeling that it hadn't been random nagged at him. Someone had done this to get at him, specifically to destroy a part of his life that was important to him.

Eleni. It always came back to Eleni. She had known how he'd enjoyed restoring the car, even the tedious sanding, the careful business of rewiring, the high of picking the car up at the paint shop after the final coat had been applied. She knew what it meant to him.

ABBY STOOD BACK, staring at the ruin that had once been a garage. She didn't follow Zach to the door, not wanting to see the corpse of the car. She didn't even know what kind of a car it had been. Not Zach's Jaguar, she assumed, or the Honda he'd rented, since it stood on the driveway in front of the house.

He turned, his gaze fixed on the house behind her, his face pale and drawn in the light of the sun.

"Zach," she whispered, wanting to go to him but somehow knowing if she did he would shatter.

"She did it."

Abby started at the rough sound of his voice behind her. She spun around so quickly the sleeve of the sweater she'd put on against the morning chill caught on a thorn. She tugged at it. Zach reached around and gently worked the thorn out of the knit without snagging the thread.

"She did it," he said again, his voice flat. "I know she did it. She's the only one who knew what that car meant to me."

"What kind of car was it?" She hazarded a glance at his face. He looked grim and determined, his eyes hard.

"An old MG I spent months working on. She was even jealous of that car. Wondered why I bothered when I could buy a dozen new ones without the rust and electrical problems."

"She was jealous of a car?"

Zach lifted one shoulder and let it fall. "Actually, that's probably not quite accurate. At that point, she nagged me about everything. The car was just another excuse to remind me I could never aspire to her level of refincment— or whatever."

"But how could she do it? Her picture's been all over the news. Somebody would have recognized her."

"Not necessarily. She wouldn't have done it herself, anyway. She would have hired someone to do her dirty work. She doesn't know which end of the can the gas comes out of. She's had servants all her life."

Sounds like a real prize, Abby thought, but kept the comment to herself.

"It doesn't matter now." Zach clamped his hand around her elbow and led her toward the house. "Come on. I'll make us some coffee."

He'd just filled the machine, which was the only appliance in the gutted kitchen other than a microwave oven and a camp stove, when the phone rang. "Yeah? Morning, David." He let out a low whistle. "News sure travels fast. It's a wonder there aren't any eager-beaver reporters here to photograph the remains." He sighed. "Yeah, they'll likely come and I can't keep them out. What's up, David?"

He listened. The news couldn't be too bad, Abby thought, as the lines bracketing his mouth relaxed marginally. He said something she didn't catch and hung up.

"What is it?"

"They've got the tests back on the samples they dug out of cracks in the hardwood floor in Eleni's house. And they've completed the analysis on the BMW."

"And?" she prompted when he paused.

"Gretchen must have been mistaken when she said there was blood all over the carpet. The stains on the floor turned out to be water, probably from a spilled vase. Everything checked out clean."

Chapter Seven

"You don't seem all that happy about it," Abby said astutely. He shouldn't have been surprised at her accurate assessment; he'd already seen her sensitivity to nuance. "Doesn't this mean you're off the hook?"

"Not necessarily," he said, wondering if he should tell her about his dreams. "She's still missing, and there is Gretchen's story. On the other hand, there's no evidence of foul play."

It finally hit him. No evidence. A bubble of relief expanded in his chest, driving out the frustration of not remembering, and making him feel light and buoyant. No blood on the floor. What he saw in his sleep must be a dream, not a memory at all. A dream conjured out of his tortured mind after being put through the wringer by Eleni.

Or wishful thinking in his subconscious, maybe, although he found the idea of killing anyone, including Eleni, completely repulsive.

"Did they find the carpet?" Abby asked.

Carpet. The buoyancy collapsed. He was sure the carpet had been there when he'd passed the open door on his way into the house that night. Yet, later, it was gone. "Not as far as I know," he said slowly. "But even Gretchen said she wasn't sure it was there that night. She had the day off, and the cleaning crew that comes once a month had been working in the house earlier. They might have taken the carpet out for cleaning.''

He rubbed his hand over his face, struggling to remember. Too much of that night remained a blur in his mind, like a collage of disjointed scenes he couldn't connect by time.

''Hasn't someone called them?'' Abby's voice jolted him back to the present.

''The office is closed for their annual summer holiday until the end of next week.''

''So that's a dead end.'' She lifted her mug and drank the last of the coffee in it. ''Guess I'd better be going. You could use some sleep, too.''

He grinned ruefully. ''Then why are we drinking coffee?''

She smiled, too, as she carried her cup to the sink. ''Nothing keeps me awake. Once I hit the bed, I'm out.''

''Lucky you,'' he muttered beneath his breath. Once upon a time, he'd been like that, too. Once, a scant week ago. Now it seemed like a lifetime. Now the dream came to visit him every night, until he'd begun to think his whole life was a nightmare.

A nightmare into which he had no right to drag Abby.

He picked up his own cup and took it to the sink. His nerve endings tingled as he inhaled the scent of her, an unidentifiable sweetness that overpowered the hospital antiseptic. He moved closer, until he nearly touched her, wanting to put his arms around her, rest his face against her neck and just absorb her essence. ''Do you have to work tonight?'' he asked, to distract himself.

''No, I'm off. Why?''

He shook his head, wanting so much he couldn't speak of. He turned on the tap, letting the cold water splash his arms. ''No reason. Just wondering.''

Just wondering if you could stay and I could hold you

until I fall asleep. He must be more punchy than he thought. Snapping off the water, he moved away from the sink and walked briskly to the door. ''I guess I'd better go take a shower. The drywall tapers will be here soon.''

''I have to go home.'' Abby paused when she reached the door. She put out her hand to take his. ''I'm really sorry about your garage and your car.''

''Thank you.'' He squeezed her hand, then on impulse, pulled her closer and covered her mouth in a gentle kiss. He released her and gave her a little push out the door. ''Go, before I do something that I can't blame on a sleepless night.''

She gave him an odd look he was too tired to interpret, then turned to leave. He stood for a moment, then followed her. On the path around the house he stopped to pick a half-open bud from the Mr. Lincoln rose she'd been admiring earlier. He ran to catch up to her. ''Here, Abby. Thanks again.''

A dimple he hadn't noticed before appeared in her cheek as she lifted the rose and sniffed the heady fragrance. A little ache pierced his heart, an awareness of his loneliness. Not that he had any right to expect her to relieve it.

''May I call you?'' he asked recklessly.

Her smile slipped. Her brown eyes met his, dark and solemn. ''If you want. Goodbye, Zach.''

She got in the car, started it, and drove away.

THE PHONE WOKE Abby out of a sound sleep. She cracked one eye open. A quarter after twelve noon. Which meant she'd just been cheated out of fifteen minutes of sleep. She reached over, turned the clock alarm off, and snagged the phone.

Before she could croak a greeting, a voice growled in her ear, ''Hey, bitch. Stay away from Zach Andros. He's poison to women.''

She came instantly wide-awake. "What? Who's this?"

For answer, she got a click and then droning dial tone.

She hung up the phone, giving it an exasperated look. Some nut, obviously. Or a practical joker. Aside from the weekend at Jane's cabin, she'd had only the most incidental contact with Zach. Why would anyone warn her against him?

Unless it was Eleni. The voice had been male but Abby recalled what Zach had said about Eleni hiring out her dirty work.

Why couldn't they find her? The police were supposedly looking, but a missing adult probably wouldn't be top priority. Now, with the car found and no sign of a struggle, the case would slip to the bottom of the stack.

Zach Andros—poison to women. The whispered words echoed in Abby's brain. Poison to women? Or only to one woman?

Distasteful as if might be, she'd have to tell him about the phone call. Someone obviously didn't like him, and it was only fair to warn him.

Abby got up and showered. She pulled on jeans and a cotton shirt. Walking past the dresser, she touched the red-velvet petals of the rose Zach had given her, which she'd put in a bud vase. The sweet fragrance perfumed the whole room. She smiled a little; she'd never expected a romantic gesture from him.

In the kitchen she made herself toast and coffee, casting a disgusted eye at the dust on top of the fridge. She had planned to clean the house today, but it was going to have to wait.

SEVERAL CARS and a van with a TV-station logo stood in the driveway when she pulled up at Zach's house. Through the open doors and windows she heard hammering and sawing. One of the workmen sang an opera aria, and another told him to shut up. There was laughter from the rest of them.

She paused for a moment. In daylight, she saw that the house was old, substantial without being overly large, two stories, and a basement with small windows along the ground. A tangled, out-of-control wisteria embraced the wide verandah.

The sound of voices drew her toward the backyard. Zach stood next to the burned-out garage, his chin jutted forward and a black scowl on his face. "I told you I have nothing to say. Now get out of here."

He wore cutoff jeans and a tank top that bared his muscular shoulders. Not exactly the tuxedoed businessman pictured in newspaper accounts of charity events he'd attended. She hadn't yet met the business persona. She had only seen him battered and bruised, dispirited, angry and frustrated. And occasionally charming.

Yellow tape still surrounded the garage, but at that moment a fire-department car drove up. A tall man in a neatly pressed white uniform shirt stepped out of it. "Zachary Andros?"

"That's me." Zach walked away from the reporters, his relief obvious. They followed in a herd, poking their microphones in the fire official's face.

He put up his hand. "No comment. And I'd appreciate it if you cleared the area. We don't need the scene corrupted."

Muttering among themselves, the reporters headed back toward their van, glancing curiously at Abby as they filed past her. One of them paused. "Do you have any comment on the fire?"

Abby gave her a thin smile. "Why would I? I'm only the gardener."

Disappointed, the woman got into her car and followed the others down the driveway.

"I heard that," Zach said, his breath warming her ear. "The gardener? At least it lets you out as a witness, since the fire happened at night."

Abby turned to meet the amusement in his eyes. "It was the only thing I could think of. Good thing they never followed you to the hospital. Did you get any sleep at all?"

"A couple of hours. The tapers were quiet but a crew of bricklayers arrived and I had to help them unload. Want to see the rest of the house in daylight? You only saw the kitchen this morning."

"Not just yet." She stepped aside as a teenage boy came out of the house for another batch of bricks from the pallet on the porch. "Is there some place we can talk?"

One of the bricks fell off the stack the boy carried, bouncing down the step and onto the lawn. "Hey, watch that, Aaron," Zach said tolerantly. "Drop them inside and you'll be sanding the floors again."

The kid groaned. "Not that again, boss. My shoulders are still sore." He grinned cheekily. "This your lady?"

The question hit Zach like a fist in the stomach. Was Abby his lady? "Sort of," he said. "Get back to work."

"Sure, man. Anything you say." He hoisted the stack of bricks onto his shoulder and sauntered back into the house, his overly long pant legs dragging on the floor.

"Kids," Zach said. "But I can't complain. They've been working hard." He laced his fingers through Abby's. "Are you my lady? Do you want to leave this drudgery and run off together?"

Abby tightened her fingers around his, warmed by his good humor. Too bad she was going to have to spoil it.

They walked to the garden shed and sat down on a bench next to it. "This okay?" Zach asked.

"Fine." She twisted her hands together in her lap, not sure whether she should hit him with the phone call right away, or work up to it. As a compromise, she said, "Has there been any news about Eleni at all?"

He shook his head, a frown darkening his brow. "No, nothing. I called David back a while ago but he says not to worry. She'll show up when she wants something. But that's not what you came to talk about, was it?"

"No." She bit her lip. "I had a phone call, warning me away from you." She repeated the caller's words as nearly as she could remember.

His frown deepened. "A man? Anything distinctive about his voice? Any accent?"

"From that short call, I couldn't really tell, but no, I don't think so."

"Did you report it to the police?"

Her brows flew up. "No. What good would it do?"

"Nothing, I guess," he admitted. "We don't even know if that call has any bearing on my situation."

"It must," Abby said. "I didn't know you before."

He clenched a fist and pounded it against his knee. "Yeah, but why should anyone care if you see me? We're both divorced, free agents. And I've dated a couple of women since the divorce and they never received warnings."

A pang stabbed her heart at the thought of him with other women. *As if he cares about you,* Abby chided herself. *He barely knows you.*

Something must have shown on her face because he took her hand and squeezed it. "Nothing serious, Abby. And it was really only one woman. I took her to a charity fundraiser as a favor to a friend. And I took one of Katie's goddaughters who was visiting from Kelowna out to dinner once."

"You don't have to explain," Abby said stiffly. "It's not my business."

"I want it to be, Abby. I don't want you to think I'm

only interested in a good time. Especially since we haven't had a very good time up to now. Maybe it'll get better once I clear up this business with Eleni.''

Her heart raced and her cheeks grew hot. "Zach, I want to help you.'' The words rushed out of her mouth before she could conjure up second thoughts.

He stared at her, saying nothing for a long moment. "Why?'' he finally asked. "It's not your problem.''

"No, but there's an old proverb that says two heads are better than one.''

"I don't know, Abby. That phone call you got—something's going on that I don't understand.''

"The police aren't doing much. And the phone call was probably a prank, maybe even from one of the people I work with.''

"Why would they care?''

"They wouldn't, but in the emergency department you're always dealing with life and death. Sometimes humor lightens things up, and a couple of people have been known to pull practical jokes.''

"So there you are.'' Katie's lilting voice brought their heads up. She stepped daintily over the muddy tracks in the lawn. "It really is a mess, isn't it?'' She put her arms around Zach's neck and hugged him. "Zachary, I'm so sorry about your car.''

"Thanks, Grandma.'' He got up from the bench. "Sit down, won't you?''

"Hello, Abby. It's nice to see you again.'' Katie sat down, crossing her shapely legs. Today she wore a cream linen suit with short sleeves and a knee-length skirt.

"Nice outfit,'' Zach commented. "Very ladies-who-lunch. What was it today, garden club?''

"Inner City Day Care,'' Katie said. "One of Eleni's pet

charities, not that she ever cared about kids in her life. It's just politically correct.''

"I don't suppose Eleni miraculously showed up, did she?''

Katie shook her head. "No. That's why I came to see you. I've talked to a lot of the people she knows and no one's seen her.''

Zach's mouth turned down. "That's not exactly news.''

Katie smiled slyly. "I know, but I saw Lance and he's apparently making deals in her name all over the place. Waving a letter giving him power of attorney.''

"Waving a letter?'' Zach said skeptically.

Katie winked at Abby, who grinned back at her. "Well, maybe not waving but I heard it from Mrs. Simmons who got it from Eleni's secretary that Eleni had been giving Lance more of a free rein lately.''

"But why? Is she planning to retire or something?''

"Not that I've heard. Rumors say she might be considering Lance as her next husband.''

"But isn't he much younger than she is?'' Abby asked. "Not that that matters, I suppose, but I didn't get the impression that there was much between them other than business when they visited Zach at the hospital.''

"Seems they keep business and pleasure separate,'' Katie said. "On the dance floor at the Opera Ball last month, they looked as if they were glued together.''

Which meant that Eleni would hardly be behind the call Abby had received, Zach thought. Too dog-in-the-manger, even for her.

He shrugged. "If I knew where she was, I'd wish her happiness.''

"And offer condolences to Lance,'' Katie said dryly.

"Oh, I imagine Lance knows what he's getting into,'' Zach said. "He's been working with her long enough.''

"Have you talked to him this past week?" Katie asked.

Zach raised his brows. "No, and it's been quite a relief not having him phoning every other day."

"Well, maybe you should. See what he's got to say about Eleni's disappearance."

"I'm sure the police have interviewed him."

"They have," Katie agreed. "They even talked to me, trying to find out more about your character, no doubt, although they were quite discreet about it."

"You're on dozens of the same committees as Eleni. You knew her well. It's logical for them to assume that you might have some idea where she'd go."

Katie sighed. "I'm afraid I haven't been much help." She glanced at the man-size gold watch on her wrist and uttered a sound of dismay. "I must run. I've got another meeting at half-past two."

She stood on her tiptoes and kissed Zach's cheek. "Don't worry. The police haven't been back, have they?" She grinned at Abby. "'Bye. I'll give you a call."

Her reassurances proved premature. Her car had barely disappeared down the driveway when a police cruiser drove in. Zach groaned, recognizing Constable Jackson, the officer in charge of the investigation into Eleni's disappearance.

Abby touched his arm, her fingers cool against his skin. "Don't jump to conclusions. It's probably routine."

Zach wasn't about to wait for the handcuffs. He marched up to the car. "Well, have you found her?"

The man smiled, his expression as fraudulent as a three-dollar bill. "Found her? Oh, you mean your ex-wife? No, we haven't."

"Are you looking?"

"We've put out an APB on her." His gaze swung over to Abby. "Mr. Andros, could we talk privately?"

Abby stepped back but Zach took hold of her arm, his eyes fixed on the cop. "This is Abby Chance, a friend of mine. I've got no secrets from her."

"Pleased to meet you, ma'am." He turned up a page and folded it around the clipboard he held, scanning the information on it. "Chance? Any connection to David Chance?"

"He's my ex-husband," Abby said.

The cop looked from Zach to Abby, and back again. Zach could almost see his smirk. "And Chance is your attorney, is that right, Mr. Andros?"

"Yes. So?" Zach drew himself up to his full height, placing his hands on his hips. "Look, I've got a lot to do. Is there a point to this?"

"I'm coming to that. Have you ever driven your ex-wife's BMW?"

"No, never," Zach said promptly. "We were already divorced when she got it."

"Have you been in it as a passenger, or perhaps loaded something into the trunk?"

"I've never touched her car."

"What about that night she disappeared? Were you anywhere near her car then?"

"Sort of, I guess. I parked next to it on her driveway when I went to see her. I'm sure it's in the report."

"You were driving a rental that night."

Zach sighed in exasperation. "Officer, I've been through this several times. I went to her house around ten and talked to her for about fifteen minutes. I didn't feel well so I left. I either slipped on the steps—it had been raining—or someone hit me on the head. I woke up to find the police all over the place and the housekeeper making all kinds of wild accusations."

The policeman's eyes narrowed. "Were they so wild? She sticks by her story, even now."

"Is that what this is about?" Zach demanded, using anger to keep the sudden terror at bay. He didn't want to go to jail, to be locked in a cell, all because Eleni had decided to disappear. "Are you going to arrest me?"

"No one's arresting you," the cop said, his voice deceptively mild as he made notes on a clean page. "At least, not yet."

Zach rocked from his heels to his toes. "Is that a threat?"

"No. If you perceive it that way, feel free to call your attorney. I can wait."

"No, I'll speak for myself. If there's a point to this."

"There is a point, Mr. Andros. Your fingerprints were found on the trunk of your ex-wife's car."

Zach felt the blood drain from his face.

The image of a dark night jumped into his head. Tripping as he went down the steps and falling against a car. Groping for his keys, finding they didn't fit. Sitting down to rest, the concrete wet beneath him. Wind roaring in the trees, not quite loud enough to drown out the screams.

Starched cloth rustled as Jackson crossed his arms over his chest. "When did you touch your ex-wife's car?"

Zach forced his mind back to the present.

Abby was glaring at the cop.

"I stumbled against the car in the dark," Zach said before Abby could be arrested for obstructing justice, or something.

"Before or after you fell against the steps and hit your head?"

Zach struggled to think. When? He shook his head, trying to remember. "I don't know. Does it matter?"

"Maybe. Maybe not. How well do you know Lance Stuart?"

"What do you mean how well do I know him?" Zach snapped. "He's Eleni's lawyer. We've been at loggerheads over the property settlement for months. But outside of that, I don't know him. Why, has something happened to him?"

"No, why would it? But Mr. Stuart says the housekeeper heard you fighting with your ex-wife that night. That you threatened to kill her."

Chapter Eight

"Well, unsubstantiated threats can't be used in court, can they?" Zach asked belligerently.

Abby wanted to warn Zach that antagonizing the law wouldn't help but she guessed he wouldn't appreciate her interference. He looked ready to take on the cop and the entire justice system.

Jackson frowned, thinking about it. "No, I guess not," he finally conceded. "If they could, we wouldn't have enough jails to hold everyone we arrested."

"All this is old news anyway," Zach said. "I admitted Eleni and I had an argument."

"But not the content."

"No, maybe not. I don't remember what we said."

Jackson scratched his chin. "Mr. Andros, you're in a peculiar position here. Apparently you were the last person to see your wife, and with the housekeeper sticking to her story, we have to wonder."

Anger painted red flags on Zach's cheekbones. "Are you saying I killed her and somehow removed her body from the house?"

"We're looking at all the angles. There was one hour between the time the housekeeper says she saw the body and the police arriving. Much could have happened in that time."

"Yeah, I made Eleni disappear into thin air and then I knocked myself over the head and lay on the wet ground waiting for the police to come." Zach's voice rose. "Come on, give me a break. If I'd done something, wouldn't I have beat it out of there?"

Jackson straightened the pages attached to his clipboard. "It's futile for me to speculate what you would do, Mr. Andros. We believe you, as far as it goes. You *were* drugged. That's a fact. But I'm warning you, if you know something you haven't reported, it could look bad for you if you don't reveal it."

Zach raked his fingers wearily through his hair. "I've told you everything that I remember. I wish you'd just get on with the investigation."

"We're working on it, Mr. Andros. You can count on it." He walked around the car and got in. "Have a good day."

"Yeah, right," Zach muttered as the engine started and the cruiser rolled down the driveway.

"Don't let 'em hassle you, Zach," Aaron said as he came out for another load of bricks.

Zach cracked a reluctant grin. "Easy for you to say."

Aaron hitched up his baggy jeans. "Experience, man. Experience."

"Not the kind of experience you should have been getting," Zach reminded him.

The kid shrugged and walked back into the house with a stack of bricks.

"Now what?" Abby asked.

"I'm going to take Katie's advice and go talk to the formidable Gretchen."

"You mean the housekeeper?"

"Yeah. I should have done it before but I kept thinking Eleni would show up. And I want to talk to Aunt Dora, as well. She lives in a wing of the house and might have seen something.''

"I'll go with you."

Zach's brows lifted. ''Abby, it's not your fight. I don't know if it's a good idea for you to get involved. That phone call you had—''

"I thought we agreed it was probably a prank," Abby cut in. ''And I offered to help, didn't I?''

"Yes, but—''

"But nothing. You need someone to help you get to the bottom of this. I don't want to meet you in Emergency again. We're friends, aren't we?''

An odd expression crossed Zach's face, half wary, half—she couldn't tell. ''Friends, yes, but I don't want to put you in danger.''

"What danger?" Abby scoffed. ''I can handle heavy breathers on the phone. *And* your dragon-lady housekeeper.''

Zach shuddered. ''Not *my* housekeeper, thanks very much.''

A smile tugged at the corner of Abby's mouth. ''Wasn't she there when you were still married?''

"Yes, but I always felt she only tolerated me. That she was just waiting for me to show my uncouth background by walking on the Aubusson rug with muddy boots.''

Once again, Abby found herself wondering what on earth had possessed Zach to marry a woman like Eleni. The thought entered her mind that maybe he had been after Eleni's money, but she shook it off. Not Zach. ''Well, after the battle-ax of a head nurse I had at the first hospital I worked in, I can handle the dragon lady.''

Grinning, Zach rested his gaze on her. ''You know, Abby, you're a special person.''

Special? Or special to him? So far he certainly hadn't given her much indication of how he regarded her, as a helpful partner or a real woman he could be attracted to. Maybe he was still hung up on Eleni. Hate could be as powerful an emotion as love. And as binding.

"I don't know why David let you escape," Zach added.

"Because I more or less let him," she said smartly, annoyed at her own indecision about Zach. "But that's neither here nor there. I'm just doing what I think is right. You'd be in jail if there was a shred more evidence."

Zach sobered. "Maybe. Okay, I'll take you along. Just hang on a minute while I get changed."

Abby passed the time by picking up a pair of pruning clippers she found on the porch and deadheading roses from the overgrown bushes around the house. Doubts crowded into her mind, but she rebuked them. She'd promised to help Zach, and she would, no matter what the outcome. If she got hurt, well, that was life.

Within ten minutes Zach was back, freshly showered and shaved, dressed in wrinkled but clean T-shirt and jeans. "Yeah, I know, the garden needs work." Gently he took the pruner from her hand. "But you're not the gardener and there's no use making a fuss until the construction is done."

"I like gardening," Abby informed him.

"Good," he said, taking her hand and leading her to the rented car. "When the house is done, I'll let you fix the garden. But I'll pay you. No taking unfair advantage of friendship."

Friendship. That word again. It nagged Abby like a sore tooth all the way down the freeway into Surrey. Was he making it clear that friendship was all he wanted from her? She couldn't ignore the fact that he had problems, Eleni's disappearance being only part of them. He had no time for relationships. And it was presumptuous of her to imagine he was interested in her any way beyond friendship.

She'd do well to remind herself of that.

She'd help him, because it intrigued her, but she'd keep her heart safe.

That heart gave a little lurch when he glanced at her and smiled. His eyes crinkled at the corners and the long lashes gave them a sleepy look, as if they hid secrets. Steeling herself against the heat that ran over her skin, she looked away and pretended an interest in the passing scenery.

Zach turned the car off the main road and onto a side street where huge houses sat at the ends of long driveways. Trees on each side of the street shaded the road, creating a cool, green tunnel.

The last driveway on the dead-end street led into a dense forest, evergreens and oaks and blackberry vines. "She left it wild near the road for privacy."

"Well, it worked," Abby said. "You can't even tell there's a house up here."

Zach rounded another curve in the narrow road. Abby gasped. The land opened up into what must be several acres of lawn. On a little rise, the house sat like a transplanted southern mansion, all pillars and porches. A weeping willow drooped its languid boughs over the lawn at one corner, in the shallow angle formed by an extra wing. Twisting the key to turn off the ignition, Zach pointed to the one-story addition. "Eleni's Aunt Dora lives there."

"How did she feel about you?"

As she pushed open the car door, Zach turned his head to stare at her. "That's the first thing you think of? Not some expression of admiration for this marble-and-stucco mausoleum?"

Abby set her lips primly. "It's interesting."

Zach's brows shot up. He gave a sharp laugh. "Interesting, huh? Eleni would be crushed. She designed it."

"And you built it?"

"Yeah, but I don't usually admit it, even under torture."

Abby laughed. "It's not that bad, if you like the antebellum look."

"Eleni did."

They got out of the car, leaving it on the circular driveway lined with precisely clipped boxwood. "As for Aunt Dora, she seemed to like me, although I might have only been someone to talk to, on the infrequent occasions we ran into each other."

"Was she here that night?"

"I don't know. She stays pretty much in her own rooms, even though technically she has the run of the house. She's family, after all. She eats in the dining room, with Eleni and whoever else happens to be here. Or by herself, if Eleni's out."

"I take it she's elderly?"

Zach shook his head. "Not that old, although it's hard to tell. Sixtyish. I don't know. Never gave it much thought. She's always just been there... She often visited before she lived in the house. She was just around."

He pushed the intercom button beside the massive oak door. Inside the house, Westminster chimes pealed a sonorous summons.

While they waited, Abby gazed over the wide lawn. As manicured as a golf green, it stretched to the edge of the surrounding woods. Only the willow, the boxwood, and a border of rhododendrons broke up the emerald perfection. "What it needs is a rose garden, right in the middle," she muttered.

"I've often thought that, too," Zach said, amused. "Too much green."

The door opened silently. For a moment, her eyes dazzled by the bright sun, Abby thought no one was there. Beside her, Zach squared his shoulders. "Hello, Gretchen."

The woman was broad and rawboned, standing an inch taller than Zach. Her steel-gray hair was drawn back into a knot at her nape, so tightly her eyebrows tilted up at the ends. Green eyes, as cold as iced emeralds, stared at them. "What are you doing here?" she finally said, her voice harsh. She stuck her hands into the pockets of her apron and effectively blocked the doorway.

"I need to talk to you."

"I've nothing to say. I don't know why you're still at large, but I guess that just shows the incompetence of our police department."

"I didn't do anything to Eleni," Zach said, fists clenching at his sides.

"Then where is she?" Gretchen shifted her gaze to Abby, her eyes sharpening. "And who is this?" She sniffed, thin nostrils flaring. Abby had the feeling she'd assessed her clothing down to the nearest penny and found her taste severely wanting. "Looks more your type."

Abby swallowed her anger, and stuck out her hand. "I'm Abby Chance."

Gretchen ignored the proffered hand.

Abby dropped her hand, her admiration for Zach going up another, dangerous notch. How had he ever lived in this house? Of course, by his own admission, he'd been away a lot on business. She didn't blame him.

Gretchen turned back to Zach. "I've known Miss Eleni since she was a child. She wouldn't just disappear like this. What have you done with her?"

"Nothing," Zach said, his own voice rising.

"She was lying on the floor in a pool of blood when I came in," Gretchen said.

"Did you check whether she was alive?" Abby asked.

Gretchen drew back, affronted. "Of course not. She must have been dead. There was a lot of blood. I didn't want to tamper with evidence."

"Gretchen has seen every episode of Columbo and Perry Mason," Zach muttered to Abby. "Several times."

"Scalp wounds bleed a lot," Abby said to Gretchen. "And wasn't it dark?"

"Not that dark." Gretchen set her lips in a thin line. "I know what I saw."

"Isn't it true that Zach had already left when you went into the living room?" Abby added.

"I didn't see him," Gretchen said, her expression hardening as she crossed her arms over her flat chest. "I'd been out—it was my day off—but I knew he was coming over that evening to see Miss Eleni. For all I know, he still has a key and could have come back into the house."

"Then why did I ring the doorbell that night?" Zach asked. "If I'd planned to do something to Eleni, I could have just walked in."

She shrugged shoulders that could have graced a linebacker. "So no one would find out."

Zach rolled his eyes. "I see we're not going to get anywhere like this. Is Aunt Dora home?"

"She's not your aunt."

"Maybe not, but I'd like to see her."

Gretchen's thin brows rose even higher. "I doubt if she's available."

"Who is it, Gretchen?" A girlish voice spoke behind the woman.

"They're just leaving," Gretchen said. "Go back to your rooms."

"I want to see." The door opened wider and a woman poked her head around it. The rest of her body followed as she took her place next to Gretchen, who frowned disapprovingly.

Abby's first thought was that the woman's light, high-pitched voice matched her appearance, if not her age. She was small and slender, looking like a child beside Gretchen. Her hair formed a froth of blond curls around a relatively unlined face, and lacy ruffles fluttered in the low neckline of her dress.

"Oh, it's Zachary," she trilled, running out and wrapping her arms around his waist. "It's been ages, you naughty boy. And who is this lovely lady?"

"Abby Chance," Zach said, his tone resigned.

Abby barely restrained an explosive sneeze as Dora enveloped her in a cloying cloud of gardenia perfume. "You must come in and have some tea. Gretchen, please bring it to my sitting room. Some of those pastries Cook made this morning, too."

Abby glanced back at Gretchen as Dora herded them into the marble-tiled hall. The housekeeper glared after them, tight-lipped and grim. A moment later, the front door slammed.

Chattering like a blond squirrel, Dora led them through a maze of corridors. Portraits of grim Greek patriarchs in black pantaloons or white wool kilts stared down from the walls. Eleni's ancestors?

How big was this place? Abby wondered. The first hospital she'd worked in, in a remote town on Vancouver Island, hadn't covered this much territory.

They reached a wide door which Dora opened, revealing a sitting room decorated in flowery chintz. "I'm so glad you came by, Zachary," Dora said happily, smoothing her dress before seating herself on a sofa upholstered in pink cabbage roses. "We don't see nearly enough of you these days."

"It is Eleni's house," Zach said dryly.

"This part is mine." Dora's determined cheer slipped for an instant. Her hands fluttered in the air like helpless birds, then dropped to her lap. "She always said so."

Zach frowned. "Is there some problem?"

Dora looked up, a smile curving her mouth. "No, no, of course not. Just Lance talking about selling the house or something. But Eleni would never put me out of my home.''

"Do you have any idea where Eleni might be?'' Zach asked.

Dora's hands twitched again, her smile slipping. "Oh, Gretchen says you've done something to her, but I don't believe her. She's always saying things. Eleni's probably just away on business. She told me she was planning a trip.''

"Did she?'' Zach said, leaning forward. "When was this?''

"Last week, I think.'' The smooth skin over her nose creased. "Oh, yes, at supper, the night of the storm. The power went off later. It was very dark. I don't like storms. So unsettling.''

She jumped up and went to the door, peering out into the hall. "I wonder where Gretchen is. She should be bringing the tea. Unless she's decided she's too busy.''

"I'm sure she'll be along,'' Zach said.

Dora pursed her lips. "Sometimes she lets me wait. Make yourselves comfortable. I'll go see what's keeping her.''

The click of her heels on the oak floor faded into the distance.

Zach got up and walked to the window, drawing aside the curtain to look out. "What is it?'' Abby asked at his elbow.

"Just checking to see whether the driveway and front steps are visible from here.''

Abby pulled the curtain wider. Zach's rented car was clearly visible on the driveway, but the boxwood hedge and a tall rhododendron blocked the view of the steps.

"Where was Eleni's BMW that night?'' Abby asked.

"Where my car is now. And I parked beside it, a little farther from the door.''

"Were there any other cars here that night?"

Zach frowned and didn't answer for a long moment. "No, there weren't," he said, but she heard a note of uncertainty in his tone. Didn't he remember? He'd hinted before at gaps in his memory, but how extensive were they?

"Are you sure?" Abby asked, willing him to level with her.

He clenched his fist on the edge of the curtain. "Of course I'm sure," he stated, but again she thought he sounded as if he were trying to convince himself.

He turned abruptly away from her, going over to the fireplace which was nearly hidden behind an enormous Boston fern. "Do you think I wouldn't remember that night, especially since the police subsequently questioned me like a criminal?"

"A concussion can do strange things," she said mildly.

"Yeah, you've told me."

"Here we are," Dora warbled in her girlish voice. She came in, pushing a loaded tea trolley.

Zach strode across the room as if he welcomed the interruption. "Let me help you with that." Taking hold of the trolley, he steered it onto the Persian carpet covering the center of the oak floor. He moved the tray from the cart to the table in front of the sofa.

Dora seated herself and poured the tea, handing each of them a cup. Abby sat down on a chair opposite the sofa, and Zach paced back to the fireplace. He set the cup on the mantel, declining a pastry from the plate Dora extended to him. "No, thanks."

"Abby?" Dora offered her the plate.

Setting her cup on the lamp table next to the chair, Abby took a pastry and a napkin. "Thank you."

"I do so like a nice tea, don't you?" Dora said, reseating herself in the middle of the sofa.

Zach cleared his throat. "What do you remember about that night we had the storm?"

The frown reappeared above Dora's nose. Her gaze skittered from Zach to Abby, to the window, and back to the tray in front of her. The spoon she used to stir her tea clattered into her saucer.

She lifted one hand to her throat, fingering the single strand of pearls around her neck. "Thunder and lightning. I was ready to go to bed when the lights went out. So difficult to orient oneself in the dark, isn't it? I couldn't even brush my teeth, and the flashlight batteries were dead."

"Did you call Gretchen?"

"I tried, but the phone didn't work."

"Which is why Gretchen had to go down the road to call the police," Zach said to Abby.

Dora shuddered, her hand shaking as she picked up her cup and drank deeply. "It was too dark, except for blue flashes of lightning. The thunder was deafening. I covered my ears and lay down on the sofa, just where I am now."

"So you didn't hear Zach leave," Abby said softly.

A shadow crossed Dora's face, and for a moment her eyes became unfocused. She blinked, shaking her head. "I heard nothing except the thunder." She frowned again. "Maybe a car. I don't know. It could have been when the police came."

"Okay." Zach rested his elbow on the mantel in a deceptively relaxed pose. Abby was sure Dora couldn't see the tension in his muscles. "Was anyone here for dinner?"

"No, just Eleni." Dora smiled. "We had a pleasant meal, the two of us. Gretchen was out. She came back later."

"How was Eleni that night? Did she seem restless or agitated?"

Dora shook her head. "She seemed very calm. Quieter

than usual. She said something about—oh, I'm not sure what—that some plan she had was going to work out. Something like that. And she said she had a surprise for me, that Lance was finalizing it."

"But Lance wasn't here that night," Zach said. "At least, not until the police came."

"He was." Dora's hands fluttered as she pleated a section of her skirt. "He came by after dinner. He asked me to go to my rooms. He said he had something important to discuss with Eleni."

Zach's eyes narrowed. "Any idea what it was?"

A delicate flush crawled up Dora's pale cheeks. "You surely don't think I would listen at keyholes?"

Zach smiled faintly. "Well, did you?"

The flush deepened. "Maybe for a moment. Eleni used to tell me everything. Now she doesn't, but I have a right to know."

"What did they talk about?"

"I couldn't hear very well. Something about a business deal that wasn't working out. Eleni changed in an instant, got really upset and called him a stupid son of a—" She broke off. "Called him a nasty word."

"So that's why she was in such a bad mood when I came by later," Zach muttered. "Dora, how do Eleni and Lance get along normally?"

Dora smiled, her eyes going misty. "They are in love. I think they were planning to get married but Eleni wanted to wait until the property settlement was finalized."

"Yeah, I bet," Zach said flatly.

"I'm sorry you had so much trouble with her. Eleni isn't usually like that." Dora sighed reminiscently. "She was such a sweet child, always so clean and well-behaved. Her parents were away so much, I thought of her as my own child."

Zach drank his tea and set down the cup. "Dora, do you

know if Gretchen walked to the store that night to use the phone? Or did she drive?''

"She started out in her car," Dora said promptly. "But there was a fallen tree just down the road. She had to walk the rest of the way to the store." She suddenly clapped her hands together. "I remember now. The car I heard was hers. I must have fallen asleep because I didn't hear her leave but I heard her coming back. I got up to see what was the matter. I met her in the hall by the kitchen. Gretchen was very wet and not happy at all. She told me to go back to bed."

"If you fell asleep, how did you know she took her car? Maybe it was some other car you heard."

"She told me the next day. We do talk, you know. And that night, not long after she got back, the police came."

"How did they get around the fallen tree?"

She wrinkled her brow. "I suppose they moved it, two big strong men. I drove past in the morning and it was in the ditch beside the road."

"Were you in the living room that evening, when the police came?"

Dora shook her head, the blond curls bouncing. "No. I stayed in my room, like Gretchen told me, but I couldn't sleep with all the fuss going on. And later a very nice policeman came to talk to me, but I didn't know anything. You were hurt that night, weren't you, Zachary? I'm so sorry."

"It's all right," he said, his tone absent. He wore a thoughtful frown. Abby could imagine his mind turning over the information, pulling it apart and rearranging it, trying to reconstruct the sequence of events.

Dora toyed with her necklace, rubbing each pearl on the string as if it were a rosary. "If I'd known you fell on the steps, I would have come out to help you. You must have been very uncomfortable, out there in the rain and wind. You could have caught your death of cold.''

"I didn't and I'm fine now," Zach assured her. He glanced across at Abby. "I suppose we should go?"

Dora jumped up, hands waving like limp bits of seaweed in a strong current. "Oh, must you? You've only just come."

"I have to see to the workmen at my house."

"Oh, of course. You're remodeling."

Zach gave an ironic smile. "That's putting it kindly."

Abby got up. She extended her hand to Dora. "Thank you for the tea."

"Oh, you must come again. We can have a longer talk. Maybe I'll remember more about that night." Dora turned to Zach. "You will come and see me again, won't you, Zachary?"

"I'll try," he said, placing a light kiss on her forehead. "Oh, by the way, which door does Gretchen use to go in and out of the house?"

"The back door, in the kitchen. She parks her car by the garage. She never uses the front." Dora hurried to the door. "I'll walk you out."

Gretchen was nowhere to be seen as they negotiated the corridors once more. Dora opened the front door and swung it wide. "Now, don't forget. Come again. You too, Abby." She looked back at the deserted hall, then grabbed Zach's arm. "Be careful, won't you, Zachary? People have been phoning here. Strange voices."

Next to her, Abby felt Zach tense. "What people?"

Dora glanced behind her again. "I don't know. They ask for Gretchen and won't talk to me. She won't tell me what's going on. I'm so worried. What if somone's kidnapped Eleni, and Gretchen is arranging the ransom?"

Zach patted her shoulder. "I'm sure they'd go to Lance rather than Gretchen."

Dora's face crumpled and a tear rolled down her cheek. "I didn't tell the police, but Eleni and Gretchen had an argument that evening. That's why Gretchen went out before dinner. It was her day off but she usually ate with us." Her voice dropped to a whisper, her eyes round and frightened. "What if Gretchen did her in?"

Abby saw Zach's mouth twist as he suppressed a smile. "Gretchen was out, remember? And she went for the police in the storm."

"Oh, that's right. She wouldn't have called them if she had something to hide." Dora smiled in relief. "Goodbye, then. Drive carefully."

"WHAT IF SHE'S RIGHT?" Abby said as soon as they were in the car.

Zach laughed. "That Gretchen did her in? Not likely. Gretchen loves Eleni. And Dora loves melodrama. She's just taking a stab at Gretchen."

At least he hoped that was all, but he couldn't shake off the feeling that Dora knew something she wasn't telling. Well, he'd give her a little time, maybe see her away from the house next time.

He drove around the curved driveway until he reached the section leading past the house to the garage. He glanced into the rearview mirror. Dora had gone back into the house. Abruptly spinning the steering wheel, he turned toward the garage. "I want to see if Eleni's car is back."

The garage, a substantial two-story building stuccoed and roofed to match the house, had space for four cars, with an apartment above. "Does anyone live up there?" Abby asked.

"Not now, I think. Eleni used to have a full-time gardener, but he retired and I don't think she's hired anyone else. Why?"

"I thought I saw the curtains move just when we turned."

"Are you sure?"

Abby shrugged. "Probably my imagination."

"Probably." Zach opened the car door. "I'll just be a minute."

One of the overhead doors stood open, the bay it revealed empty. Zach came back shortly. "No, the BMW's not there."

"The police might still have it," Abby suggested. "And if it's declared a write-off, it'll go straight to the wrecker's."

"I guess." Zach was about to get into the Honda when a red Porsche roared up the driveway, tires squealing as the driver braked next to them. "Well, if it isn't the boy toy, Lance," Zach muttered.

He waited, feet apart, arms crossed over his chest. Abby, not wanting to miss anything, got out and stood with her arms resting on the roof of the car.

Lance got out of the Porsche and strode over to them, bristling with anger. "What are you doing here, Andros? Eleni doesn't want you hanging around."

"Well, she's not here to say anything about it, is she?" Zach said evenly, slamming a lid on his own irritation. "I'm not under a restraining order."

"No, but maybe that can be arranged."

Zach thrust out his chin. "Try it and see how far you get. I don't suppose you've heard from Eleni."

"No, and I'm surprised you're still free. I thought the police would have arrested you by now."

"On what charge? I had nothing to do with Eleni's disappearance."

"Didn't you? That's not what Gretchen says."

"Gretchen is mistaken. And I gather you were here after dinner that night."

"I'm Eleni's lawyer. Why wouldn't I come here? We had business to discuss. And I left before you arrived."

"Did you?" Zach tossed out the challenge. Lance could have been anywhere in the house, his car down by the garage where Zach wouldn't have seen it.

Lance stared at him, his face stony. He jerked one hand in the air. "Just beat it, and take your friend with you. Or maybe I'll call the police and have you arrested for trespassing."

"Really?" Zach sneered. "Don't forget that the settlement is still up in the air. I may get half of this place yet. Not that I want it, but a claim could make things interesting."

"It'll soon be settled," Lance said, fists clenched. "Maybe sooner than you think."

Chapter Nine

"Not exactly friends, are you?" Abby said dryly moments later as Zach gunned the Honda down the driveway. "Or was that only testosterone talking?"

Zach gave a humorless laugh. "Little of each, I'd say. Lance is very ambitious but sometimes I wonder if his brains measure up to his aspirations."

"If he's in charge of much of Eleni's business, I wouldn't underestimate him." Abby shifted in her seat. "Gretchen mentioned keys. Do you have a key to the garage apartment?"

He glanced down at the ring of keys dangling from the ignition. "Yeah, I think I still have it. Why, did you see something else?"

"Just the curtain. It moved again while you were facing off with Lance."

"It would be stupid for Eleni to be hiding out there, so close to home. Somebody would have noticed something."

"Even if they noticed, would they say anything if they were in on it?"

He gnawed on his lower lip. "Probably not. Gretchen is fiercely loyal, as we've already seen. And Dora—well, Dora probably wouldn't notice an elephant in the garden unless she tripped over it."

"So you can get in there to check it out, if you want?"

"I could, if I wanted to. But I don't think it's a good idea to try in daylight. Gretchen would call the police. She's itching to have me arrested. It'd be the perfect excuse."

"Or she'd come out and bop you with a frying pan. The last thing you need is another concussion. Zach, how well do you know Dora?"

"Pretty well. She was around all the time after we moved into the house."

"But you didn't live in the house much after it was finished, did you?"

Zach glanced at her, his mouth kicking up at the corner. "Anyone ever tell you you'd make a good lawyer? You've got the art of cross-examination down as well as anybody."

Abby felt a little rush of pleasure at his words. "That's what David used to say. He'd run a situation past me sometimes—no names, of course. That would violate client confidentiality. He said I had a knack of cutting through the crap and seeing the real picture."

"Well put. No, I didn't live in that house much. But I saw quite a lot of Dora whenever I was there. I hope you're not suspecting her of anything. She's as transparent as water."

"Is she?" Abby asked pointedly. "Or does she just want you to think that?"

"No," Zach insisted. "She's kind of flaky and fluttery. Not quite with it. Why would you think otherwise?"

"No reason. Just a feeling. And she warned you."

"Very obliquely. She often told me to be careful, worried about me. Why? Do you think she knows more about that night than she's saying?"

Abby squirmed under the dark look he gave her. "Maybe. It just seems that she's too vague about what went on. She says the storm frightened her and then she fell asleep. If you were scared, would you fall asleep in the middle of a storm, especially when the power was off? Wouldn't you go to another part of the house where you knew someone else could keep you company?''

''Yeah. I guess. But maybe she was scared to leave, to walk down the dark halls.''

''Maybe,'' Abby said, but deep inside, she didn't buy it. Nor the story about the dead flashlight batteries. In a house in the country, surrounded by trees, people usually made darn sure they had an alternate source of light. ''By the way,'' she added, ''back to what Gretchen said, do you have a key to the house?''

Zach ran the keys through his fingers. He finally picked one. ''Yeah, actually I think I do. But only to the back door and I wasn't anywhere near it that night.''

''OH, NO,'' Zach groaned when they pulled up next to the workmen's vans in front of his house. ''David's here.''

''Is that what he drives these days?'' Abby eyed the red Lexus with a twinge of envy. ''He used to have a Peugeot.''

''I think his wife still drives that.''

''I'm glad he kept it. He offered it to me but I didn't want to take the car he'd had since high school.''

Halfway out of the car, Zach glanced back at her, an odd expression on his face. ''You didn't take any kind of settlement from him, did you?''

She shrugged. ''Why should I? I was making a good living on my own. I didn't need his money.''

''That's not what most women would have said.'' Abruptly, he stood, slamming the car door closed.

Abby got out on her side, muttering, ''Then maybe you've been meeting the wrong women.'' Excess baggage. Hadn't Jane warned her he came with too much of it? She'd do well to remember it.

David burst out of the house and cleared the steps in one flying leap, as if he'd been waiting for them to return. Waiting, and nursing his anger until it spewed from him like lava from a volcano. "Zach, what the hell do you think you were doing going over to Eleni's house? Do you want to blow this case straight to hell?"

Zach put up his hands as if to ward off a blow. "David, I just went to see Eleni's Aunt Dora."

"Fat chance," David blurted. He glared at Abby. "It wasn't your idea, was it? One of your investigations?"

"No, it wasn't," Zach stated before Abby could say a word. "It was my idea. I wanted to know if Dora had seen anything that night."

"And she saw nothing. Isn't that what you found out?"

"So you've already talked to her, have you?" Zach asked. "Would have been nice if you'd told me. And how did you find out I was there? Have you got someone following me?"

"Don't you just wish. I got a call from Gretchen. Something about harassment."

Abby laughed. She couldn't help it. "Gretchen wasn't exactly welcoming, but what did she expect Zach to do, torture her and Dora for information? Give me a break. Gretchen could handle a brace of mercenaries armed with machine guns."

David burst out laughing and a moment later Zach joined in. "I see you've met the valiant Gretchen," David said, gasping for breath. "Defender of home and hearth and Eleni. She was her nanny, you know. They've been together all of Eleni's life."

No wonder Eleni grew a little twisted, Abby thought with disconcerting clarity. Of course, she only had other people's word for what Eleni was like. And Dora had painted a different picture, of a little girl in starched pinafores and curls.

"Yeah, even if Eleni committed murder, I think Gretchen

would find a way to give her an alibi," Zach said. "Even to the point of lying."

"Just stay away from the house," David warned him, laughter forgotten. "It's bad enough that the police think you had something to do with her disappearance, without you doing something that might jeopardize the settlement."

Zach's eyes met Abby's and he winked, very faintly. David, busy pulling papers out of his briefcase, obviously didn't notice Zach had made no promises. "I've got some stuff here for you to sign. Do you want to take it inside and look it over?"

Zach took the papers, his mouth twisting in distaste. "Okay. Don't leave, Abby. I'll take you out to dinner."

Abby should have given herself a moment to think, but as usual, impulse won. "I'll be here. Those roses need more work anyway."

Zach groaned. "I told you not to bother."

"No bother at all. Just run along and get your papers done."

Zach strode into the house. Abby heard him calling greetings to the workers inside. She looked up to find David still on the steps, a frown creasing his brow. "Are you sure you know what you're getting into, Abby?" he asked quietly.

Her cheeks grew hot, even though she tried to turn off the vague guilt that invaded her. "What do you mean?"

"Zach's got a lot of problems right now. I don't think he's ready for a relationship, not so soon after Eleni."

"It's been over with Eleni for years."

"Is that what he says, Abby?"

She suppressed a shiver, the hot flush fading. Wasn't that what she had thought at times, when he seemed to come on to her and then abruptly back off? But she wasn't about to let David see her niggling doubts.

"Him, and lots of other people who know them," she

said firmly. "Besides, he is divorced. He can do what he wants." *And so can I,* she added silently. Make my own mistakes.

"Eleni could show up again and make things difficult for you."

The inner chill deepened. Abby thought of the heavy breather on the phone who'd warned her about Zach. "Why should she?" She didn't recognize her own voice. Something constricted her throat, making it difficult to speak.

She hoped David wouldn't notice, but of course he knew her far too well. "Abby, what's wrong? Has something happened?"

She hugged her arms around her chest. "I suppose I might as well tell you. I got a phone call today. It woke me up just after noon."

"A phone call?" He straightened, squaring his shoulders. She could just see his mental wheels spinning into lawyer mode. "What kind of a phone call?"

"The usual heavy-breathing-pervert kind of call. What other kind is there? He—it sounded like a man—warned me about Zach. Stupid, of course. I've only known Zach a couple of weeks. There's nothing between us."

"Isn't there?" David said flatly. "Is that all the caller said?"

"Yes, that's all." She repeated the words as well as she could remember. Not that they weren't emblazoned in her brain but she'd been doing her best this afternoon to slam them into a secret compartment where they wouldn't be able to haunt her.

"Why didn't you try to trace it, you know, push *69?"

"David, it woke me out of a sound sleep. I didn't think of it."

"Maybe it's not too late. Did anyone else phone you after the call?"

"Yes, a telemarketer selling frozen food."

"Well, next time, get the number."

"I'll try, but it'll probably turn out to be a pay phone, which won't do us any good. You think there'll be a next time?"

"If you insist on staying around Zach, and especially snooping into his former life with Eleni, I wouldn't be surprised. If it happened once, it'll happen again. It could be someone connected with Eleni. In fact, Eleni herself phoned me right after Zach hired me. Said some pretty stupid stuff, not exactly threats, but insulting stuff about Zach's character and honesty. The gist of it is she seems to want to isolate him."

Abby had a mental picture of a lioness separating an antelope from a herd to attack it. Eleni sounded like a real prize. No wonder she'd decided to disappear. Probably needed to catch her breath from alienating everyone around her.

Except Lance, it appeared.

"At least Lance is loyal to her. He warned Zach off the property."

David scowled. "That's why I want him to stay away. I don't want him to talk to Lance under any circumstances. Lance is a slippery character, clever and inventive. Who knows how he might twist anything Zach says."

Abby bit her lip, restraining herself from telling him how the two men had almost come to blows.

"Why are you in this, anyway, Abby?" David said in a calmer tone. "Is it another one of your projects, the kind you used to get into with kids at the hospital? Is Zach another stray you feel needs nurturing?"

Abby glared at him. "Back to that, are we? You always resented the extra work I did."

David shook his head. "Not resented, exactly. I hated to see you breaking your heart over lost causes."

Abby shrugged. "Zach isn't a lost cause. He looked like

he could use a friend. And I was curious. Something's going on. He's had too many mishaps to dismiss as mere coincidence. And now the threat of a murder charge is hanging over his head." She heard the lengthy explanation and wondered if she was really trying to convince herself.

David frowned in a way that was all too familiar. She'd seen that look often enough during their marriage. Renewed irritation flared up in her. "Don't give me that look, David. I can take care of myself."

"I hope so," he said soberly.

Abby picked up the pruning clippers from the steps, aware of David's troubled eyes on her. "Just go in and see to your business with Zach." She raised one hand and touched his cheek, inhaling the familiar scent of Old Spice. "And don't worry, I'll be careful."

Shaking his head, he bounded up the steps. Abby found a bucket that had once held drywall compound, and set it next to the nearest rosebush. She cut off the spent blossoms and dropped them in the bucket, emptying it in the compost bin next to the garden shed when it was full.

She had progressed to the back of the house when the sound of engines and the shouts of the workmen told her they were leaving for the day. She finished the last rosebush, averting her gaze from the ruined garage. She breathed in the rich scent of the Mr. Lincoln blooms, thankful that it overpowered the odor of burned wood and fried paint and rubber.

She dumped the last of the debris in the compost and walked around to the front of the house. David's car still stood there next to Zach's rented sedan and her own little economy model.

Glancing at her watch, she was surprised to find that two hours had passed. She scanned the rosebed, a sense of accomplishment filling her. At least the roses looked less neglected than before.

And she had managed to keep her mind off Zach for a while. Most of her mind, at least. He'd sneaked in every now and then, but she'd firmly shut him out.

She laid down the clippers, rinsed her hands under the hose and entered the house, looking for a cold drink. Since there was no fridge in the kitchen, she figured there must be a cooler somewhere. She found it in the middle of the living room, sitting on the heavy tarp that protected the newly sanded floor. The bricklayers had been busy here, rebuilding the fireplace.

She popped the top on a can of soda and took a long drink before going into the kitchen. David and Zach sat at the table with their heads together, poring over a stack of papers. As she came in, Zach closed the file folder with a snap. "Let's hope we get a marginally progressive judge. Maybe I'll come out of this with at least my underwear intact."

"More than that, if I have my way," David said. "Oh, hi, Abby. Sorry we were so long."

"No problem. I just finished." She held up the can. "Want some?"

"I wouldn't mind," David said. "How about you, Zach?"

"Sure," he said absently, nimble fingers riffling through another file.

Abby brought two more cans. She set one in front of David and handed the other to Zach, who had let his chair tip back as he clawed his hands through his hair. "Trouble?" she asked.

"No more than before," he said tiredly. "Thanks." He took the can from her, his eyes widening as he looked at her hands. Setting down the can, he took them in both of his, running his thumbs gently over the scratches. "You've hurt yourself."

She laughed. "This is nothing."

"I'll say," David agreed. "She used to spend every summer covered with scratches when we lived in Vancouver. That's how she got into roses. The house we had there came with an enormous rose garden, gone totally wild. She had it whipped into shape by the first summer."

He stood, gathering the papers and files into his briefcase and snapping it closed. "Well, guys, I've got to go. Lillian and the kids'll be waiting."

The room seemed silent and somehow far too intimate when the front door closed behind him. Draining her soda can, Abby hazarded a glance at Zach. He sat on the tipped-back chair, an odd look on his face.

Abby sighed and sent the can clattering into the blue recycling bin. "Yeah, I know. So conventional. So domestic. Work all day and go home to the wife and kids. Picket fence and all."

"At least he doesn't drive a minivan," Zach said. "You know, I wanted that once. When I married Eleni."

"When you married Eleni?" Abby said incredulously. "Wasn't Eleni already in business then?"

"Sure she was. But I had some fool notion that she heard her biological clock ticking and would take some time off to have babies. She sure put me straight in a hurry."

"Come on, Zach. You weren't that young or that naive."

He shrugged. "I guess I was, and the people around us, her family and mine, perpetuated the idea. Never mind. It's a dead issue. Or will be when all the financial stuff is settled."

"When does it go to court?"

"In a couple of weeks, if there are no more delays." He let the chair settle on its four legs, and lobbed his empty can at the blue bin, landing it neatly inside. "Do you want to go home and change, or shall we go somewhere casual?"

Abby wiped her hands down her jeans. "You don't have to feel obligated. I can go home now, meet you later."

"No, I promised to buy you dinner. Pizza okay?"

"Yes, but—"

Getting up, he sauntered over and laid a finger against her lips. "No arguments." He shoved his hands into his pockets. "And after dinner, I'm going to have a look at that garage flat at Eleni's."

Abby stared at him. "Are you sure that's a good idea?"

"Good or not, I'm doing it. You thought you saw something. We're going to check it out."

The phone rang. Zach picked it up and punched the On button. "Hello? Hello, is anyone there?" A scowl deepened on his face.

With a snap of his wrist, he clicked off the phone and thumped it down on the counter. "Wrong number, I guess. I hate when people do that and don't say anything."

An eerie chill crept over Abby's skin. "Has it happened often?"

Zach shook his head. "Only once or twice since I've been staying here. Usually in the middle of the night. Well, maybe more than twice, although once somebody did speak, some drunk trying to get a taxi. Why?"

Abby tried for a casual laugh. "No reason, I guess."

"You're thinking of the call you had."

"Maybe. Could there be a connection?"

"No, probably not," he agreed.

Then why did the words sound so hollow?

"ARE YOU SURE this is such a good idea?" Abby whispered as they pushed through the thicket of rhododendrons that surrounded Eleni's garage. Overhead, a nearly full moon hung in the sky, making deep shadows that both helped and hindered them.

"Why, are you getting cold feet?" Zach fingered the key in his hand, recklessness surging through his body. After the hours struggling over the legal documents with David this afternoon and realizing how much it would cost him if he lost, he almost wished they would meet Eleni. David would probably kill him afterwards but a direct confrontation might satisfy his need for action.

"No. Actually, I'm too hot," Abby muttered. "I should have never worn this black turtleneck in the middle of summer."

"Adrenaline. Raises your body temperature."

"Whatever. Just remember what David said. You can get into trouble just for being here."

"I'm thinking of David all the time," he assured her. "He's the ultimate nag, isn't he?"

In the dim light it was hard to tell, but he thought a look of horror crossed her face, followed at once by wry amusement. "Yes, he can be that. I should know."

"I gather his present wife adores him, though."

"Yes, and I'm happy for him."

"No latent yearnings for the minivan and the picket fence?" Zach said slyly.

"No, but I don't want to be arrested for trespassing or breaking and entering, either."

He flicked the key near her nose. "Abby, my dear, it's not breaking when I have a key." He gave her a little push. "Shall we get on with it?"

She crept forward, casting a wary glance over her shoulder at the house. Suddenly she stopped so quickly he bumped into her, his heightened senses registering firm but resilient hips and a faint rose perfume. For a moment, he wanted to stay where he was, pressed against her, and forget their mission. But just in time, just as his body began to tingle and react to her nearness, he pulled back, putting a fraction of an inch between them. "What? Did you see something?"

"No," she whispered. "I just remembered there's probably a security light. Will it come on and give us away?"

"Not likely. Bulb's burned-out."

"How do you know?"

"I walked back here one night when I had to meet Eleni." One of their more acrimonious meetings, several weeks ago, he recalled. Why did she summon him to the house for their "discussions" instead of to her office?

"They could have replaced it."

"I don't think so. Too hard to reach, and since the gardener's gone, nobody's living here anyway."

"Okay, I'll take your word for it. Here goes nothing."

She moved ahead again, but he laid a hand on her arm, restraining her. "Abby, you can wait here if you want."

"No, I'll come. If you find anything, at least you'll have a witness."

He held his breath as he moved in front of her, into the open. He wasn't nearly as sure about the light as he'd let on. But to his relief, nothing happened. No spotlight flooding the stairs.

Silently, on sneakered feet, they climbed the steps. Not that anyone was likely to be there. They'd gone by the house twice after it got dark. And if anyone had seen them turn off the main road, they'd assume they were looking for an address. He'd seen headlights behind them, but the vehicle had continued straight on after he'd turned down Eleni's street.

Finally everyone had gone to bed. Dora's living-room lamp had been the last to go out, surprising him. From what he knew of her habits, she usually went to bed early.

No light had shone from the garage apartment during either of their drive-bys.

They'd left the car on the road, beneath the boughs of an evergreen, hidden from all but the keenest scrutiny. To enter the grounds, they'd climbed over a low spot in the wall where the bricks had crumbled, and cut across the lawn. A crisscross pattern of animal tracks on the dew-covered grass assured him their footprints wouldn't likely be noticed. Besides, the dew would have dried long before anyone in the house got up in the morning.

The key fitted smoothly in the lock. Zach let out his breath, feeling the sweat cool on his face. He swiped the sleeve of his shirt across his cheek. Abby was right. This was a dumb idea.

But some macho need not to lose face in front of her drove him on. He pushed open the door, peering around it before stepping inside. Abby came up behind him, her hand on his arm. He could hear her quick, shallow breathing. She was no more at ease than he was.

He closed the door quietly. Empty darkness yawned around them.

Covering his flashlight with his fingers, he turned it on, shining the reddish light around the room. He saw only bare carpet with a vacuum cleaner sitting in one corner. In the kitchen alcove, a bucket and mop stood on a square of tiled floor.

"Do we dare turn on a light?" Abby whispered.

Zach walked over to a window and checked the curtains. "Not the overhead light. This cloth isn't very thick, and the last thing we want is to alert some passing cop on patrol. This place is supposed to be vacant, remember."

"It's not hooked up to the house security system."

"No." He gestured toward the kitchen cupboards. "Do you want to start there?"

"Sure." Shielding her own flashlight with her fingers, she started opening doors and peering inside.

Zach checked out the cabinets below the built-in bookshelves. Nothing, not even dust. Going into the bedroom, he flashed the dim light around. Some furniture remained, an old brass bed with a bare mattress, and in the corner a desk. The drawers proved empty, one grating on misaligned runners, the sharp sound making him jump.

A tangle of plastic and metal hangers populated the closet, and someone had forgotten a Jets baseball cap on the top shelf.

He moved into the adjoining bathroom. A lone tube of hand cream sat on the shelf in the medicine cabinet. He opened the linen cupboard built in next to the bathtub. It was full, shelves holding blankets and sheets and pillows, another stacked full of towels. He was about to close the doors when it occurred to him what a good hiding place this would be for small items.

Standing on his toes, he slid his hands between the blankets. The cupboard wasn't deep and he could reach the far end. Nothing. Neither was there anything among the pillows.

Between the towels, his fingers encountered a thin, hard object. "Bingo," he muttered.

He pulled out a computer disk. Rummaging farther, he found another. He should have known. Eleni was paranoid about losing data, kept disks everywhere. Of course, he had no way of determining if these had been hidden last week or last year.

As he slipped them into his back pocket, he froze. Was that a sound in the other room? The fine hairs rose on his neck. Abby! He ran to the door.

Abby stood next to the window overlooking the driveway. Alone. Her shoulders were shaking. It took him a second to realize she was laughing. "What is it?" he whispered harshly.

"Remember I thought somebody was up here this afternoon? I nearly jumped out of my skin just now. Look."

Turning off her flashlight, she pulled the curtain aside. He could see that the window was open a crack, not enough to be visible from outside, but enough to move the curtain. "It was just the draft."

Not Eleni, then, Zach thought, adrenaline draining away. No, it wouldn't be that simple.

"Find anything?" Abby asked.

"Maybe," he said, going back to the closet and straightening the towels. He shone the light under the bottom shelf but only disturbed a couple of dust bunnies.

Zach cast a final look around, making sure they hadn't missed anything. Satisfied, he turned off the flashlight. A thin shaft of moonlight shining between the curtains drew a line across the floor. It hadn't earlier; the moon had moved lower in the sky. Urgency gripped him. "Let's get out of here."

He carefully locked the door behind them, pausing at the top of the stairs to scan the area below. Nothing moved, only that damned moon, making the yard as bright as day, and the shadows as deep as black holes in space. Crickets sang in the shrubbery.

They had reached the bottom of the stairs when Abby stiffened beside him. "Did you hear that?"

"What?"

"I don't know. Some kind of noise, breathing or something."

"Breathing?" Half-amused, he looked at her.

A metallic clatter sliced through the night, silencing the chirr of the crickets. As if their minds had fused together, sharing the same thought, they both dove into the rhododendrons.

Chapter Ten

Another clatter and a couple of thumps. Zach pushed Abby farther into the shadows. "What is it?" she breathed against his ear.

"Sshh," he hissed.

They huddled together, hearing nothing more, except each other's breathing. Zach wrapped his arm protectively around her, her fragrance sweet in his nostrils. The pungent scent of wet earth rose from the ground. Someone must have watered the plants earlier.

No sound disturbed the night. The crickets resumed their monotonous song. Abby shifted but Zach found he couldn't let her go, even when his muscles began to cramp. He wanted her even closer. He wanted that soft body lying beneath his.

His arm was caught just under her breasts, his thighs and groin snugged firmly against her hips. He stifled a groan as his body reacted predictably, hardening, seeking. She must have become aware of it the same moment he did, for the rhythm of her heartbeat sped up. His own heart pounded in his ears, and a deep erotic heat flooded him.

He squelched it firmly, before it could overwhelm his shredding common sense. They were in a precarious position here. At any moment someone might come by, or

Gretchen or Dora might wake up, look outside, and see them sneaking around the yard.

He eased himself up, letting his arm slide away from her. Turning slightly, he adjusted the uncomfortable tightness of his jeans. Abby stood next to him, holding her breath as she listened, head up, her lower lip caught between her teeth.

A slice of moonlight illuminated her face, making it as translucent as porcelain. He gazed at her, lost in the pure beauty of her profile. As if in a trance, he brushed back a strand of her hair. He longed to sink his fingers into the cool silk of it, but was frustrated by her sensible ponytail.

Her lips parted as if she was about to speak, luscious and pink. No lipstick, just bare, moist skin.

His own breath stuck in his throat. As if he'd fallen under a moon-spell, he lowered his head toward her, covering her mouth with his. Her lips moved softly beneath his, her breath rushing hot and sweet into his mouth. As she opened her mouth to him, a fierce pleasure surged through him.

Spreading both hands over her slender bottom, he pressed her closer. His heart stopped, tripped, then resumed when she moved against him, with slow, sinuous promise. He dragged in a deep gulp of air, then kissed her again, featherlight caresses over her downswept eyelids, across her cheeks, back to her mouth, where she again welcomed him inside. He tightened his arms, glorying in the rich taste of her, wanting more, wanting all of her.

Finally, breathless, he lifted his head, his gaze boring into hers. "I'm—going—crazy," he said, fighting for control, for sanity. "You make me crazy. And I don't know what the hell I'm going to do about it. I'm usually so sure of myself, but you—I don't know what hit me." He broke off, shaking his head.

"I know," she said quietly, too quietly.

"You feel it, too." Again he didn't know what to think,

his emotions a turmoil in his chest. He gripped her arms, holding her away, resisting the urge to pull her against him. "We have to get out of here," he said, silently calling himself twenty kinds of coward.

She stiffened, her eyes wide as she gazed at him. "Yeah, I guess we should." But she made no move to step back. Women weren't cowards, he remembered reading somewhere, not when it came to something they wanted, needed.

Could Abby ever need him?

He'd shied away from the question. He felt stupid and elated, confused, yet seeing her with devastating clarity, all at the same time.

This couldn't go on. He was suspected of kidnapping, if not murder. Abby was his partner, but only until he got to the bottom of this. Nothing more. They had no future. It would be unconscionable to drag her into the whole dirty business of the property settlement. Who knew what Eleni might do, just for revenge?

ABBY SAW the cold resolution come into his eyes, and knew the interlude, whatever she might think of it, was over. What had made him stop? Not the danger of their situation, she figured. Not the thought of getting caught. He'd remembered Eleni and her treachery. Abby was sure of it.

Telling herself she should be grateful—she'd be wise to think about this before it went further—she pushed aside the rhododendrons. "Wait," Zach cautioned her, catching her arm.

He edged in front of her and peered around the garage. Suddenly he chuckled. "There's our intruder."

At the corner of the garage, a furry mound with a black burglar's mask crouched beside the overturned garbage can. "Someone forgot to put the can inside the garage and this opportunist decided to take advantage of it. Shoo!"

He lightly clapped his hands, and the raccoon trundled

off across the lawn, its thick body making remarkable time. It vanished into the row of trees next to the wall enclosing the property.

"Okay, it's our turn to get out of here."

Abby glanced at the house. All the windows appeared dark but that didn't mean that a wakeful person wasn't watching from behind a curtain. She quickened her pace, until she was almost running. Zach lengthened his strides to keep up with her.

Her feet squished in her shoes, the heavy dew soaking through the canvas. She shivered, hugging her arms around her, recalling how hot she'd been earlier.

How hot she'd been five minutes ago. *No,* she told her all-too-responsive body, *I'll think about that kiss later, especially if it's all I'm ever going to get from him.*

"Come on," Zach urged her. "Just a quick hop over the wall and we can get the car."

He turned on the heater as soon as he'd started the car. Abby leaned forward and held out her hands to the warm air streaming from the vents.

Zach lifted his hips from the seat to get at his back pocket. Grinning triumphantly, he held up the computer disks. "So you did find something," Abby said. "Think they're important?"

"Maybe." He turned onto a wider road, passing the convenience store Gretchen must have phoned the police from the night Eleni disappeared. Closed now. A lone vehicle sat in the shadows beside the building. "Eleni always saved everything on disks in case of hard-drive failure, so they might be old ones."

"Why would they be up there?"

Zach frowned as he steered the car through the deserted township toward the freeway. "I don't know. Maybe she was helping with the cleanup after the gardener retired."

"Not everything was cleared out, I noticed, although the kitchen was as bare as Mother Hubbard's cupboard."

"No." He downshifted as he turned at the freeway ramp, accelerating onto the highway. Only a semitrailer far ahead of them winked red taillights. But—was that another car just coming onto the ramp behind him? He hadn't noticed it earlier.

"Actually, the place was furnished, but I think the living-room carpet needs to be replaced so that furniture was moved out. You see, the garage was already there when we built the house. We just left it except for some remodeling. There had been a house there, too, but it burned down in a drug raid."

"Nice neighborhood," Abby murmured drowsily.

"It is, now. But the isolation made it great for someone who had something to hide. We got a super deal on the land, and built the house from the ground up."

His words washed over her, a soothing murmur that allowed her to pretend that only this moment existed. She leaned back against the headrest, her tired brain shutting down.

Zach patted her knee as her head lolled to one side. "Sleep, Abby. I'll shut up."

She smiled faintly, and let herself drift.

She started awake when he spoke again. "Damn it, what does that guy want with his high beams on? Must be drunk."

He rolled down the window and stuck out his arm, gesturing for the other vehicle to pull around him. Abby craned her neck to look back. The car—no, truck, Abby guessed from the height of the lights—remained where it was. The beams glared like spotlights in the mirrors, effectively blinding all rear vision.

"Bloody hell," Zach burst out, winding up the window. "I'm going to try to shake him. Is your seat belt buckled?"

Abby straightened and thumbed the belt across her chest. It snapped tight on the automatic tensioner. "Maybe if you pull over—" she suggested, shaking her head to clear the fuzziness in her brain. She was never at her best just after waking, and she must have really been asleep.

"If I pull over, he might follow and run us off the road. Hold on. Here he comes."

The car lurched violently as the truck bumped it, bucking ahead and veering off to the right as if it had suddenly developed a mind of its own. Swearing, Zach let the wheel slide through his hands until the vehicle stabilized. He pushed on the accelerator. The car plunged forward as though projected from a rubber band.

The truck fell back. But not for long. In a moment, the headlights filled the mirror once more.

Another jolt, and the crunch of something breaking. "Taillight out," Zach said. "Hang on. We've got to get more speed out of this thing. If I can make it to 264th Street, we'll shake him."

Abby gripped the armrest, her fingers cramping. The car's engine screamed as Zach pushed it to maximum revs. But to Abby's dismay, the truck again ate up the lead they'd briefly gained.

It struck their rear again. Something clattered off the car and onto the highway. Abby didn't dare look back to see if they'd lost half of the trunk. Poor Zach, another car damaged. She choked back a hysterical laugh.

"What's so funny?" Zach snapped. "I don't see anything at all amusing about dodging some psycho driver at two in the morning when there's not a cop in sight."

"It's not funny at all," Abby said, another uncontrollable giggle rising up her throat. "Your insurance is going to go through the roof."

"No kidding. Easy for you to laugh about it."

"More a case that if I don't laugh, I'll scream."

"Brace yourself," he suddenly shouted. "He's coming again. And we're turning off."

She saw the big green sign for the exit looming on the right, flashing by. At the last second, before hitting the cement divider, Zach wrenched the steering wheel around and, tires squealing, careened into the exit. He braked, and gravel went spinning as the wheels hit the unpaved shoulder.

The truck, unable to follow, shot by down the highway. Its horn wailed as the driver leaned on it, fading into the distance as the taillights grew smaller. Moments later they vanished as the vehicle topped the hill and disappeared over it.

"I don't suppose you got the license number?" Zach asked, breathing rapidly. "I know I didn't."

Abby shook her head. "It was muddy. I couldn't even see if he had one on the front with the lights glaring like that."

"Doesn't matter," Zach said, putting the car into motion once more, heading south. "The truck was probably stolen, anyway. They'll find it abandoned in a gravel pit or something in the morning."

Abby tapped her fingers on the armrest. "Question is, was it some kid with a few beers under his belt randomly trying to scare us, or were we the target?"

"And the second question is, do we report it? Or is it not worth the trouble?"

"I don't know," Abby said slowly. "Do you think the police will do anything?"

"Not much. They haven't been able to find Eleni—why should they care if some drunk or lunatic nearly drove us off the road." He paused, dragged in a breath. "On the other hand, if the truck is stolen and they find it, maybe they can dust it for fingerprints and see if any of them match those found in Eleni's car. Yeah, I guess we'd better report it. At least we know the make and model.''

He reached into the glove compartment and pulled out a cell phone.

AN HOUR LATER Zach stopped in front of Abby's house. He turned off the engine, and swung around to face her. "I can't believe they made us come all the way to the police station. And reporting that truck was probably a big waste of time. They had no record of it being stolen and without the license number, no way to trace it.''

"Its owner probably hasn't missed it yet," Abby said. "I mean, how many times at night do you go out to check if your car is still parked at home?''

"I'll call the police back in the morning." He touched her cheek with one fingertip. His hand was warm and she almost snuggled her face into it.

Almost.

"I'm sorry, Abby," he said. "I didn't mean to keep you out so late.''

"At least I can sleep in tomorrow." She yawned widely, patting her mouth with her open hand.

"When do you work next?''

"Tomorrow night. Is that Friday night? Whatever. I'm too tired to think." She fumbled for the door handle. "Good night.''

"Wait." She paused, turning her head questioningly. He lifted his hand and tucked it under her hair. Half of it had worked loose from the ponytail and hung down her neck. She must look a mess, she thought, makeup long gone, her hair as tangled as if she'd been dragged through a blackberry hedge.

His fingers sifted through the long strands, brushing her nape. Unconsciously she tensed her muscles, and he tightened his grip, kneading gently.

She rocked her head from side to side. "Ah, that feels good." *Keep it impersonal, Abby. Don't think about the heat.*

"Abby." His breath feathered her mouth, then his lips came down, gently but firmly, a kiss of promise rather than passion. "Abby, I hope this won't scare you off. I want to see you again but maybe we should wait a little, at least until the police give me a report."

She pushed at him, half playful, half serious. "Oh, no, you don't. You can't shut me out." No matter what, she had to see it through. "I want to know the minute you find out what's on those disks, as well. But don't call before noon."

"I won't be alive before noon." He bent toward her again, but before he could kiss her, she had opened the door and jumped out.

She poked her face back into the car. "Good night, Zach."

Something tightened in his chest, gripped his vocal cords. She had more courage than most soldiers going into battle. Loyalty and tenacity, too. "Good night, Abby," he said, nearly choking on the words.

He turned the key in the ignition. The engine leaped to life and he quickly engaged the gear and drove away.

Abby stood there until the taillights, one the proper red and the other shining white through the broken glass, disappeared down the street.

A SHRILL SCREAM pierced the dream. Zach threw his arms over his head, covering his eyes. Searing lights drilled into his brain. He couldn't shut them out. They came closer, closer. *No.* He tried to call out a warning. A warning to whom? He couldn't remember. He had to get away.

Another shriek. He jerked upright, nearly falling off the cot as the sheets tangled around his legs. Fire alarm?

Adrenaline pumped through him. He ripped aside the sheets, his feet hitting the cold floor.

He tore across the room to the window. No fire. The skeleton of the garage cast grotesque moon shadows on the lawn.

Another strident screech. He barked out a harsh laugh as he grabbed the ringing phone.

"I'm going to get you. You can't escape." The eerie whisper sent ice down his spine. "You'd better watch your back every second of the day. You'll never know where I am."

Zach collapsed onto the tumbled bed. "What? Who are you?"

"Someone who's watching you."

A click told him the line had disconnected. He punched Number Recall. A disembodied voice recited a number. Snatching up a pen, he scribbled it on the back of an envelope. He disconnected and dialed the number. As he'd expected, he got another recording: "The number you have dialed cannot be completed. If you have a problem, please dial zero for the operator."

He swore in frustration. A pay phone, naturally. What else?

Slamming down the phone, he straightened the sheets and threw himself back onto the cot. He linked his hands behind his head and stared up at the ceiling. His brain was running on permanent overload. He'd never sleep now.

What he hadn't told Abby this afternoon was that he'd had several calls in the middle of the night, the kind you dismiss as a drunk or a wrong number. No one speaking, just the hollow silence of an open line. Lately, it had become a nightly occurrence. Between the calls and his nightmares, he wasn't getting much sleep.

At least this time the caller had spoken. Not that it made much difference. The sinister whisper could have been male or female, or a machine—like Abby's caller yesterday. The caller hadn't addressed him by name but he suspected it wasn't a wrong number.

Just as that truck earlier, which had turned up again to haunt his nightmares, hadn't picked them as a random target for highway harassment.

The phone rang again. Zach stared at it, daring it to ring a second time. It did. When a third ring pealed out, he jerked it to his ear. "Talk, damn you."

Nothing. Only silence. Then he heard a breath, long, drawn-out, then another, and another, until it sounded like a dog panting on a hot day. "Oh, hell," Zach yelled into the phone. "That is so trite. Can't you think of anything more original?"

Obviously, crank callers couldn't. Furthermore, he'd obviously insulted him/her. The connection was broken abruptly, filling his ear with a dial tone.

Giving up on the idea of sleep, Zach sat up and pulled on a pair of boxer shorts. He flicked on the light, blinking in the sudden glare. Picking up his keys, he crossed the room. He stuck one into the lock of a steel-bound trunk in the corner. It didn't turn. He frowned. Had he forgotten to lock it?

Must have. He lifted the lid, heart thumping. To his relief, the laptop computer was still there. He took it out and carried it back to the cot, vowing to be more careful.

Piling pillows against the wall, he propped the computer on his thighs and turned it on. He inserted one of the disks he'd found in the garage closet.

A row of words and numbers materialized on the screen. Leaning forward, Zach began to study them.

BY NOON, Abby's phone had rung twice. The first was a wrong number, some child speaking to Big Mama in Punjabi. Abby had gently told her she'd better try again. She had just dropped back to sleep when a telemarketer offered her the deal of the decade on carpet cleaning. Abby barely restrained herself from rudely telling off the perky girl, managing to mumble, "Not interested."

So much for sleeping. At least she'd gotten five hours. She was surprised she'd slept at all, after the evening's excitement, but her brain had turned off the minute her head hit the pillow. No nightmares about being chased by a psycho pickup truck. And in the light of day, she found it easier to dismiss the incident as a drunk driver having a little fun at their expense.

She decided she might as well get up and get some work done. She needed to grocery shop as well.

The phone rang again as she was getting out of the shower. Wrapping a towel around her dripping body, she padded into the kitchen to pick it up. "Hello?"

"Abby, can you meet me for lunch?" Zach asked without preliminaries. "I'd ask you to come here but there's nothing to eat and it's even noisier than it's been."

"Sure," Abby said, figuring she could get basic groceries on the way. Housecleaning, a job she detested, could wait.

"Okay. Do you like Chinese?"

"Great. How about the Fortune Cookie?"

"Fine. In about an hour, then."

ABBY REACHED the restaurant only five minutes late. She parked on the street and locked the car, brushing back her hair. Hot and flustered after a flying trip through the supermarket, she drew in a long breath and composed her face, hoping she didn't look as flushed as she felt.

A blast of air-conditioning hit her when she walked in the door, welcome after the heat outside. The place was crowded with lunchers, attesting to its popularity.

She spotted Zach at once. He'd managed to snag a window table, which meant he'd likely been early.

She rushed over and sat down before he could get up and pull out her chair. "I'm not that late, am I?"

"Not worth mentioning." He grinned, but his eyes looked tired, the lines at the corners etched more deeply than usual. He obviously hadn't slept well, dark circles underscoring the shadows in his eyes.

Abby opened her mouth to ask him if anything else had happened when the waitress came up with glasses of water and an order pad. "The Number One lunch special," Abby said without looking at the menu.

"And for you, sir?"

"I'll have the same." He handed the girl both menus and she hurried off.

He folded his hands on the table, his eyes meeting Abby's. "Okay. Do you want the good news, the bad news, or the I'm-not-sure-how-to-interpret-it news?"

"Might as well start with the bad and get it over with," Abby said, the flippant tone belying the sudden knot in her stomach.

"The car-rental company took a very dim view of the damage to the Honda."

"Won't your insurance cover it?"

"It will, I think, except for the deductible. But I have to wait until next Monday before I can see anybody, so I'm still driving it until then. I may have a bit of talking to do, because they're always suspicious of supposed hit-and-run accidents. Not to mention two accidents in less than a month. They're going to wonder what kind of driver I am."

"But neither of them were your fault," Abby said indignantly.

"I know," he said gloomily. "But it does strain credulity. Good thing we reported last night's incident to the police, if only to get it on record."

"Yes, good thing. So that's the bad. What's the good news?"

This time his grin was real. "I can pick up my own Jaguar whenever I want. They've got it all back together and repainted."

Abby smiled back at him. "Where will you park it, since you no longer have a garage? You wouldn't want anything else to happen to it."

"I'll park it in front of the house and leave the outside lights on all night. At least it'll be visible from the road and no one will be likely to tamper with it."

The waitress returned in a few moments and placed their plates in front of them. "Enjoy your lunch."

"Thank you," Zach said.

Abby picked up her fork and dug into the sweet-and-sour pork, chow mein and rice. She chewed for a moment, then asked, "Okay, what's the other news?"

Zach set down his fork and poured Chinese tea from the pot he'd ordered earlier. "It's complicated. I called the police and they found a truck that fits the description of the one that rammed us last night. One broken headlight—score one for us—scraped bumper, dented fender, and no stereo. Yes, it was stolen. The owner reported it in the morning. Must have been some joyrider."

"Maybe." Abby thought of the successive crashes into their car. Once could have been an accident, a moment's inattention by a drunk driver. But three or four? Not likely.

"You don't believe that, do you?" Zach said.

"No, I don't. Do you?"

"No."

"More to the point, do the police?"

Zach shrugged. "I don't know. I couldn't tell. These cases have very low priority because of the minimal chances of solving them. But the fact that we were hit more than once might help my case with the insurance and the rental company.''

''What else?''

Zach paused, his face animated, his eyes dancing. ''I checked out the disks we found.''

''You must have been busy. That's why you didn't sleep.''

A shutter came over his face, leaving it stony and drawn. ''I didn't sleep because the phone woke me up. First a vague threat, followed by a heavy breather.''

The food turned to lead in Abby's stomach and she pushed away the half empty plate. She wrapped her hands around the bowl of tea, seized by an urge to warm her icy fingers. ''Like mine.''

''Probably. You didn't get any more calls, did you?''

Abby laughed shakily. ''I slept so soundly I probably wouldn't have heard the phone anyway. I had a couple of calls this morning, a wrong number and a carpet cleaning service, the usual crap.''

''Wrong number?''

''Not our heavy breather, unless it's a Sikh child talking to Grandma.''

''Oh, a *real* wrong number.''

''Yes. For sure. What did you find on the disks?''

''A lot of stuff that you could only understand in its proper context. And one significant thing which may or may not be important. It appears that Eleni's business enterprises are not doing as well as they used to.''

Chapter Eleven

Abby shifted in her chair, her eyes fixed on a bit of tea leaf floating in the pale liquid. "Does that mean she's not looking after it the way she should? Or did this start in the past week?"

"Don't I wish?" Zach said with a grim smile. "If those disks had been updated in the past week, no one would have to worry that Eleni has met with foul play. No, the last entry is nearly a month old." He frowned. "Although there is something peculiar about the dates. I couldn't figure everything out, but I'll have another go at it later."

"When did Lance start taking over more of the workload?"

"I don't know. Katie might have an idea."

"But Eleni's business is large and diverse, isn't it?" Abby said. "From what I understand, she's got real estate, a retail store selling cosmetics, even a place where they make plastic pipe. It wouldn't all just start failing at once, would it?" She made a self-deprecating gesture. "But what do I know about business, anyway?"

"Probably more than you think," Zach said seriously. "You run a household, however small. Same idea. Income has to equal or exceed outflow."

"Of course."

"Well, any business has to operate on the same principles. You can have outstanding debts, but they shouldn't add up to more than a certain percentage of total income. In the last six months or so, Eleni's enterprises have gone awfully close to the danger level in accounts outstanding. Cash-flow problem, mainly.''

"Shouldn't Lance be looking after that?"

"Yes. If she's left him in charge, he should be either cutting expenses somewhere, or putting more pressure on creditors to pay their accounts promptly."

"Is this the case in every area of her business?"

Zach frowned. "Not everything was on those disks, of course, but yes, profits are down and outstanding debt up everywhere."

"Isn't that unusual? Surely economic factors couldn't affect all of it the same way at the same time."

Zach grinned. "You should go into business, Abby. That's exactly right. Not all of it should be affected at once."

"Does that mean Lance is incompetent?"

His grin broadened. "I'd like to think so, because if he shows the same level of competence in the property settlement case, David will run circles around him." He sobered. "But I can't dismiss him that easily as a self-important doorknob. He may be hampered by Eleni's interference much of the time, but the last proposal he made on the property settlement, which he must have calculated since she disappeared, was more astute than previous ones."

"Is it possible that he's behind Eleni's disappearance?"

Zach pursed his mouth, tapping his fingers on the table. "I'd say not likely. And if the rumor is true that Eleni was planning to marry him, he would have every reason to keep her around."

Abby sipped her tea, the wheels going around in her head. "There is another possibility," she suggested, setting down her tea cup. "Maybe Eleni went off somewhere to get away from the stress of business. Don't forget what Dora said about Eleni and Lance arguing about some deal not working out. Anything about that on the disks?''

Zach shook his head. ''Must have been something initiated more recently. I wonder if David can find out what it was.''

The waitress set a small tray with fortune cookies and their bill on the table. ''May I take your plates?''

''Yes, we're done,'' Zach said. He handed Abby a fortune cookie.

She broke it open, unfolded the little slip of paper. '''Fortune will smile on you,''' she read aloud. ''That's encouraging. What does yours say?''

''Something I hope isn't too prophetic. 'Dark clouds are gathering on your horizon but the sun will soon shine.''' He tossed it down, and picked up the bill. ''Let's go. People are waiting for the table.''

In the car, Zach made no move to turn on the ignition. He stared morosely out of the windshield. Abby rolled down the window at her side as sweat trickled down her neck. A breeze rustled the leaves of a nearby tree, but did little to relieve the heat condensing inside the car.

''You're not letting a fortune-cookie message spoil your day, are you?'' Abby said at last.

He started, as if he'd been so lost in his thoughts that he'd forgotten her presence. ''Cookie?'' He laughed humorlessly. ''No, of course not.''

He leaned forward and twisted the key. The engine started, cool air pouring from the vents. ''I'm sorry,'' Zach said. ''I didn't realize it was so hot.''

Didn't realize? Abby would have laughed if he hadn't been wearing that black scowl. Little beads of sweat stood out on his upper lip and his hair clung damply to his temples. He glanced at her as he pulled into the street. ''Do you want me to drop you somewhere, or do you want to come along?''

''Come along where?''

''That's what I was trying to figure out. I should see David and ask him about Eleni's business. And after that— I don't know.''

He braked at a red light. ''Remember that night you rescued me from the side of the road?''

''Yes?'' How could she forget? That was when she'd been forced to see him as much more than her patient.

''Well, that cabin I was heading for...I wonder if Eleni might have gone there. Not that camping was ever her thing, but if she wanted to get away—'' His voice trailed off.

Abby sat up straighter. ''Yes, except that the road was washed out.''

''The night we were up there, it was.'' Zach reminded her. ''It would have been okay the day before, or even earlier the same day, before the storm. She could have gone up then.''

''What about her car? She couldn't have walked all that way.''

''Why? I was planning to.'' He flashed her a quick grin, which just as quickly slid away. ''No, not likely. Eleni isn't the athletic sort. But she could have borrowed or rented another car. Or better yet, a four-wheel drive.''

''Or somebody could have given her a lift there.''

''Yes. Maybe even Lance, never mind that he denies having seen her since that night.''

He pulled into a parking lot next to a nondescript brick building. ''Here's David's office. Do you want to come in? It's bound to be cooler in the waiting room than in the car.''

THE FIRST PERSON they saw upon entering the second floor office was Katie. David, shirtsleeves rolled up to his elbows, his tie hanging loose under his unbuttoned collar, held the door for her. "I'll take care of it, Mrs. Andros. You don't have to worry about a thing."

"Thank you." She turned, saw Zach and Abby. Surprise sent her delicately penciled brows up, but she quickly smiled and hugged Zach, leaning over to kiss the air next to Abby's cheek. "Abby, Zachary, what brings you here in the heat of the day? You should go out to White Rock. The sea must be lovely today."

"Work, Katie," Zach said. "Some of us have to work. And I might ask the same of you."

She smiled archly. "Just a slight amendment to my will."

"Leaving it all to a charity for homeless cats?" Zach teased.

Katie playfully pinched his cheek. "You know better than that, Zachary. I donate mainly to human charities. Not that our furry friends don't deserve our concern, but people have to come first. By the way, have you ever changed your will since the divorce?"

Zach frowned. "No, but—"

"The property has to be settled first," David cut in. "Call me Monday, Mrs. Andros. I'll be able to tell you when to come in to sign the documents."

"I'll do that." She smiled, adjusting her sun hat. "And thank you, David."

"David, could I see you for a moment?" Zach asked. He glanced at the vacant reception desk. "Are you all by yourself?"

"She's out for lunch. Come into my office. Abby, help yourself to some coffee, if you want."

"Thanks."

"Abby and I will be fine," Katie said, tucking her hand into the crook of Abby's elbow.

As soon as the door of David's office closed behind the

men, Katie drew Abby down to a seat on the sofa in the waiting area. "How are you and Zachary doing, Abby?"

Abby felt a blush climb up her neck and fervently hoped it wouldn't reach her face. "Fine. We aren't making much progress, though." Her face burned as a knowing look crept into Katie's eyes. "I mean, with finding Eleni and clearing Zach of suspicion."

Katie's eyes twinkled. "That's what I meant, too. You saw Gretchen and Dora, did you?"

"Yes." Abby hesitated for a second, then plunged ahead. "Do you know Dora well?"

"Not all that well, but yes, I know her." Katie smoothed her hair under the brim of her hat. "Don't be taken in by that poor-little-me act of hers. Dora's not helpless at all. One has to admire her. She never married, never worked. She had a small inheritance from her parents, but she's always managed to live with one relative or another. The last few years it's been Eleni because almost everyone else has died. Eleni's family has become rather sparse in this generation. Dora tried to hint to me one day that she wouldn't mind visiting me for a while, that there was nothing to do out in Surrey and she'd like to work for some of my charities here in Abbotsford, but I managed to steer the conversation to a different track."

"Surely she didn't think she could live with you?" Abby said. "I understand from Zach that you only have a small place."

"Two bedrooms, but I use one as an office for my volunteer work. I don't have a spare bed. And I don't have an obligation to Dora. She's Eleni's relative, not mine. And no reputable charity wants her help anymore. If that woman adds a row of numbers five times, she comes up with five different answers."

Abby laughed. "Yes, I can see that."

"Don't be fooled, though. Dora has backbone and more

nerve than a matador. She always lands on her feet, usually in someone else's guest room.'' Katie patted Abby's hand. ''Well, I must be off. I'll call you.''

"ELENI'S AUNT DORA would have a motive for getting Eleni out of the way," Abby mused aloud when she and Zach were back in the car. "If Eleni was tired of her living in her house, she might have been thinking of kicking her out. And Dora wouldn't have had a place to go."

Zach threw back his head and shouted with laughter. "Eleni and Dora used to argue sometimes, but they always made it up again. I think they enjoy it. Eleni likes the power she has over Dora, and Dora likes to feel she's the helpless victim. Seems illogical, but there it is."

"But what if Eleni meant it this time?"

"Don't worry about it, Abby. What would Dora do? Murder Eleni and somehow transport the body some place where it wouldn't be found? She's not strong enough, nor aggressive enough to even dream of such a thing. No, Abby, I don't know what kind of stuff Katie's been putting into your head, but this time you're barking up the wrong tree."

"Maybe," Abby muttered, not willing to give up the idea that quickly. Motive was something they hadn't looked at closely. Eleni's motive for disappearing. Or anyone else's motive for making her disappear....

"Now, Katie," Zach added speculatively. "Katie would be strong enough to kill Eleni and smart enough to hide it. And she never could stand Eleni. Not to mention that lately she's been livid over the way Eleni is trying to get my business. Katie could have done it."

"No, she couldn't have," Abby stated positively, shooting him a withering look. "She wouldn't have risked having you in a position where you'd be a suspect. And she wouldn't have done it in a sneaky fashion."

"No, she would have gotten a gun and shot her on the main street at high noon." He grinned at Abby. "See how absurd that idea is. We *are* going crazy, suspecting everyone."

Abby sighed. "Are we going to pick up your car?"

"Not yet," Zach said. "They want the paint to dry a little longer. That's why I'm keeping the rental until tomorrow morning." He frowned. "Just remembered. Your car is still at the restaurant. But it'll be okay until we get back."

"Sure," Abby said. "We can pick it up later."

"You're sure you have time to go up to the cabin?"

"Of course. Unless you don't want me to come."

He shot her a look from narrowed eyes. "I want you," he said, his voice low and deep. "Believe me, I want you."

Awareness raced through Abby, settling in a simmering pool in her abdomen. She stared out the window at her side, trying to suppress the way he made her feel, hot and needful, faintly wicked and too conscious of herself as a woman. No matter how she might deny it, keeping their search as a buffer between them, no man had made her feel like this, not even David.

An hour later, Zach turned onto the mountain road. She remained silent, choosing to pretend she hadn't sensed the hidden meaning behind his words. She was a coward, lying to herself. And indirectly, to him.

It was safer that way. They were drawn together by their quest, but what would happen afterwards, when real life resumed? Could she bear it if she let herself love him and then he walked away?

Sun and shade dappled the road through the forest. A couple of crows flew in front of the car, squawking raucously. "That looks like the spot where you picked me up in the storm," Zach said casually. "See that big hemlock? I'm pretty sure that's where I fell asleep."

"Passed out, you mean," she said, forcing a lightness she didn't feel.

"Yeah, probably. Good thing you came along. Do you always pick up strangers along the road?"

"Only if it's storming. And you weren't a stranger."

"I was until after you'd stopped. You couldn't have recognized me in the dark."

"That's true."

"So you picked up a stranger."

"Call me the last fool of the twentieth century," Abby said. "David was always on my case because of it. Although I never picked up anyone beside the road before. Jane thinks it's romantic."

"Yeah, Jane would. She thinks everyone should be paired up, like on Noah's ark."

"Yes, I forgot. You know her, don't you?"

"We've met at a few of Eleni's gatherings."

A faint bitterness in his tone drew her attention. "Obviously, you didn't enjoy Eleni's gatherings," she said lightly.

"Not much, although I enjoyed Jane. I know, I know, you're going to ask what Eleni and I ever saw in each other. Truth is, it beats me." He slanted her another glance. "Now you and I—I have a feeling we're on the same wavelength. And it must mean something that Katie likes you. She didn't like Eleni, even when Eleni was on her best behavior."

Was he flirting with her? Abby wondered. Maybe, but Eleni still stood between them, and the excess baggage Zach carried around as a result of his disastrous marriage to her. He had to end one phase of his life before he could start another. Abby would be crazy to get deeply involved with him until Eleni was well and truly relegated to his past. Which meant they had to find her first.

"There's the driveway," Zach said. "You can just see the house between the trees."

The shutters over the upper windows were closed, a sure sign no one was there. Of course, Jane was working, but sometimes one or another of her children would use the house. Not this week, apparently.

"Quite a contrast from that night," Abby commented idly. "All sunshine today."

The road forked. Zach took the left one, which rapidly began to climb. A black squirrel bounded across in front of the car, scolding shrilly as it leaped into a tree.

Zach pointed ahead of them. "There. That must be where the road washed out."

Abby gazed down into a deep ravine as he steered the car slowly onto a makeshift wooden bridge that crossed the washout. Far below, massive boulders lay in a pile, an infant mountain that could have buried Abby's car that night if she'd continued on. She shuddered as she imagined the rumble of sliding earth, sweeping trees and shrubs out of its path.

The hiss of tires on the wooden ties changed to a crunch as they reached the gravel road on the other side. "Safe," Abby whispered.

His eyes met hers, dark and somber. "Yes, safe. And don't worry, it's not going to storm tonight."

He gunned the engine up the steep slope. "I had an interesting talk with David, about the computer disks."

"Oh?"

"Yeah. The timing of some of the entries. I hired David about six weeks ago when my previous attorney quit. She was fed up with Eleni's increasingly extravagant demands, said she'd never seen a case like this."

Abby raised her brows. "That must have been interesting, having a woman as your lawyer in the case against your ex-wife."

Zach shrugged. "She was highly recommended as a property-settlement expert, but Eleni was too much for her. Too bad. I had confidence in her, but at least now I have David and he may be on to something. The demands increased about the time Eleni's business started going downhill."

"So she needed money."

"It appears that way, but I don't understand why. If she was in trouble she could have still come to me for a loan."

"You would have loaned her money?" Abby asked incredulously.

"Sure. Strictly business, properly drawn up and notarized. It would have been a good investment, since Eleni is an astute businesswoman. Something must have happened to cause this downturn, but I'm betting in a few months she'll have the problems solved and be on the right track again."

With Zach's money, if the property settlement went in her favor, Abby thought cynically.

Poor Zach was too generous by far.

"I know what you're thinking," Zach said, interrupting her increasingly dismal thoughts.

"How clever of you," she said dryly.

A fleeting smile touched his lips. "Not so clever. You're thinking I'm a glutton for punishment. I just want to assure you I'm not. I'd lend her money if it seemed like a good business deal but that doesn't mean I'll let her take everything I worked for because of some community-property crap."

His face hardened, a muscle tensing in his jaw. "I worked bloody hard for my business. She had her own business and she should have understood. But, in fact, she resented much of the time I put into it. No way am I just going to hand it over to her. Not without a fight."

THE CABIN sat at the end of an open meadow, neatly fenced with white painted boards. A small herd of Black Angus cattle grazed on the rippling grass. "Yours?" Abby asked, still a little stunned by his last passionate declaration. "Or is that another of Eleni's enterprises?"

Zach shook his head. "There's a cattle ranch down near the lake. This is their land. I lease the section the cabin's built on." His eyes narrowed against the sun slanting across the meadow. "Doesn't look as if anyone's here."

"Or been here," Abby said. "The grass in the middle of the track is too high. No one's driven over it in weeks, I'd say."

The cattle eyed them curiously as they drove by, one hanging its head over the fence, yellow and white daisies dangling from its jaws. Abby laughed, waving jauntily. The cow jumped back and sauntered off, tail twitching in annoyance.

Zach produced a key from the ring he carried and opened the cabin door. Heat greeted them, along with a musky cedar smell. Ghostly white sheets covered the furniture. Zach slapped at the back of a chair. Dust rose into the air, shimmering in the shaft of light from the window Abby pushed open.

"Big waste of time, coming up here," Zach grumbled. He walked down the hall, peering into the bathroom, which smelled damp and a bit moldy. In the room beyond it, the bed lay smooth and untouched under a quilt Katie had given him for Christmas the year he bought the cabin.

He pushed away the memory. He'd come up here alone that year, seeking solitude. Eleni had gone on a cruise to Mexico, arranging it without consulting him. They'd fought about it. He had business obligations he couldn't leave; she pouted, then raged that he didn't care about her.

At that time, two years into their marriage, he hadn't cared, numbed by the constant friction. Nothing pleased

Eleni. They'd gone to Hawaii the month before, in an effort to make things work. A total fiasco, especially when a storm warning had kept them inside the hotel, bickering, for two days. It wasn't the second honeymoon he'd naively envisioned.

"No one's been here," Abby said behind him, jolting him back to the present. "There's no food and the fridge is turned off. How would you have managed if you'd come up last week?"

He shrugged, shaking off the weight of past memories, past regrets. "Starved, I guess. You're right about head injuries. They addle your brain. I sure wasn't thinking that day."

To distract himself, he leaned closer to her, brushing back a strand of her hair with one finger. When he came near her, she filled his senses, leaving no room for the past. "I'm no good for you, Abby."

"I know," she said softly, although a little frown creased her brow. She closed her eyes and turned her face into his palm. Perspiration lay in a moist sheen on her skin. He cupped his hand around her cheek. Cool. Soft as that peach silk shirt she'd worn the other day.

"Abby," he whispered. "Tell me to go away. I'm only going to hurt you." His thumb rested on her throat. Her pulse sped up, galloping into high gear, matching the pounding of his.

She tilted up her face. He gazed at her for a long, breathless moment. Her lashes lay in dark crescents against the pale skin. A delicate flush painted her cheekbones.

He dipped his head, covering her mouth with his, breathing in her fragrance, a complex bouquet of warm woman and meadow flowers. Her lips parted, resilient and responsive under his, her teeth sharp and smooth against his tongue. He clasped her tightly against him, wanting to absorb her into his skin, his being, so that he wouldn't be able to tell where he left off and she began. So not a single memory could sneak between them.

He tangled his fingers in the cool silk of her hair. Today it smelled of coconut, lush and tropical. He spread it over her shoulders, wishing he could see it spread on a pillow, himself above her, joining with her.

Lost.

His hand delved beneath the silky waves, shaping her skull, ranging down to her nape, sliding over her ear, around the delicate shell.

The room faded away, his senses centered on the taste of her, the feel of her softness against his hard body. Gasping for breath, he opened his eyes. The sun dazzled him, slanting its rays into the window as it sank toward the forest.

His palm clung to her skin, sticky and moist. Suddenly he was back in Eleni's house. Darkness mercifully cloaked the blood spilled on the floor. His hands, sticky, clammy.

He stiffened, letting go of her so abruptly that for a second Abby swayed against him, off-balance. He shook his head, trying to drive out the picture of Eleni lying on the Aubusson rug, lightning glinting off her mahogany-colored hair. Blood pooling around her.

Had he killed her?

Half fearfully, he looked at Abby. She glared at him, her lips set in a straight line. "I suppose that was another experiment," she said scathingly. "Well, I'm tired of these games."

Chapter Twelve

She spun away from him, running for the door. Zach snagged her wrist, pulling her back to him. They stood facing each other, sudden adversaries. Her eyes blazed, and her chest heaved with every breath she took.

Zach lowered his head until his forehead rested against hers. She jerked back, twisting her arm in his grasp. He braced himself for a kick in the shins but apparently solitary children of middle-aged parents never learn to fight dirty. She glared at him, her face flushed with temper and exertion. A trickle of sweat slipped down her temple and over her cheek. She swiped it away with her free hand.

"No, this isn't a game, Abby," Zach said quietly, his heart aching. If only he were free. If only he could let himself love her. If only he could be sure he hadn't killed Eleni. "I'm sorry."

Letting her go, he turned away, scrubbing his palms over his face. As soon as he closed his eyes, he saw the woman lying on the blood-stained carpet, heard someone screaming. Tension gripped his head in a vise, and his temples throbbed. He dug the heels of his hands into them, willing the pain to go away.

His vision blurred, and he stumbled into the bathroom, nearly slamming his head into the mirror before he wrenched the cabinet open. A open roll of antacids sat on the shelf, along with a bottle of aspirin. He picked it up, squinting at the expiration date. Last month.

Good enough. Unscrewing the cap, he shook three of the white tablets into his palm. He tossed them into his mouth, nearly gagging on the bitter taste as he swallowed them dry. He recapped the bottle and set it on the shelf.

He found Abby sitting on the steps, holding a pinecone and trying to coax a squirrel to take it from her hand. At the sound of his footsteps, the shy creature chattered shrilly and ran off.

Abby looked up at him, her face closed, expressionless. His heart sank. He locked the door, flipping the key ring between his thumb and forefinger. He winced as the metallic jingle clashed against his eardrums. "Let's go."

She stood up and stalked to the car, back straight as a fashion model's.

"Abby, I'm sorry," he said once he'd settled behind the steering wheel and started the car. The headache subsided to a dull, rhythmic beat as the aspirin began to work.

She set her mouth in a mutinous line, obviously determined not to speak. The odd thing was, he wasn't completely sure what he'd done wrong. He'd kissed her. She had responded; he knew he wasn't mistaken. Then the dreams, memories, or whatever they were, had crowded into his head. He'd stopped, letting her go. What else could he have done? It was as if Eleni was a silent witness, cynically observing them.

In some corner of his mind he was glad he'd stopped. Call him a romantic, but he didn't want the first time he made love with Abby to be a hurried grope in a mountain cabin with all of its limited conveniences turned off.

Make love? Hadn't he told himself they couldn't? Not until his life was settled. But when he kissed her, all his uncertainties dissolved like smoke. He wanted her. He needed her.

"Abby." He tried again. "I didn't mean to hurt you."

Her hands balled into white-knuckled fists on her knees. "I hate this," she burst out.

Astonished by the words ringing in his ears, he jerked the steering wheel, nearly sending the car off the road. It lurched as he corrected the skid on the gravel surface. "Hate what?"

"The way you blow hot and cold. One minute you're kissing me, the next you go off into some mental fugue and I don't know where you are. And you're positively obsessed with Eleni. But you say you want me. Make up your bloody mind." She yelled the last words at a volume an opera diva would have envied.

"Abby—" He started to lay a calming hand on her arm but she yanked it out of his reach, crowding close to the door. He stared at her in amazement. Abby, usually so unruffled, her composure learned in the hectic pace of the emergency ward, was angry. And not just angry. Royally pissed. He couldn't believe it.

On the other hand, maybe he should have expected it. She was right. Uncertain of his own feelings, he must have communicated that to her.

"I'm fed up to the eyeballs with you twisting me around," she said, fingers clenching on the armrest.

"I haven't."

"You—are—crazy, do you know that?" she declared angrily.

"I know." He suddenly sobered. "In more ways than one."

"At least you admit it," she said, her voice ripe with satisfaction.

"I've got a headache, too, not that that's an excuse."

She stared at him, all concern at once. "Maybe it explains the way you seem to blank out. Are you sure you shouldn't see the doctor again? Maybe there was more damage than they first thought.''

"No, it's okay. Just a lot on my mind.''

The car hummed across the wooden bridge, suspended precariously over thin air. This time Abby didn't seem to notice. She bit at a thumbnail, her forehead creased. "I don't understand you, Zach. Maybe that's why Jane warned me about getting involved with you.''

Yeah, Jane would have, he thought, then the rest of Abby's statement hit him. "Involved? Are we involved?''

She gestured impatiently and for a second he thought she'd sock his arm again. "Aren't we? What do you think?''

He considered it, a warm feeling circling his heart. "Yeah, I guess we are, since you made clearing my name your project.''

"It isn't fair. I don't like injustice.''

"Yeah, so David told me.''

"They had no right to suspect you. And that policeman, Jackson, coming after you like he's only waiting for Eleni's body to surface before he snaps the handcuffs on you.''

"He can't do anything unless he's prepared to charge me. And so far there's no evidence that Eleni's met with foul play.''

"Then where is she? A person might be able to hide out for a couple of days, but it's been over a week.''

"Out of the country, maybe. Or just holed up at some friend's,'' Zach said. "Sooner or later she'll come out. She can't possibly do without shopping for much longer.''

BACK AT THE Fortune Cookie, Abby silently got out of the car. "Goodbye, Zach,'' she said formally.

His heart sank. That sounded final. Did it mean she'd given up her campaign? "Abby,'' he said, his voice cracking, "it can't end like this.''

She turned, her face composed, her eyes half-hidden behind downswept lashes. "Why not? There doesn't seem to be much more I can do. I might as well let you continue on your own."

He couldn't. More to the point, he didn't want to. The thought of not seeing her knotted a lump of pain in his chest. "Can I phone you? I'm going to have another look at those computer disks." He leaned into his car and retrieved them from the glove box.

Abby shrugged, unlocking her own car. "Do what you want."

"You work tomorrow, don't you?"

"The evening shift." The corner of her mouth tilted slightly. "I don't want to see you come in with another injury."

"Don't worry. I'll be careful."

He stood there, staring down the street long after her car had chugged out of sight. The sun beat down on his head, worsening his headache again. He'd had nothing to drink for hours. No wonder he felt so lousy.

Telling himself it was dehydration and not Abby's leaving that made him feel a hundred years old, he headed back home.

When he arrived, the workers had gone for the day. The house lay silent around him, dust motes dancing in the sunlight that slanted through the windows. Going into the kitchen he drew a glass of water from the cooler, gulping it down. It hit his stomach like a benediction. Just for good measure, he drank another, then filled the glass a third time and set it beside the camp stove.

In the picnic cooler where he kept perishables, he found a couple of eggs left in the carton. He scrambled them, and piled them between two slices of toast, carrying the plate and more water upstairs.

He took out the computer and turned it on, eating absently while the program booted up. He pushed one of the disks into the disk drive and brought it up on the screen. Then he put in a blank disk and copied the data. He did the same for the second disk. Sticking both disks into an envelope, he scribbled the address of his office in town on it and added a couple of stamps. He'd put them in the mail first thing in the morning.

He worked half the night, staring at the screen until his eyes felt as if he'd rubbed sand into them. He slept for a couple of hours, restlessly, images of blood haunting his subconscious mind.

The phone rang at three, a drunk giving a slurred spiel about a great party. Or was it? After he hung up, he stared at it, thinking there was something odd about the voice. He didn't bother with Number Recall. Whoever it was, they would have likely used a pay phone anyway.

It rang again at five, waking him from the now-familiar nightmare. No one on the line, not even the requisite heavy breathing.

The workmen arrived at seven, with their attendant noise and commotion. Zach gave up on the idea of sleeping. Punchy, his mouth tasting like a sewer, he staggered into the bathroom, nearly scaring himself when he glanced into the mirror. He looked like hell. Maybe he'd landed there permanently.

The thought was not cheering.

ABBY FINISHED her shift at midnight. The parking lot behind the hospital was half-empty when she went out. Plenty of standard lights made it bright, but because of the congestion in midafternoon, she'd been forced to park her car at the far edge near a stand of trees.

Threading her keys between her fingers, she strode purposefully across the lot. The car sat in a pool of darkness. She stilled for an instant, holding her breath, when the bushes rustled next to it. A small black shape darted into the air above her head, emitting a high-pitched chirp. She laughed nervously. A bat, of course. On summer evenings, there were often four or five of them swooping over the lot, catching insects on the fly.

The sound of voices snapped her head around. Three teenage boys went by on the adjacent street, two walking, shoving at each other and laughing. The third rode a skateboard. The wheels clacked on the asphalt as he made a jump.

A moment later they were gone, laughter and the sound of the skateboard fading into the quiet summer night. Abby bent to insert the key into the lock.

And froze where she stood.

She stared at the car, sure she'd locked the door. The glow of the street lamp spread just far enough for her to see the door wasn't quite closed. Not open enough to activate the interior light, but definitely not locked.

She reached out her hand to try it, then pulled back. Fingerprints, not that they were ever much use.

Casting a wary eye around, she saw nothing. No one was hidden between the sparsely parked cars. She leaned down and checked the inside of the car. The stereo, a cheap model, sat in its usual place in the dash. The glove box hung open, maps and papers scattered on the floor and the passenger seat.

Anger flared in her. The culprit had probably been looking for money or cigarettes. She straightened and moved around the car, checking the insurance decal on the license plate as she passed the back of it. Still intact. That was a surprise. For some reason there had been a rash of decal thefts lately.

Deep shadow hid the far side of the car. She glanced at the passenger door. It appeared closed. She turned to head back to the hospital to call the police.

A flurry of movement had her spinning around, but it was too late. A hard object landed on the back of her head and she fell heavily onto the asphalt.

She lay there, stunned, unable to find the strength to gather her knees under her and push herself up. Wincing at the pain in her head, she cracked one eye open. A pair of dingy white running shoes stood next to her face. She saw only a blur as a hand, encased in a pale surgical glove, grabbed her keys from the ground where they'd fallen. He also snatched up her purse.

"Hey," she tried to yell, but all that came out was a feeble croak.

The thud of running feet told her he was gone.

She struggled to her knees, letting her head hang down until the world stopped spinning. Wasn't there anyone around? She tried to turn, groping for the car bumper. Her knees burned as if they'd been seared. She glanced down at her stockings, hanging in shreds down her shins. New stockings, too, damn it.

"What happened?" a gruff voice shouted, slicing through the pain in her head. More running feet. A pair of thick-soled oxfords stopped next to her, hands reaching out to her. Heavy breathing near her ear, then the hot lap of a long, pink tongue across her face. "Down, Chester. Leave the lady alone. Just hang on, ma'am. I'll get someone out here from Emergency."

"No need," she croaked. "Just help me up."

"I don't know, ma'am," he said dubiously. Beside him, the dog, a brown spaniel, gave a helpful bark.

"I'm a nurse. I'm not badly hurt. Did you get a look at him?"

"Sorry, ma'am. All I saw was a dark figure running off down the street."

And the spaniel, on a leash, hadn't been able to give chase, even if it had been so inclined. "Please help me up,'' Abby said in her firmest nurse's voice. "I'm all right.''

Liar. Her head felt as if someone was performing brain surgery without an anesthetic, and she was dreadfully afraid she might throw up all over the kind man's shoes.

"Okay," the man said dubiously, holding out a hand gnarled by arthritis. She took it as gently as she could and hauled herself to her feet. For a second she swayed, stomach heaving. She swallowed hard, willing herself to breathe deeply. In, out. In, out. The nausea passed, the coffee she'd drunk ten minutes ago burning like toxic waste. Elbows and knees stinging, she managed to stand alone.

A commotion rose from the road. The three boys she'd seen earlier came around the end of the trees, the skateboarder in the lead. "This your purse, lady?"

Relief flooded her, made her dizzy. She propped herself against the car fender, shaking her head to clear it. "Yes, thank you."

"You okay, lady?" the skateboarder eyed her closely. "Want me to fetch a doc or somebody?"

"I already offered," the elderly man at her side said. "She doesn't want any help."

The other two boys came up, panting. "Sorry. We couldn't catch him. George nearly did, but the guy dropped the purse and took off across that vacant lot opposite the church. No place for a skateboard. Man, could he run."

"He's got my keys," Abby said dismally. "Could one of you phone 911 and report this?" Goose bumps broke out on her skin, clammy sweat running down her sides. Her teeth chattered like castanets. She slumped against the car.

The two kids each grabbed one of her arms to steady her. "Maybe I should go into Emergency, just to clean these scrapes," Abby said. She smiled weakly at the old man. "I guess I could use some help."

The skateboarder had already headed out for a phone.

The other two boys stayed close to her side as she walked gingerly across the lot, trailed by the old man and his dog.

"What happened to you?" Jane exclaimed the moment she stepped into the bright light of the emergency waiting room.

"Truck ran over me, I think." She turned to the people around her. "Thank you. You've been very kind."

"Stick around, guys," Jane said. "The police will want to talk to you. Has someone called them?"

"They're on the way." The skateboarder glided in through the automatic doors, against all regulations. Twisting his body, he braked, deftly flipping his board up into his hand.

Feeling as if the tendons in her knees had been severed, Abby sank down into the wheelchair Jane set behind her. She turned her head tiredly toward the double doors leading outside. A white police cruiser, roof lights flashing an iridescent red and blue, pulled into the lot. Pain lanced through her eyes and into her head, throbbing in sync with the lights. She closed her eyes and let Jane wheel her into the treatment area.

Abby's arms and legs flopped like a rag doll's when she tried to climb on the bed. Jane clicked her tongue, and heaved her up. She lay there, trembling with shock and chagrin. Nothing like this had ever happened to her.

"I told you to take a security guard with you to the car," Jane scolded gently. Forcing open each eyelid, she shone a light into Abby's eyes. "How's your head? Were you out at all?"

Abby shook her head. Bad idea. Her brain must be loose in her skull. "No, only stunned."

Jane probed the lump on the back of her head. "Skin's not broken. It's only a little bump."

"I'd hate to think what a big bump would feel like."

"Like your skull's being drilled with an auger," Jane said sympathetically.

"Well, this only feels like a gremlin with a sledgehammer."

Jane chuckled. "At least you're coherent. We'll assume there's no lasting damage. Can you get your stockings off or do I cut them? Not that they're worth saving."

"I'll do it." Grunting with the effort, Abby released the garter tabs and pushed the stockings down. She gasped in pain when the shredded nylon stuck on her lacerated skin. Jane pressed a wet cloth on first one knee and then the other to loosen the tatters. Gritting her teeth, Abby pulled the hose down to her ankles. "You do the rest," she mumbled, lying back, panting and exhausted.

"You've sure done a number on your knees, haven't you?" Jane muttered as she wiped them with a soft cloth soaked in warm water.

"Hands, too," Abby said faintly. "And I think I bashed one elbow."

She drew in a hissing breath as Jane applied an antiseptic cream to the scrapes and wrapped them in sterile gauze. "Hey, take it easy," Abby grumbled. "Is this what it's like to be a patient?"

"Don't you know by now that medical staff make the worst patients?" Jane efficiently cleaned Abby's hands. At least they hadn't suffered as badly as her knees. Her palms were raw and bruised but only one abrasion had broken the skin. Her elbow also turned out to be only bruised, a little stiff but painful only if she put pressure on it.

A harried-looking doctor Abby knew only slightly came in and poked and prodded her. After checking her pupils for the second time, he patted her on the shoulder. "I'm giving you some painkillers. You can go home, but take it easy. And don't drive. Are you on for tomorrow?"

"Yes."

"Call in sick." He gave her a faint smile. "It won't hurt for once."

"Too bad you're in relatively good shape," Jane said with typical black humor after he left. "You don't even get to spend the night in these luxurious quarters." She peered around the edge of the curtain. "There's a handsome cop standing out here. Are you up to talking to him?"

Abby shifted on the bed, wincing as she acquainted herself with a dozen more aches. "Guess I might as well get it over with."

SHE DIDN'T KNOW which was worse, the doctor's probing of her body earlier, or the policeman's probing of her mind and memory. "I didn't see him," she said wearily for the third time. "Only his running shoes, dirty and white, some cheap brand, and his hands in surgical gloves. Wouldn't you normally send a woman on this kind of case?" she added peevishly.

"We would, but there wasn't one available. Friday night, you know. We're spread pretty thin."

A picture of a group of uniformed officers as flat as roadkill in a cartoon flipped into her mind. She almost laughed aloud. Between exhaustion, shock, and the painkiller Jane had insisted she actually swallow, she felt as punchy as if she'd gone three rounds with the world heavy weight champion.

"The hands," the cop said. "Could you tell if it was a man or a woman?"

That threw her for an instant. Man or woman? Her woolly brain tried to zero in on the image. Thick hands. Heavy knuckles straining against the latex, stretching it thin and transparent. "A man's hands," she said. "And he ran like a man, too. Something about the motion. A heavyset man, I think, although I never got a good look at him."

The officer nodded. "That's what the kids thought, too."

"Oh, are they still here? I want to thank them again."

"No, I sent them home. Kids that age shouldn't be out on the street this late." He closed his notebook. "I guess that will be all, Mrs. Chance." He handed Abby his card. "Call me tomorrow evening, and I'll give you the names of the kids in case you'd like to contact them later."

"I'll do that." She tucked the card into her uniform pocket. "Thank you."

He set his cap back on his head. "I do have to tell you, in a mugging like this we rarely catch the culprit. You're lucky your purse is intact but you'd better get your locks changed. Good night, Mrs. Chance."

When he was gone, Abby struggled to sit up, swinging her feet over the side of the bed. "Not on your own, my girl," Jane said, coming around the corner with the wheelchair. "Not with that codeine in you. Is there someone you can call to drive you home?"

Zach. His name jumped into her head. No, she couldn't call him, not at two in the morning. Not ever again. She was off his case, for good. "Call me a taxi," she said, resigned, depression settling in like a month of rain.

THE TAXI DRIVER dropped her off at her house, silently handing her change from a twenty. "Want me to check first?" he asked, his English heavily accented.

The house looked normal, the streetlight illuminating the front door. Without her purse, the mugger didn't have her address and couldn't know where she lived. "No, I'll be all right," she assured him, handing him a generous tip.

He grinned, his teeth white against his brown skin. "Thank you, ma'am. Good night."

No wheelchair here, she thought as she dragged her feet up the walk. No key, she realized as she reached the front door.

Go to the back. Find the spare key.

She sat down on the step to rest for a moment. It was tempting to just lie down and sleep there, but her elderly neighbor across the street would have a heart attack if she got up in the morning and saw a body lying on Abby's porch.

Hanging onto the rail, she struggled up, forcing one foot to move, then the other, as she shuffled through the side gate and around the house. The back lay in darkness, but when she reached the door, the security light came on. Must remember to adjust the angle so that it lights a little farther out, she told herself hazily.

She groped in the corner of the roof overhang, standing on her tiptoes to reach and nearly passing out from holding her head at an awkward angle. She found the key, the metal cool between her fingers.

Corroded from lack of use, the key refused to turn at first. She wiggled it in the lock. Finally it moved, metal grating on metal. The door opened. She nearly fell through it, propping herself against the kitchen counter as she pushed it closed and turned the lock.

She flipped up the light switch next to the door.

A little whimper escaped from her mouth, while a scream echoed through her head. The key dropped from her nerveless fingers and clattered to the floor. Her knees gave out and she slid down the side of the cabinets, bare thighs scraping against the sugar that lay like fresh snow on the tiles.

The car registration, she thought, with one clear moment of insight. He did have the address.

And he had destroyed her house.

Chapter Thirteen

Tears spurted from Abby's eyes, splashing down on her bandaged knees. As if from a distance, she heard little animal sounds, and realized they came from her mouth. Clamping her lips shut, she rubbed her hands over her face, trying to stop the flood. It was as if a dam had broken.

And no wonder. First the argument with Zach, the realization she'd probably never see him again. Then the mugging at the end of an exhausting shift. And now this.

Through a blur of tears she saw the ceramic dinosaur one of the kids in pediatrics had made for her years ago—a child who had later died of leukemia—smashed on the floor.

"No! No! No!" Covering her face with her hands she drew her knees to her chest and curled up in the corner. Flour, sugar, syrup, and soya sauce littered the tiles, but somehow the broken dinosaur seemed the ultimate violation.

A sound penetrated the numb acceptance that mercifully settled over her. She lifted her head, heart pounding so loudly she thought she'd heard an echo. Or was the burglar still in the house?

Anger surged through her, hot and volatile. If she found him, she would kill him.

The anger faded as quickly as it had come. If the intruder

was the man from the parking lot, he outweighed her by fifty pounds and would likely kill *her*.

She scrambled across the floor, sugar grating under her bandaged knees. She had to get to the door. The street-proofing course she'd taken came back to her. She'd done exactly the wrong thing, returning to the house.

Her fingernails scraped on the painted wood as she groped for the lock. She turned it, pulled the door open, sliding it past her body. She tumbled out on the porch.

All at once she saw what the sound had been, a stray dog snuffling around the compost bin at the end of the garden.

Grasping the rail, she heaved herself to her feet, swaying drunkenly. The security light winked on, illuminating the backyard. The dog raised its head, gave a quick woof and trotted off, tail waving jauntily.

She had to call the police. The neighborhood slept, all the windows dark. She'd have to use her own phone. Where had she left it? The living room, most likely. Which meant she had to reenter the ravaged house.

She shuffled back into the house. Leaving the door open in case she needed a quick getaway, she crossed the kitchen, arming herself with the conviction that the burglar must be gone. If the intruder had hung around until she came home, waiting to do her in, he'd had his chance while she lay whimpering on the kitchen floor. She was still alive; therefore he couldn't be here.

The cordless phone lay on the carpet, dead as the roses spilled from the vase lying shattered on the hearth. She picked it up, along with its base. The cord dangled, fortunately undamaged. She plugged it back into the wall jack and lifted the phone. A dial tone droned reassuringly in her ear.

Quickly punching out 911, she waited, holding her breath

and listening for any noise, while it rang. "What service do you require?" a nasal voice said.

"The police, please." She gave her name and address and received the dispassionate promise that the police would be there shortly.

The living room showed the same wreckage as the kitchen. Bright yellow mustard had been squirted on the walls. Stuffing protruded from torn sofa cushions. Her plants lay in disarray, soil ground into the carpet. She glanced toward the cabinet which normally housed her TV and VCR. The shelves gaped vacantly.

She began to laugh, the sound more hysterical than humorous, but she couldn't stop it. Her electronics wouldn't be of much benefit to the thief. The TV was fifteen years old and the VCR ten, offering only the most basic channels. No market for that kind of thing now, she was sure.

Oddly, her stereo and CD collection still sat in the bottom of the cabinet. She could only conclude that the burglar either didn't like music or his tastes were different from hers.

Depression settled over her like a soggy blanket. Mindful that the police would probably scold her for being in the burglarized house, she stumbled across the room to the front door. Pulling it open, she sat down on the step, thinking she should have followed her first impulse and just slept there. She wouldn't have found out about the break-in until morning.

It was nearly light, she realized, seeing the man who delivered the morning papers driving slowly down the street, his son running out of the car and up the walks to the houses. The boy skidded to a stop when he saw her. "What are you doing outside, Mrs. Chance?" he asked. "Or did you just get home?"

"Somebody broke into my house," she said, her voice trembling.

The kid's eyes grew round. "Did he attack you? Have you called the police? I can get my dad—"

Abby touched the bandages on her knees. "No, this happened earlier. The police are on the way."

"I can wait with you until they come. I'll just go tell my dad."

Abby's eyes stung as fresh tears threatened. For the second time that night, a kid dressed in an oversized T-shirt and baggy jeans had offered to help her. "No, I'll be okay. You just go ahead with your route."

He shuffled his feet. "Well, if you're sure—"

She forced a smile. "Yes, go on." Headlights strafed them as a police car turned at the corner and came slowly down the street. "See, here they are."

The kid nodded and ran back to his father's car. The officer, getting out of his cruiser, paused and had a word with them, then came up her walk. Abby saw he was the same cop who'd interviewed her at the hospital.

"I didn't think I'd see you again," Abby said, getting to her feet.

"Just doing my job, ma'am. The call came and I recognized your name. What's happened?"

"Burglary." Her voice hitched, pressure clogging her throat. She was sure she'd be screaming if she didn't feel so numb and exhausted. "Probably the mugger, using my keys."

The cop's gaze sharpened. "Why do you say that?"

"The doors weren't forced and no windows are broken, at least as far as I can see. He locked the door after he left." She shivered, hugging her arms around her waist.

The officer gently touched her back. "Shall we go inside? You look like you could use a chair and maybe something hot to drink."

He gave a low whistle as he saw the living room. "Wait till you see the kitchen. It's much worse," Abby said.

He shook his head sympathetically. "I trust you've got insurance."

"Of course, but it'll never be the same, will it?" The memory of the invasion of her home would remain like a ghost. She set her jaw. No, she wouldn't move. She liked the house and the neighborhood. Once she'd changed the locks and replaced the missing or damaged items, and repainted, she'd be okay.

"No, but you can take measures to make it harder for a burglar next time."

She laughed bitterly. "Like not get mugged and let someone take my keys."

The cop looked at her with warm brown eyes. "It's not your fault, Mrs. Chance. Victims always blame themselves, but it really isn't your fault." He picked up a jar from the floor. "Instant coffee. It's about the only thing not broken."

The microwave still worked, too. Too old or too heavy to steal, she guessed. In short order Constable McGuire had made her coffee. She was forced to drink it black since all the sugar lay on the floor, and the milk carton had been dumped into the sink. It wasn't the first time; on long night shifts she'd learned to make do with what she could get. The bitter liquid sank down to her stomach, jolting her with caffeine.

The anger she'd felt earlier rushed back. And with it, coherent thought. "I don't understand this. Why didn't he just steal my car? He'd gotten into it. But it looks like he waited for me, in order to set up this break-in."

"We don't know for sure that it was the same man," Constable McGuire cautioned.

"Who else? It's too much of a coincidence. He had my keys and he knew I'd be delayed at least an hour, having my scrapes patched up."

"You may be right." He pulled out a notebook. "Can you tell me what's missing?"

"The TV and VCR." Her fingers tightened around the mug. "I haven't looked in the other rooms."

He nodded. "Wise of you. Actually, you shouldn't have come into the house at all."

"I didn't notice anything wrong until I turned on the light. I told you he relocked the doors. And I had to use the phone to call 911."

"Okay." He scribbled in the notebook. "Full name, street address and phone number?"

She supplied them, sipping at the bitter coffee. "It's almost as bad as hospital coffee."

"You haven't tasted police-station coffee." He pulled on a pair of thin rubber gloves. "Do you want to look through the other rooms?"

Not really, she thought. She wasn't sure she could face more destruction without a good night's sleep. Despite the coffee, she was running on empty.

To her relief, the two bedrooms were untouched. "He might have been interrupted, or didn't want to take more time," McGuire suggested. "What about the bathroom?"

Abby braced herself as McGuire grasped the doorknob. Just the fact that the door was closed when she usually left it ajar warned her that she wouldn't like what she saw. He pushed the door open. Talcum powder dusted the floor, but the fixtures appeared intact.

Pushing past the burly cop, she moved farther into the room. "Don't touch anything," he warned. "The fingerprint crew is on the way."

A silent scream rose in her throat as she saw the mirror. "No." The word emerged as a strangled gasp.

"Oh, sh—" the cop said behind her. "I'm sorry. I should have checked it out first."

Stark red letters covered the mirror, written in lipstick. The tube, its contents mashed into a ragged mushroom, lay in the sink.

Keep your nose out of other peopuls bisness.

"An illiterate burglar," Abby said, sure she was about to dissolve in hysterics. The suddenly too sweet perfume of the honeysuckle talc rose around her, making her stomach churn. She swallowed the sick feeling, breathing deeply.

What next? At least she now knew this was connected with the phone call she'd had, and with Zachary Andros. There couldn't be any doubt.

The giddy feeling of standing on a precipice faded as her brain began to work again. Should she tell McGuire her suspicions, or would he just laugh at her?

She thought of Zach, considered a suspect in his wife's disappearance, even if it hadn't been formally spelled out. This message could only refer to her and Zach's admittedly amateurish investigation. Somebody was getting nervous. And Zach might well be this person's next target.

She turned to the cop. "You've heard of Eleni Mavrakis?"

He kept on writing in his notebook. "The lady who disappeared?"

"Yes. Well, I know her ex-husband. We've been asking questions about her and we've both had vaguely threatening phone calls. I think this is connected."

His pen stopped in midword. "Are your sure? Seems farfetched to me. We've discussed the case down at the station and the general consensus is that the lady took off on her own and didn't want anyone to know. There's no evidence of foul play."

"So you don't suspect Zach of doing her in."

"If we did, we would have arrested him."

She walked out of the bathroom, swallowing her rage. She went back into the kitchen and heated more water for coffee, slamming the microwave door with unwonted force. So Zach wasn't a suspect. Then why had that cop Jackson come around with his attitude? Shades of Columbo? Make a suspect nervous enough that he eventually confesses? Except that Columbo was always nice about it, the good-natured bumbling detective, not hard-eyed and hostile like Jackson.

The slamming of car doors told her the fingerprint crew had arrived. "I'll let them in," McGuire called.

For the next two hours McGuire made notes, and his crew sprinkled practically every surface with gray fingerprint dust. At least they kept their questions to a minimum. For the most part, she just sat in the kitchen, numbly drinking the dreadful coffee.

When they finally left, she locked the doors, grimly wondering what good it would do when someone had her keys. She felt as if she was sleepwalking, wading through a heavy fog that made her limbs weigh tons. She braced a chair against each outside door for good measure but at the same time she wondered if she really cared.

Going into the garage, she dug a hammer out of the toolbox Jane's husband had given her as a housewarming gift last year when she'd bought the house. She carried it back into the house and laid it next to the pillow. Fully clothed, she stretched out on the bed, her hand on the hard rubber handle of the hammer. If the burglar came back, he was in for a rude surprise.

She didn't think she'd sleep but she must have because the next thing she knew, the sound of the doorbell pealed through the house. She sat up too fast, nearly dropping the hammer on her toe as she swung her legs off the bed. It fell with a clunk on the floor, echoing through her aching head as the room spun around her.

Full daylight had come, the light searing her eyes, making red and yellow and black spots dance before them. Every muscle in her body protested painfully as she tried to stand.

The doorbell rang again. Abby squinted at the clock radio, belatedly realizing it hadn't been stolen. Seven forty-eight. Moving like an old woman, she hobbled to the front door, keeping her gaze away from the devastated rooms.

She'd removed the chair blocking the door before she had the presence of mind to look through the peephole. A blurry face above a pale blue uniform. Jane.

Unlocking the dead bolt, she pulled open the door. She flung herself into Jane's arms. "Oh, I'm so glad you came by."

Jane hugged her tightly, then leaned back to look into her face. "You do look a bit the worse for wear. But we'll fix that right up." She held up the bag she carried in one hand. "Honey crullers. Your favorite. And two large coffees."

She let Abby go and stepped past her into the hall. "I figured I'd stop by and see how you were before I went home. Oh, no, what happened here?"

Before Abby could answer, Jane grabbed Abby's shoulder. "That same creep, I bet. Used your keys. What do the police say?"

"Same as they said at the hospital, that they're not likely to catch him. Unless he's done it a lot and they catch him trying to sell the stolen goods. He got the TV and the VCR."

"Lucky him," Jane said dryly. "He'll get a lot for them, the age they were."

"You haven't seen the bathroom."

Jane thrust out her jaw pugnaciously. "Why, did he tear it apart?"

"No, he left a message."

Jane walked into the bathroom and contemplated the red scrawl on the mirror. "I told you Zachary Andros might be trouble," she said slowly. "This has to be about him."

"Just what I thought, but the police are skeptical."

"They're always skeptical. That's their job."

Jane thrust the bag of crullers at Abby. "Here, eat one of these and drink the coffee while I phone home. Then we'll start on the cleanup. The police didn't want to check out anything else, do they?"

Abby shook her head. "No, they suggested I get a cleaning service."

"That's a good idea, but let's get some of this swept up first. And I'll clean the bathroom mirror."

At the reminder, the knot in Abby's stomach tightened. "I guess I'd better call Zach."

Jane spun away from the sink which she'd been filling with soapy water. "I thought you'd finished with him."

"I have to warn him. This person may come after him next."

"You think so?" Jane's raised her brows skeptically. "Why would they? If someone wants to implicate Zach for doing away with Eleni, they need him alive and well."

"What about wrecking his car with a forklift?"

"Could have been an accident. And that was before he met you."

"And someone rammed us on the highway the other night."

"A drunk."

"Maybe. Maybe not. But I'm not taking any chances. I'm going to call him."

Jane laughed. "You just want an excuse."

Did she? Abby asked herself that as she picked up the phone.

He answered on the second ring. "Hello?"

"Zach, something's happened that I thought you might want to know about."

"Abby." His voice was cool, controlled.

Not encouraging, but what had she expected? "Yes," she rushed on. "I was mugged and my house—"

"*What?*" The single syllable exploded in her ear. "Abby, are you all right? Are you hurt? Why didn't you call me?" All semblance of indifference evaporated as his frantic questions tumbled over one another.

"I'm okay," she said, warmth driving out some of her uncertainty. She did care about him, whether it was a good idea or not. And he cared about her.

"Are you sure?" he asked.

"Yes, I'm sure. I've only got scraped knees and a bump on my head."

"Are you home?"

"Of course I'm home. Jane's here and—"

"Don't do anything. I'm coming over." He slammed down the phone.

Bemused, Abby hung up the phone. "Jane," she said. "Don't clean the mirror. I want Zach to see it."

Jane gave her a knowing look. "So he's coming over, is he? Ready to dash in as the hero the minute he hears you're in trouble."

"Is that bad?"

"No, actually, it's good. I think Zach may have possibilities, once he gets rid of Eleni for good."

"I'm so glad you think so. A moment ago you were telling me I was better off without him."

Jane sniffed delicately. "I didn't realize he cared."

They drank the coffee, discussing possibilities. "I think Eleni is behind this, to get back at Zach," Jane declared. "Or else someone's holding her hostage and somehow trying to frame Zach."

"But why?"

Jane shrugged. "I guess that's what you have to find out."

The screech of tires in the street sent them both to the window. "A shame to treat a Jaguar like that, but I guess they're sturdy enough to take it," Jane said as Zach pulled up at the curb and jumped out of the car almost before it stopped. "Quick, go and comb your hair. I'll let him in."

Abby's hands flew to her hair. She couldn't let him see her like this, hair matted at the back of her head and straggling around her face. She ran into the bathroom, coming up short as the letters on the mirror hit her. Ducking her head, she ran water into the basin and rinsed her face, rubbing away the last traces of mascara. She should take a shower, but he was already inside, judging by the voices drifting down the short hall.

And coming closer.

Eyes closed, face dripping, she groped for a towel. Nothing. All of them lay in a heap on the floor, mixed with talcum powder. Never mind, her skin would dry. She headed for the door, dragging a brush through her hair, flinching as it grazed the lump on her head.

"Here." Zach stuck a towel into her hand and took the brush gently from her. "You dry your face. I'll get your hair."

Hiding her face in the towel Jane must have found in the linen cupboard, she bent her head as he carefully untangled her hair. His fingers roved delicately over the lump on her scalp. "Is this where he hit you?"

Abby met his eyes over the edge of the towel. His face was scored with lines of suppressed rage, his eyes hard, as cold and glittering as sapphires. His hand clenched into a fist. "If I catch the son of a bitch who did this, I'll kill him."

"I'll help, for what he did to my house."

His eyes softened as he searched her face. "Abby, are you really all right?"

Inexplicable tears filled her eyes at the tenderness in his voice. "I will be, Zach." Her voice wobbled. "I will be."

His arms closed around her and she laid her head on his chest, breathing in the warm scent that was uniquely his.

He lifted her face and kissed her, his mouth soft, almost tentative, as if he'd suddenly realized she was fragile.

In other circumstances she would never have admitted it, but the comfort of his embrace felt good, just what she needed right now. She allowed herself to accept it. Time enough later to reassert her independence.

"Ahem." The sound of Jane clearing her throat drew them apart, although Zach kept his arm around Abby's shoulders. "I made more coffee and it's getting cold."

"We'll be there in a minute," Abby said. "First I have to show Zach the mirror."

He stared at the lurid letters, a scowl darkening his brow. "Yeah, I'd say it's all connected. Has to be."

"The police took prints, but of course it's a question of matching them to somebody. If this person has a record, they might get him. If not—" She shrugged. "Then I guess I don't get my geriatric TV back."

He turned back to her, brushing back a strand of her hair with one finger. "You're taking this awfully well."

"Am I?" Abby folded her arms over her chest. "You should have seen me last night. I just fell apart."

"You're allowed to, you know." His voice was low and gentle, his hand softly cupping the back of her head.

"Even now I want to be screaming and yelling but I know it won't do any good. So I figure I might as well clean up and go on."

Zach pulled her close to his chest. "That's it, Abby. That's the attitude you've had since you picked me up by the road. It helped me a lot. You don't know how much."

"Coffee, guys," Jane called from the kitchen.

Jane had swept up the flour and other debris from the floor and mopped it down. Except for the empty spaces in cupboards and fridge, it looked almost normal.

"Where's your phone, Abby?" Zach asked when the coffee was down to dregs and the crullers reduced to a few crumbs. "First thing to do is call your insurance company and then a cleaning service. The house could be presentable again by evening, tomorrow at the latest. In the meantime, you can stay with me."

Jane raised her brows at that, but Abby shot her a quelling look. "Don't say a word," she mouthed as Zach strode into the living room.

He brought back the cordless phone and handed it to her. "Thanks."

BY NOON, the insurance rep had finished his assessment, and the cleaning service Zach recommended had begun the cleanup. Jane had gone home long ago, to a much-needed sleep. Abby had had to practically push her out the door. "Don't be such a mother hen. I'll be all right."

"Okay, but don't stay in the house until you change the locks."

"That'll be done this afternoon."

"Let's go for lunch," Zach said now. "The cleaners can manage on their own for a while. And the locksmith can start whenever he comes."

Now that he mentioned it, it had been a long time since she'd eaten the crullers. Echoing her thought, her stomach growled. "Okay. But someplace simple."

After a word to the cleaning crew, they walked out to the Jaguar. Abby ran a hand over the glossy silver paint. "I see you got it back."

"Yeah, yesterday. They did a good job on the repairs."

He opened the door for her. The cushy seat enfolded her like an embrace. She wriggled a little, enjoying the feel of glove-soft leather. "This is nice. Oops, what was that?"

Lifting her hips, she felt around the crease where the back joined the seat. A thin sharp object pricked her fingers and she pulled it out. She held up a gold circle with what looked like a diamond threaded on it, winking in the sunlight. "An earring? I'm surprised, Zach. It doesn't look quite your style."

He sat, hands on the steering wheel, not moving. His face looked pale, suddenly cast in stone. "It's not," he said tonelessly. "It's Eleni's."

Chapter Fourteen

"Eleni's?" Abby said slowly. "I thought you weren't on the sort of terms that she would ride in your car."

Zach's fist tightened around the steering wheel. "Eleni has never been in this car."

"Then how did her earring get in here?" Abby carefully laid the earring on the dash. Was he lying? She cast a sidelong glance at him. No, he looked as stunned as she felt, and as bewildered.

"I don't know."

"You don't know? Who has access to this car? Not just anybody, I'll bet. It's not the sort of car you'd leave unlocked on the street."

"It was at the body shop for several weeks. Someone could have walked in and planted something in it."

"Is that what you think happened?"

"No." His jaw was set like a granite cliff.

"Then what? Damn it, Zach. Talk to me. There must be something."

"I killed her and when I was disposing of the body, her earring fell off. Or it caught in my clothes and fell on the seat."

The scenario was so absurd she would have laughed, except for the ghastly pallor of his skin and the tormented agony in his eyes. "Not possible," she said flatly.

"Why not? Everyone else is already thinking I killed her."

"You didn't transport her in this car. You couldn't have. It was in the body shop days before. You had the accident with the forklift some time before Eleni disappeared, remember?"

"I remember." The haunted look remained.

Abby reached out her hand and touched his forearm. The muscles felt as hard as alloy cables, his skin faintly moist with sweat beaded in the soft hair covering it. "Please, Zach, tell me. There's something, isn't there?"

"Nobody would believe it." He turned his head toward her and her heart contracted at the pain in his eyes. "Jackson thinks I killed her and hit myself on the head."

"The rest of the police department doesn't think that. Constable McGuire says you're not any more of a suspect than anyone else who knew Eleni."

"I suppose he's the one who answered the burglary call?"

"Yes, and he doesn't believe Eleni is dead because there's no evidence."

"That's the only reason I haven't been arrested," Zach said dismally.

Abby couldn't argue with that. It was true. She wondered what the police would do if Eleni stayed away much longer.

"Where is she, damn it?" Zach pounded his fist on the armrest at his side. "The fact is, Jackson's closer to the truth than he knows, for all his groping in the dark."

A cold lump sank through Abby's stomach. "What do you mean?" she asked through lips that felt frozen.

"What I mean is that I can't remember what happened that night. And I know she slipped me a mickey, as they say, but it was the sort of drug that doesn't render you totally incapacitated."

Abby's mouth opened and closed several times. *Zachary*

Andros is poison to women. The words her crank caller had used resounded through her brain. A logical part of her mind told her to get out of the car and take her chances with returning burglars, to run as far as possible from Zachary Andros. She gulped in a breath, steadying herself. "What about the story you told the police, about her being alive when you left?"

"I made it up. Can't you see? If I told them I couldn't remember, I'd be locked up now."

She caught her bottom lip between her teeth and bit down hard, her mind racing. He'd been found outside, apparently dazed. According to Jane, when he'd been brought into emergency that night, he'd had a bump on the head, not likely self-inflicted. The housekeeper had seen a body on the floor in the dark house, and gone for the police. Out the back door, so she hadn't seen Zach, or noted his condition.

And he'd been drugged. She'd heard of the drug; it interfered with memory, perception and judgment. Under its influence, could Zach have been coherent enough to kill Eleni, wait until Gretchen left, take the body somewhere, and then come back and fake his own injury?

"You couldn't have done it," she said.

"I could have had an accomplice. I could be lying about everything."

"Liars never admit they might be lying. No, something's odd about this whole thing."

He gave a short laugh. "You mean you've just noticed that now?"

She shot him a look that she normally used to subdue aggressive drunks in emergency. "I've seen it all along. That's why I got involved."

"And then you walked out."

"You mean, that bothered you?"

"I tried not to let it, but yes, it did bother me." This was said in a low voice she could barely hear.

"Well, I'm back in now. I can't ignore what happened last night. We have to get to the bottom of it."

"What if I did kill her?"

"You didn't. There's the time element, for one thing. Where could you have taken the body and got back that fast, with the power off and trees down everywhere? I presume the police searched all of Eleni's property."

"Of course, urged on by Lance and Gretchen standing there yelling that I was a killer."

"You mean Lance was there when the police came?"

He frowned. "Yeah, he was. Didn't I tell you that before? Gretchen must have called him."

"But what if she didn't? What if he was there all along? What if he had something to do with it?"

"Sorry, but that doesn't wash. He says he left before I came. And he had every reason to keep Eleni alive. She was his bread and butter, after all."

"Depends how much that so-called power of attorney gives him. And he could have lied about leaving. Besides, he might not have killed her. He could be holding her somewhere."

Zach made a derisive sound. "Shows how well you know Eleni."

"I *don't* know her."

"That's just the point. If you did, you'd realize she wouldn't let some little snot like Lance tell her what to do or have any control over her. Whatever latitude she's given him, she did out of some motive."

"Then how do you explain the state of her business?"

His shoulders slumped. "I can't."

"Unless Lance is stealing from her."

"Not likely. He doesn't have that much access to the really big stuff."

"What about Gretchen?"

"What about her? She's not involved in the business."

"Personally, I mean."

"She loves Eleni like a daughter. You heard her."

"Yes, but maybe she's lying. Maybe she's become disillusioned. And Dora didn't seem too happy, either. Maybe Eleni threatened to kick her out. She sort of hinted at something like that."

Zach reached forward and turned the ignition key. "This is all speculation. Even if we come up with a viable suspect, we can't prove anything. And Eleni is still missing."

"We could talk to Lance."

He steered the car into the street. "Yeah, I guess we could. But first let's eat."

THEY BOUGHT chicken burgers and drinks from a take-out window, eating them in the car. Using his cell phone, Zach called David, who wasn't too pleased to be disturbed at home on a Saturday. "I'll make it up to you," Zach said. "Do you have Lance's address?"

"Yes, but what are you planning to do with it?"

"Sending him a bomb is tempting," Zach said. "Naw, wouldn't do any good. Eleni would just hire someone else. David, give. I just want to talk to him."

"That's against my advice. You should be staying away from him. Every time you meet, you get into a fight."

"No fights, I promise," Zach said. "And it's not about the property settlement. You know I wouldn't lie to you."

"Okay, but you owe me." David rattled off the name of a town-house complex. "Do you know where it is?"

"Yeah. I should. We had some of the finishing contracts when it was built. Thanks, David."

He put down the phone, throwing Abby a triumphant grin. "Got it. Now we'll see."

They drove out to the east end of town where the luxury

town houses spread over a hillside, artfully arranged around a beautifully designed lake, which looked natural. "Oh, one of those," Abby said when they pulled up at the locked gate. "Maximum security."

"No problem. I'll buzz him."

He got out of the car and pushed the intercom button. Waited. Pushed again. Finally, he walked back to the car, hands deep in his pockets. "No answer." He glanced around. "I still want to check out his place."

Running his gaze over the real-estate signs next to the gate, he snapped his fingers. "Gotcha. Open House from one to four."

He walked back and buzzed the number. A voice crackled over the intercom. "Yes? May I help you?"

"I'd like to see the unit."

"Come on in."

He ran back to the car, driving it through the gates, which slid slowly open.

"We're not really going to look at the unit, are we?" Abby asked.

"Sure, we are," he said, the innocence in his eyes at odds with the circles under them and two day's worth of black stubble on his chin. "Lance's place is right across from it."

The Jaguar must have impressed the real-estate agent. She came out to greet them, her lacquered blond hair bouncing. "This is one of our finest units," she gushed before they were even out of the car. She handed each of them a card and a sheet of paper detailing the house.

Zach, who had hastily finger-combed his hair, looked critically at the outside of the town house, then at the sun. "I'm sorry. I'm afraid it would be a waste of time. It faces west. I hate houses that face west. Too hot in summer."

Her smile slipped a little. "The trees, which the developer carefully preserved, do shade it in the afternoon. And it's very bright—that's important in winter.''

The real-estate business must be going through a low spell, Abby thought, hearing the desperation in the sales pitch.

''Now that one,'' Zach said, pointing to the unit where Lance apparently lived. ''That might do better. It's a bit lower, closer to the trees and borders on the lake.''

''I'm afraid it's not for sale,'' the real-estate woman said. ''In fact, the owner only moved in a couple of months ago.''

''He wouldn't be there right now, would he?'' Zach put on a winning smile, one Abby figured no woman could resist.

The real-estate agent, despite being old enough to be Zach's mother, was not immune. She smiled back, perfect teeth gleaming. Her hand reached up to pat her hair. Abby expected the glossy helmet to ring like a brass flowerpot. ''No, he went out shortly after I arrived.''

''Big place for one person. Lives alone, does he?''

''Yes, I believe so. Of course I'm not here every day, but I've never seen him with anyone.''

''Not even lately?''

Her eyes narrowed, as if she suspected she was being interrogated. ''No, no one's been around.''

''Comes and goes quite a bit, does he?'' Zach shifted from one foot to the other. ''I'd like to catch up to him, maybe talk to him about selling.''

Seeing the possibility of a commission after all, the agent leaned closer to Zach. ''I could talk to him for you. He may be back later. I could handle the approach for you.''

''Do you mind if I just walk around the place?'' Zach asked.

''No, go ahead. The paths are for the use of all the residents. Will you leave me your card?''

Zach patted his T-shirt and his jeans pockets. "Oh, I'm so sorry. I don't seem to have any with me. But I have yours. I'll be in touch."

He grabbed Abby's hand and dragged her up the driveway of Lance's town house. The path along the side also served as the walkway to the lake, leading downward to a set of stairs. Safely out of the curious real-estate agent's sight, Zach crept up to the downstairs windows of Lance's place. They were fortunately not curtained, but all they saw was a large unfinished expanse of concrete basement.

"Well, she's not here," Abby said, disappointed. Until that moment, she hadn't realized how much she was counting on finding Eleni here and resolving this whole business.

"No, and I'd say if she'd been around at all, that real-estate agent would have noticed. I've a feeling she doesn't miss much."

They checked out the other lower windows, even testing a door and finding it locked. No sign of life. Going back up the stairs, they walked back to the Jaguar. Luckily the agent was involved with a potential buyer and didn't try another variation of the sales pitch on them.

"What are we going to do about the earring?" Abby asked as they drove through the gates and onto the road.

The pseudo-affability he'd shown at the open house fell away from him like a discarded coat. New worry creased his brow. "I don't know. What do you think?"

"I think we should hang on to it for now. It doesn't prove or disprove anything." She fidgeted with the seat belt, settling deeper into the leather seat. "I think someone's trying to frame you."

"Yeah, but who?"

That was the question they pondered as they drove back to Abby's house. The cleaning crew had finished washing the walls and were wiping out the inside of the kitchen cabinets. A carpet cleaner's van stood outside the front door, a long hose extending into the living room, motor humming.

"Has the locksmith come?" Abby asked.

The carpet cleaner and his assistant exchanged glances. "Haven't seen anyone."

One of the cleaning crew spoke up from the kitchen doorway. "They phoned. They had an emergency and can't come until Monday morning. They're really sorry."

"So they should be," Zach muttered at Abby's side. "Not that your burglar is likely to be back."

"I can put chairs to block the doors again, like last night, or rather, this morning," Abby said, not that she looked forward to spending the whole night in a house with someone out there who had her keys. Someone destructive. Last night the cops had kept her occupied until nearly daylight; tonight would be different, just her and the darkness.

"No, you won't," Zach said firmly. "If I'd known what happened last night, you wouldn't have been alone then."

Abby arched one brow. "I've been on my own for a long time, Zach."

"I'm not trying to infringe on your independence. I just want you to be safe."

She sighed. "I know. But I can't leave the house like this either."

"No problem. Have you got a hammer and a length of lumber?"

"Must be something in the garage. Wait a minute, where are you suggesting I sleep, if not here? Your house isn't even finished."

He winked at her. "With me? No, I guess not," he added in a comically disappointed tone. "I've got a cot in one of the other bedrooms. All it needs is some sheets and you'll be all set."

"Okay." She wasn't sure why she agreed but it seemed to mean a lot to him and she owed him an apology for the other day when she'd walked out on him, breaking her promise to help. Not to mention her uneasy feeling about her own, suddenly vulnerable house.

"We're done here, Mrs. Chance." The woman in charge of the cleaning crew came into the hall where they were standing.

Abby checked out the kitchen and the bathroom. All signs of the break-in had been erased, to her profound relief. Maybe she could stand to stay in the house again without feeling violated.

She paid the maid service, writing a check. By the time they drove away, the carpet cleaners had finished. She wrote them a check as well. "Thank you, Mrs. Chance. You can move the furniture back in tomorrow. Leave a window open a crack overnight and it'll dry faster."

"Okay. Thank you."

They drove away. Abby walked through all the rooms of the house, trying to chase away the faint disorientation that seemed to plague her. She supposed everyone whose house had been broken in to felt that way, as if their home had somehow been contaminated.

"I found the wood and the tools." Zach's voice behind her startled her. "We can secure the doors. Go and pack something for overnight."

Abby listened to the sound of him hammering a board across the inside of the back door while she threw underwear and a change of clothes into a duffel bag. She ran her hands over a skimpy silk nightgown that Jane had given her for her thirtieth birthday a couple of years ago, with the injunction that she find someone to wear it for. She hadn't, but maybe the time had come.

No, she told herself firmly. Not with Zach, no matter how tempting. Not right now, when his whole life was in a turmoil.

She shoved the nightgown to the back of the drawer and

gathered up the long T-shirt she usually slept in. Not glamorous, but it would do.

Going into the bathroom, she collected a makeup kit. Zipping up the bag, she carried it into the hall.

Zach stood there, hammer in hand. "We'll lock up, then nail this board on the outside of the front door. At least it'll slow him down if he comes back, and he'll be visible from the street if he tries to take off the board. You've got spare keys, haven't you?"

She held them up. "Not that they're much use once the locks are changed." She started out the door. "I'll load this stuff into my car."

ZACH'S YARD was deserted when they drove in, one car behind the other. Abby got out of her car. "No one working today?"

"Saturday," Zach said. "The bricklayers were supposed to come and finish up but they have a key. I didn't need to be here to let them in."

Unlocking the front door, he went straight into the living room. The fireplace was finished, the dust and debris swept up. The bricklayers had folded the tarp protecting the floor. The oak planks gleamed with a gentle patina.

"It's coming along, isn't it?" Abby said.

"Not bad," he admitted. "Should be all finished by fall."

The sound of car doors slamming sent them to the window. A marked police car and another with no lights or insignia, but the same make and model, stood next to their cars. "Oh, hell," Zach muttered. "Here's Jackson again."

A fist pounded on the front door. Zach braced himself.

Feet dragging, his stomach knotting, he went to the door and pulled it open. He forced a smile. "Well, if it isn't my favorite cop. What brings you here this time, Jackson? Have you found Eleni?"

"No, but we received a message."

Zach quirked one brow, belying the sinking feeling in his guts. "An anonymous message?" When Constable Jackson nodded, he said, "Constable, I'm surprised at you, taking an anonymous message seriously."

Jackson didn't crack a smile. If anything, his expression became more grim, matching that of his two companions. "You'd be surprised how many anonymous tips work out." He pulled a folded paper from an inside pocket. "I have a search warrant here. Mind if we come in?"

Fragments of his nightmare flashed through Zach's head and an icy chill ran over his skin. With an effort, he kept his face composed, even friendly. He gestured expansively with one hand. "Feel free. Never let it be said that I interfered with an officer doing his duty."

The three cops walked past him, their heavy shoes thumping on the newly sanded floors. Zach thought of movies of the Nazis walking through conquered cities with just that cadence. He pulled at the neck of his T-shirt, as if he felt a noose tightening. Did they still hang murderers? Maybe not, but that didn't make him feel any better.

The thought of being locked up in prison, never living in his house on which he'd worked so hard, never seeing Abby again—he ground the heels of his hands into his eyes. Maybe he should run now. Just get into the Jag and keep driving.

Maybe she'd go with him.

"What do they want?"

He jumped. He hadn't noticed her coming back into the hall. "Just routine, I'm sure," he said as steadily as he could. "They've got a search warrant."

Abby's brown eyes scanned his face. He tried to give her a reassuring smile but somehow he couldn't twist his facial muscles into the right shape.

She tucked her hand into his, squeezing hard. "You're scared, aren't you?"

He started to deny it. But seeing the concern and caring in her face, he bent his head, closing his eyes. "Yes, I'm scared."

She stepped forward and he wrapped his arms around her. She clasped hers around his waist, and laid her head against him, the gesture as simple and natural as breathing. How long they stood there, he didn't know.

But Jackson's return shattered the moment of comfort. "Mr. Andros, do you have any idea how this got into your toolbox?"

Jackson held up a small brass urn Zach recognized as having once adorned the hearth in Eleni's living room. Its heavy bottom showed a small dent. And around the dent, he could see rusty stains.

Chapter Fifteen

Zach turned slowly, his arm still around Abby's waist. "No, I can't explain how it got there. Which toolbox did you find it in? Maybe it wasn't mine."

"It was in your room, in that wooden box," Jackson said. "My men are going through the rest of the house."

"They won't find anything," Zach said, but the words sounded uncertain even to his own ears. His head buzzed, an ache lurking at his temples that threatened to become full blown pain. Someone hated him. Someone was framing him.

He swallowed bitter saliva. "Look, Jackson, I used that toolbox only yesterday. That urn wasn't in there then. And any of the workers here had access to the room. They would have seen it if it had been there. Besides, if I killed her, would I be so stupid as to keep the weapon around?"

"That and the fact that we have no body is the only thing that's keeping me from arresting you, Mr. Andros," Jackson said stolidly. "I'm planning to talk to your workers. Would you mind giving me their names?"

One of the other cops came downstairs. "There's a trunk in Mr. Andros's room that's locked. We can't get into it."

Zach, resigned to the inevitable, dug in his pocket for his keys. He threw them so hard they hit the cop in the chest and clattered to the floor. "Here. Look inside it, but be careful with my computer.'' His voice rose. ''Look at anything you want. The garden shed is outside. There's a key for it there. Look all over the house. Tear up the floor-boards if you want. How many times do I have to tell you I didn't kill Eleni?''

He broke off, breathing hard, gratified that even Jackson, the impassive cop, looked taken aback by his outburst. At his side, Abby tightened her fingers around his. The irony of her unwavering support didn't escape him. Just when his life was going to hell, he'd met a woman he could love.

A woman he wanted to love. When he had no future to offer her. And possibly no future of his own.

''Go on,'' Jackson said, scooping the keys from the floor and handing them to his fellow officer. He turned back to Zach. ''Have you remembered anything else about that eve-ning, Mr. Andros?'' he asked in a solicitous tone.

''After all that's happened, would I keep it from you?'' Zach demanded. He wasn't fooled a bit by Jackson's ap-parent softening. It was just part of the game of good cop/bad cop, with only one player. He had no doubt that Jack-son could play both parts with ease. ''I want to clear my name so I can get on with my life.''

''Have you questioned Eleni's lawyer, Lance Stuart?'' Abby asked.

''We've talked to him. He was at Ms. Mavrakis's house early that evening, but he left before Mr. Andros arrived, and came back later to find the police there and the house-keeper in hysterics. He confirms that you were dazed, Mr. Andros, but he doesn't give you an alibi.''

''He wouldn't, even if he'd been sitting on me the whole time,'' Zach muttered. ''You must know by now that we're opponents in a property settlement as the result of my di-vorce from Eleni.''

Jackson put up his hand. ''Mr. Andros, I must warn you. Don't say anything that might incriminate you. We are aware that the property settlement case was acrimonious enough that some might construe that as a motive for getting rid of your ex-wife.''

"The whole world knows it," Zach said, scowling. "That doesn't mean I killed her or even wanted to. Half of my assets are better than nothing, which is what I'd have if I were rotting in jail.''

"True, but jails are full of people declaring their innocence." The two cops clumped down the stairs. "Well?" Jackson asked.

"Nothing. By the way, Mr. Andros, the floor in that front room is pretty rotten. Looks like there was a water leak at some time. I see you've put tape around it, but maybe you should put up a sign so no one will walk there and fall through.''

"That's why the door was closed," Zach said testily. "And I've got carpenters coming on Monday to start working on the repairs.''

They nodded. "Okay. We'll go out to check the shed.''

"You won't find anything there." Zach sent the words after them like arrows.

"Let's hope so, Mr. Andros. It wouldn't be the first time a murderer hid a body in a garden shed.''

"Now just a minute," Abby cut in. "I was in that shed a couple of days ago, getting out tools. There was no one in there, nothing except watering cans, spades and clippers, and a lawn mower. No body, and Eleni had disappeared several days before that.''

Jackson gave her a measuring look. "Admirable of you to support Mr. Andros, but bodies can be moved, you know.''

"Yes, I know, and maybe you've been watching too much TV," Abby retorted, at the end of her patience.

The situation might have deteriorated further but at that

moment Jackson's two colleagues returned, shaking their heads. "There, are you satisfied now?" Abby said nastily.

Jackson made a production of handing Zach the keys. "Maybe. Maybe not." He picked up the plastic bag containing the urn. "We'll see after we test this item. If we find your ex-wife's blood on it, Mr. Andros, I'd suggest you have your lawyer present next time we speak."

Zach made a mock bow. "I'll remember that, Constable Jackson. Goodbye."

He slammed the door shut as they went out, nearly catching their heels. "And good riddance."

He leaned back on the door, his eyes meeting Abby's "Did it occur to you that you could be arrested as an accomplice?"

"For what? Defending you?" She raked her hands through her hair. "He makes me so mad. He's such a pompous ass."

"Well, we showed him." He chuckled, and the chuckle rapidly turned into a full-fledged laugh.

After one startled look at him, Abby began to laugh, too. They stood in the middle of the hall, hanging onto each other and laughing like idiots. Hardly noticing the slight tone of desperation that tinged their mirth.

But as the echoes died, the laughter turned to something else. Passion, long suppressed, flared to life. Zach's mouth suddenly covered hers with a hunger that sent sensation flashing along her nerve endings. She clung to him, barely able to stand on legs that had turned liquid, warm as melting wax.

One of his hands locked to the back of her head, holding her while his mouth avidly explored all the contours of her face. The other slid down to her hips, tightening to bring her close to him. Abby reveled in the feel of his arousal hot and hard, thrusting against her through their clothes

Her body burned with the need to be closer still, naked in his arms, without clothes between them.

Without pretense. Without the dark clouds that hovered over him, coming closer with every passing hour.

"Abby, Abby, I need you," he groaned. "Please don't say no. For once, don't think."

She laughed breathlessly. "I can't think, not when you're kissing me."

He tensed, leaning back and staring at her. "Then why did you always push me away?"

She shrugged. "Beats me. Right now, I can't think of a single reason. Caution, I guess, but it doesn't seem to make sense now. And you pushed me away a few times, too."

"I must have been insane. I promise I won't do it again."

"Promise," she whispered, gazing into his eyes, seeing the tenderness there. She tangled her fingers in the crisp hair at his nape. "Forget it. Just kiss me some more. I don't want to think."

"Neither do I. I just want to feel."

She gave a little shriek as he swung her into this arms, carrying her up the stairs as if she weighed nothing. She looped her arm around his neck, feeling the hard muscles of his shoulder flex under her hand.

He took her to his room, glancing around as he set her down next to the cot. "At least they didn't wreck anything."

He cupped her cheeks between his hands, rubbing his thumbs against the corners of her mouth. His breath drifted over her face, warm, minty, quick and shallow. "Out of practice," he muttered. "I'll have to do that more often, get back in shape."

Shape. The reality of what they were doing hit her. He worked with his hands, up and down roofs and ladders all day long. Her only exercise was walking hospital corridors and shifting patients. Would he compare her thirty-two-year-old body to some young chick who had nothing better to do than work out at a gym? Oh, why hadn't she tried harder to lose that five pounds she'd gained last winter?

He began to kiss her again, deep passionate kisses that reached into her soul, driving all doubts from her mind. She inhaled his scent, woodsy aftershave and hot summer day. She yanked at his T-shirt, trying to pull it off, but was frustrated when she'd rolled it as far as his underarms. Giving up, she ran her hands over the skin she had bared, hot, faintly moist, rough with hair. Ducking her head, she nuzzled him, molding herself to his hard body, as if she could absorb his essence into herself, make them one.

He stilled under her palms, scarcely breathing, his heartbeat thunderous. Almost shyly, she looked up. His eyes were as blue as a deep lake, gentle, yet tinged with uncertainty. "Abby, after all that's happened, are you sure?"

She knew in that moment that she loved him. Permanently. Irrevocably. He'd imbedded himself in her heart, and she finally understood why it had never worked with David. What she felt for Zach made her fondness for David seem like a pale, insubstantial ghost of love.

"I've never been more sure of anything in my life," she said. She tugged at his shirt. "Could we get rid of this?"

He smiled, eyes twinkling. "I will, if you will."

Laughing like naughty children, they stripped off their clothes, and fell onto the cot. It swayed and creaked ominously, but fortunately didn't collapse. "This bed's too small," Zach said, frowning, apologetic. "I never expected to share it."

"Doesn't matter."

Pressed together in the narrow space, they lay for a moment, breathing deeply. Zach traced one finger along Abby's hairline, across her brows, smoothing them.

'You're so beautiful,'' he whispered. ''I've dreamed of this moment for so long.''

''We've only known each other a couple of weeks,'' Abby reminded him.

''Feels like forever.'' He sighed in contentment. ''I've never felt like this with anyone, Abby. I want you to know that. Whatever happens, remember this moment.''

And she would. Even if she never saw him again, she would have this memory to warm her lonely nights.

He shifted so that he leaned over her, one arm on either side of her head. Abby tasted his breath as he came closer, sweet, intoxicating, and she opened her mouth in eager anticipation. ''Abby, do you want me?''

Deep inside her body, heat coiled in a relentless torment. *Want* was too mild a word. She craved him more than her next breath. She'd die if she didn't have him soon. She met his gaze, her eyes open and aware. ''Yes, Zach, I want you. Please come to me now.''

She wrapped her hands around his head. Her lips moved under his, her tongue entering his mouth, rubbing gently over his teeth at first, then dancing along his tongue.

Fire flashed through her body as he cupped her breasts, running his thumbs over her nipples. Turning her head, she nipped his shoulder, tasting the saltiness of his skin, savoring the firmness of the hard muscle. She writhed against him, striving for closer contact, her thighs shifting restlessly as his fingers delved between them.

Zach, I love you. I want you. The words echoed through her mind as he paused to dig in the shaving kit under the cot. Sitting up, she took the condom from him, laughing when he groaned as she made a game of rolling it on him. She stroked him with loving hands, his chest, his belly, his thighs, and finally back to the center where his erection jutted out of a nest of dense black hair.

He gritted his teeth, swearing beneath his breath as her

touch grew more intimate, more arousing. She laughed softly. "Now you know how you made me feel."

Taking mercy on him, she lay back, stretching her arms over her head. She waited, tense as a spring. He stared at her, his eyes dark and intent, as if he wanted to memorize her. At least he moved, touching her again, and heat rushed through her body.

Kneeling before her, he covered her mouth with a kiss as he slowly entered her. Abby, driven to near frenzy by the heated probing of his body against her sensitized skin, thrust her hips upward. His tender entry became a powerful surge, spinning her into a whirlpool of pleasure. Her head fell back and her legs clamped his waist. She gave an ecstatic cry as the blazing fulfillment engulfed her. A moment later, Zach stiffened against her, eyes closed in profound pleasure. "Abby," he whispered raggedly, and collapsed upon her.

She lay there, clasping him in her arms even when he made a move to get up. "I'm too heavy," he groaned, gasping for breath.

"Just right. Stay." She held onto him with the last vestiges of strength in her. Her thoughts drifted hazily, fading in and out. She wanted to savor the moment, but sleep descended like a heavy blanket.

Fighting to stay awake a moment longer, she dimly felt Zach pull away, but her arms were too limp to hold him. She let them drop, missing him already. Cool air caressed her body, drying her skin. She stretched voluptuously, embracing the sense of well-being that filled her.

He came back. She sighed, draped herself over his chest and let sleep take her.

Zach, for the first time in weeks, slept deeply and dreamlessly. No ghosts of Eleni. No fractured memories of the hours he couldn't remember.

At one point he woke for a moment to find the room

filled with a twilight glow that turned Abby's skin to gold. Wonder filled him. She was here. She had made love with him. Snuggling her closer to his body, he breathed in her flower perfume, honeysuckle again.

Somewhere in the house, a floorboard creaked. He stiffened, listening, but heard nothing further. The day had been hot, the evening cool enough that he pulled the sheet, which had fallen on the floor, up to cover them. Sighing, wanting to preserve this moment for the rest of his life, he slept.

"WHAT WAS THAT?" Abby's sleepy voice barely brought him out of a pleasant dream.

"Zach, I heard a noise." Abby's insistence jarred him fully awake. Around them, the room was dim, lit only by a swath of moonlight. He glanced at the clock radio. After midnight.

"What kind of a noise? This is an old house. It often shifts at night."

Despite his reassuring words, her worried frown remained.

"I thought I heard a car."

Zach yawned, pulling her down and burrowing his head between her breasts. "At night, sound carries. It was probably on the road."

The phone rang. They both jumped, the cot squeaking. Zach tensed. It rang a second time, its intrusive shriek destroying the quiet night. She saw the relaxed planes of his face harden into grim lines.

"Zach, what is it?"

"The damn phone. I should have shut off the ringer."

He sat up and snatched it from the table, stabbing the On button. "Yes?"

He listened for a moment, then pushed the button again. His fist clenched around the phone, his shoulder muscles bulging. For an instant, she thought he'd hurl it across the room. Instead he laid it down very gently on the floor next to the cot.

The smile he cast her looked glued on, and not very securely at that. "Just the usual heavy breather."

Alarm skittered through her, icy footprints up her spine. "Has this been happening often?"

He shrugged, settling himself next to her and pulling her into his arms. "Often enough, but I always get a pay phone if I use the number-recall feature." He rested his chin on the top of her head, his breath stirring her hair. "Go back to sleep, Abby. I turned it off now. Call Answer will get it, if he tries again."

Her stomach growled. "Excuse me," Abby muttered, embarrassed.

He jerked upright again. "I just remembered. We never ate any dinner."

"We were too busy."

Even in the dim light, she could see the gleam in his eyes. "Yeah, we were. Want to get busy again?"

"After you've fed me."

His mouth turned down in pretended disappointment. "Hang on. I've got some granola bars here somewhere. I'm afraid there's not much else to eat in the house." He got up, unselfconscious in his nudity, and turned on the table lamp. Rummaging in a grocery bag, he came up with a half dozen bars.

In companionable silence, they sat on the cot and munched. "I've never had a midnight picnic before," Abby said.

"We'll do it again sometime," Zach promised. "With real food and champagne." He tossed the wrappers back into the bag and switched off the light.

He snuggled down beside her. "So, now that you've been re-invigorated…"

Electricity sizzled through her veins as he bent his head.

Opening her mouth under his, she gave herself up to the pleasure.

"No! No! Go away!" Zach's moans catapulted Abby out of a sound sleep. Pre-dawn shadows filled the room. Enough light came through the window that she could see his tortured expression, his eyes open, glazed with horror.

His arm swung out, hitting the wall next to her head. She ducked under it, shaking his shoulder.

"Zach, you're dreaming. Wake up."

His body jerked as if he'd touched a live wire, then he collapsed, his eyes falling closed. He groped for her, clamping his arm around her waist, holding on as if she were an anchor in an angry sea.

Abby stroked her fingers across his brow, combing back the damp hair, soothing him. His breathing gradually returned to normal, his face growing calmer.

"Tell me about it," she said. "Sometimes it helps to talk about nightmares. Defuses them."

He smiled faintly. "Did you learn that in nursing school?"

"Yes, but it actually does work, you know."

He said nothing for a long time. The room slowly lightened, gray turning to rose as the sun climbed into the sky. Abby let her mind drift, enjoying the heat of his body in the morning chill. Enjoying holding him in this gentle nurturing way.

She'd almost fallen asleep again when he spoke. "It's the blood. I see her lying on the carpet, in a pool of blood. It smells like scorched metal, and feels sticky. It's all over my hands and I can't get it off."

She smoothed his frown away. "It's a dream, Zach. If the police had found blood on your hands, you'd be under arrest."

"I know, but it seems so real."

"The police went over that whole room, didn't they? And found nothing, not even traces of blood between the floorboards. I know enough from what David used to tell me that forensics can find even microscopic traces and identify them. There was nothing, so this has to be a dream."

He flopped back, covering his face with his arm. "That's what I've been trying to tell myself. But Gretchen swears she saw Eleni on the floor."

"Shadows," Abby stated. "The power was off and it spooked her. She saw something between the flashes of lightning and imagined the worst. She wouldn't deliberately get you in trouble, would she?"

"With Gretchen, who knows?" Zach said flatly. "She never liked me much, said I wasn't good enough for her darling Eleni."

"Not good enough? Is she crazy?"

Zach shifted his arm so that he could fix an eye on her. "Thanks for the vote of confidence. You might not be so understanding if you knew the rest."

"The rest?"

"Yeah. It's not only at night that I have these dreams. I've had flashes of the same images in the daytime, just out of the blue."

Abby frowned thoughtfully, sitting up and wrapping her arms around her raised knees, still encased in bandages, now rather grubby. She rolled her head. Her neck was a bit stiff from her encounter with the mugger, but it was nothing she couldn't live with. If it hadn't been for doctor's orders, she could have been at work.

And missed this. She hid a smug smile. It was the best time she'd ever had in bed. "The brain is a funny thing," she said, turning back to the pragmatic. "If you witness some traumatic event, it keeps replaying. I know. I've been there, with some of the kids."

Zach lifted his hand to touch her face. "Abby—"

She smiled a little sadly. "It's in the past now. I hardly ever dream about them any more."

"What about the accident victims in Emergency?"

"Oddly enough, you sort of get used to it. And they're mostly adults, often victims of their own stupidity. I still hate it when the kids come in, though. And once we had a house explosion in which a child died." She hugged her arms tighter. "In Emergency, you don't spend a lot of time with them, so you don't get emotionally involved."

She jumped up from the cot, quickly turning her back as she searched for her clothes. "Never mind, Zach. I can handle it, and if I can't, I'll transfer to another department. Or take a long holiday."

She pulled on her shirt, tugging it down over her hips. She clutched her underwear and jeans to her chest as she headed for the bathroom. Her muscles had stiffened up overnight—falls always felt worse the second day—but a shower would take care of it.

She ripped off the tape and unrolled the bandages from her knees, probing gently with her fingertip. Dry and healing, no sign of infection. She tossed the bandages in the wastebasket and turned on the shower.

The house had plenty of hot water, she was pleased to note. She tried to shut off her thoughts under the steaming spray but it didn't work. What was going on in Zach's head? The time element didn't make it possible for him to have killed Eleni and disposed of the body, but what if someone else had? Or faked the murder, to frame Zach?

But who? Gretchen might have hated him, but she wouldn't have killed Eleni. She'd practically brought her up while her parents were too busy for a child.

Lance? He could have. He'd been at the house, but again, he had no motive. As Zach had pointed out once, his financial security depended upon Eleni staying alive.

Dora? Not likely. Her fluttery vagueness might be an act, but Dora couldn't have cold-bloodedly planned a murder that required split-second timing.

That left only some stranger who just happened to come in off the street when there were numerous people in the house, who had killed Eleni and gotten rid of the body in such a way that no one had yet found her.

And that was preposterous.

Which meant Eleni couldn't be dead.

She finally shut off the shower and got out, drying herself on one of the thick towels hanging next to the tub. Belatedly, she remembered that her overnight bag was still downstairs somewhere. She pulled on the same clothes. She'd change later.

Zach's room was empty, the cot neatly made. Her skin warmed as she remembered their lovemaking, the feeling that they had truly connected in ways that far surpassed the physical.

No time for that now, she told herself, and started briskly down the stairs.

At the bottom, she paused, listening. Zach should be down here but she didn't hear any sounds coming from the kitchen. Where had he gone?

The living-room door stood slightly ajar. Strange. It had been wide open last night. All the doors were kept open to allow air to circulate freely to dry plaster and mortar.

Must have been a draft or something, she decided. She'd taken another three steps toward the kitchen when a sound stopped her in her tracks.

A low moaning, more like a whimper, came from the living room. Holding her breath, she listened again. Yes, soft crying and an eerie bumping sound—definitely in the living room.

She pushed against the door with one finger, stepping

into the doorway. A scream stuck in her throat, making her feel as if she couldn't breathe.

Zach sat on the floor, rocking back and forth, his head thumping rhythmically against the wall behind him. The monotonous keening contained words. "I knew it. I knew it. I killed her. I killed her."

Next to him lay a woman's body, a pool of blood spreading under her onto the beautiful Aubusson rug.

Chapter Sixteen

"Zach, you didn't." Abby grasped his shoulder and he looked up at her, his eyes glazed. "You didn't. The body is cold. It happened hours ago. It wasn't you."

"She's still dead," he said raggedly.

"But you didn't do it. Hang on, I'm going to call 911."

Within minutes of Abby's call, the place was full of police. Zach, his face as pale as chalk, sat on an overturned plaster bucket, his head in his hands. Her heart wrenched in her chest, and she wanted to hug him to her, to shield him from the horror. She contented herself with pulling up another bucket, sitting down, and holding his hand.

He squeezed her hand in return. "Are you all right?" she asked.

A shudder ran through his body and he lifted his head. "Yeah, I guess so. At least, I will be."

Constable Jackson came toward them, the customary spiral notebook in his hand. "Can you answer some questions, Mr. Andros?" His tone was unusually solicitous, raising Abby's hackles.

"Is he a suspect?" she asked curtly. "Because if he is, you'll have to wait until his lawyer gets here."

Jackson's grizzled brow rose. "You've called him, at this hour?"

"David's an early riser, even on Sundays, and I thought

he'd like to know. He didn't answer but I left a message so he should be getting back to us soon."

"I don't think there's any reason to postpone this. Just a few questions." He held his pen, poised. "You were together all night?"

"Yes," Abby said. "And around midnight I thought I heard a car."

Jackson nodded. "Who has access to this house, Mr. Andros?"

"Uh, the—" Zach's voice hitched, and a muscle tightened in his jaw. He cleared his throat. "The contractor, the drywallers, and the carpenters. They all have excellent references."

"I've no doubt," Jackson said. "In fact, I've already checked out some of the names you gave me yesterday."

Without turning his head, Zach gestured toward Eleni, her body obscenely lit by the sunlight streaming into the windows. "Is she—I mean, has she been dead long? Was she killed here?" His voice sounded strangled, as if he had to force the words up from somewhere deep inside him.

"I appears she wasn't killed here. And I would judge from the condition of the blood and the body that she died sometime before midnight last night." He set his gaze on Abby. "That car you heard might have belonged to the killer."

Abby felt the blood drain out of her face. The thought had occurred to her earlier, but to have Jackson confirm it somehow made it real. A murderer in the house while they slept upstairs. Of course, the idea must have been to frame Zach. If he'd been alone, he would have had no alibi.

"I'm his alibi," she said aloud.

"Yes, but I'm not sure how critical that is. My men have already searched the house again and found no murder weapon."

"How did she die?" This from Zach, a low whisper, hoarse with anguish.

"We'll know more once forensics is through but it appears she died from knife wounds, one to the chest, the other to the jugular vein. That one caused most of the blood on her clothes, but either of them could have killed her."

Loud voices erupted from the door. "I don't care if this is the scene of a crime. I have a right to see my client, and he has a right to legal representation."

Abby's shoulders sagged in relief. *David.* At least he would make sure the situation remained under control.

He rushed into the room, carrying a briefcase but incongruously dressed in a tank top and shorts. Abby had called him right after she'd phoned the police but had gotten his answering machine. Her first thought had been to wonder where he was but she'd recalled that he liked to go running first thing in the morning. In summer that meant right after dawn, when it was still cool. And he'd mentioned the other day that his wife and children had gone to visit relatives for a few days.

"Have you answered any questions, Zach? Hi, Abby." He shot Jackson a glare. "Jackson."

"Mr. Andros is not an immediate suspect," Jackson said stiffly. "Mrs. Chance confirms that he was here all night, and the evidence indicates that Ms. Mavrakis died elsewhere."

David's eyes popped. "You mean someone broke into the house and brought her body here?"

"So it would appear. Our conclusions are only speculative, of course." He looked at Zach. Abby thought she detected a glimmer of compassion in his eyes. "Mr. Andros, the preliminary report is back on the urn we found in your toolbox. The nature of the stains has not been determined but they are definitely not blood. And there is no sign of a head injury on the body."

Zach's drawn face flooded with relief, eyes clearing. His mouth set in a tight line, and Abby knew he was well on the way back to his decisive self. "Then I presume you'll do everything you can to find her killer."

Jackson inclined his head. "We will. In the meantime, be careful. In view of the phone calls you've been receiving and the attempts to cast suspicion on you, it's possible that you're also a target of this killer."

He walked across the room to have a word with the ambulance attendants who were loading Eleni's body onto a stretcher. Zach kept his head down, but Abby and David watched silently as they wheeled her out.

"Too bad," David muttered. "She was driving me crazy about the settlement but I'll miss her. And so will a lot of other people, her employees and the charities she raised funds for."

"Some parts of her business were in trouble," Abby said.

"Yeah, I kind of suspected that," David said. "Lately she was pushing for a large cash settlement. Well, it's all over now. Unless Lance can take up where she left off."

"Yeah, Lance," Zach said in a hard voice. He got up from the bucket. "Jackson, you might check Lance Stuart's alibi for last night. Rumor had it they were closer than lawyer and client. Maybe Lance does stand to benefit from her death."

"We'll check it out, Mr. Andros," Jackson said with his usual austerity. "This room will be off-limits for a while, at least until tomorrow. We're going to check all the evidence but we may have to come back."

"Is it all right if I stay in the house?"

"If you want to. Some people don't feel comfortable in a house after a crime has been committed."

"We can stay at my house for tonight," Abby said, putting her hand on Zach's arm.

"That might be better," Jackson said. "By tomorrow, the house will be all yours again. In the meantime, we'll seal off this room. My men are leaving now. You can go whenever you're ready. By the way, maybe you'd like to leave me a key?"

"Sure." Zach went into the kitchen, his steps a little slow and unsteady. He came back with one of his spare keys. He turned it over in his palm, his brow creased. "That's funny. This is the last one. There should have been at least two there."

"Which means absolutely anyone could have come into the house during the day when the workers were here and taken one," Abby said thoughtfully.

"We'll check it out," Jackson promised, attaching a sticky label to the key and writing a code on it.

David shook Zach's hand and gave Abby a quick hug. "I'm going now. I'd suggest both of you go somewhere and lie low for a few days. The media are going to be all over you as soon as this gets out."

THE HOUSE SEEMED strangely silent after the police and forensics crew left. Zach and Abby stood in the hall for a long moment, face-to-face, their arms around each other. Zach nuzzled Abby's hair, breathing in the scent of his own soap and shampoo that clung to her, while trying to ignore the bright yellow police tape stretched across the doorway to the living room.

He closed his eyes. Was he going to be able to live in this house, after all? Forget the traumatic events of the past few days and go back to a normal life? He didn't know. If he found it intolerable, he supposed he could always sell.

"We should call Katie," Abby said quietly.

"Yeah. I wouldn't want her to find out by reading it in the headlines of tomorrow's paper." He reluctantly un-folded his arms, letting her go with a soft kiss on her forehead. He felt wrung out, drained so dry he thought if he moved too fast he'd blow away. If it hadn't been for Abby's presence this morning, he was sure he'd now be in some ward for psychotics, screaming gibberish.

They climbed the stairs, going into his room. Abby smoothed the blanket on the cot, which had been roughly searched by the police. Zach picked up the phone and sat down on the edge of the cot, patting the spot beside him. He punched out Katie's number, slinging his other arm over Abby's shoulder when she sat down.

She answered after the fifth ring, sounding annoyed. "Hello?"

"Grandma, it's me, Zach. Sorry to bother you but something's happened."

"I trust it's something important for you to disturb me in the bath."

He closed his eyes for an instant, his fingers tightening in Abby's hair. He loosened them when he realized what he was doing. "Zachary, are you still there?" Katie said impatiently. "I suppose this is about Eleni. Has she run off with some sheik to Morocco or something?"

"Grandma, this is going to be a shock," Zach said, wishing he'd decided to drop by her place rather than use the phone.

Katie laughed shortly. "At my age, nothing can be too much of a shock. I've seen or heard it all. Come on, spit it out."

He swallowed, the phone slippery in his hand as he began to sweat again. "Eleni's dead," he said starkly.

For a moment the line hummed vacantly. But Katie wasn't one to sit in silence for long. "I'm sorry to hear that." An odd note had come into her voice, too nebulous to interpret. "How did it happen?"

"She was murdered and her body left in my living room."

"Oh." He heard her swallow. "Do you need bail money? Is there anything I can do?"

Zach nearly choked on a laugh. "Katie, don't always expect the worst. I haven't been arrested. I had an alibi."

"Abby, I suppose." Katie sounded composed again, her old self. "It's about time you got serious. Bring her over for dinner next week."

"If I'm not in jail."

"You won't be," Katie said sturdily. "Do the police have any suspects or are they doing their usual bumbling in the dark?"

"I don't know," Zach said wearily. He wound a lock of Abby's hair around his fingers, finding the motion soothing. "I don't know what to think any more."

"Find out who benefits from her death. Greed is a prime motive. Kill Eleni, frame you, and they're home free. Get David to check her will."

"I will, Grandma. I'm sure he's thought of that, too."

"Just be careful then. And take good care of Abby."

He set the phone on the table. "Let's get out of here."

He unlocked the storage trunk in the corner and took out his laptop computer. Pulling the trunk away from the wall, he pried up a loose floorboard, and retrieved Eleni's computer disks from their hiding place.

Frowning suddenly, he tapped them against his palm. "These disks—remember I told you that something didn't look right about the files and the dates."

"Didn't you compare the data?"

"Yeah, I did. Some of the files seemed to be duplicates of others but what if they aren't? You can do some weird things with computer data these days." He put the disks into the backpack, adding a change of clothes and his shaving kit. "You met Aaron, one of the kids I have working here. I think I'll have him take a look. He's a whiz at computers, believe it or not."

Abby looked skeptical. "Won't he be in bed at this hour?"

"Then I'll wake him." Picking up the cell phone, he dialed the number. "Aaron, can you look at something for me? I'll be there in five minutes." He clicked off the phone. "Hadn't gone to bed yet. You know these computer nerds, play all night and sleep all day. Let's go. Your bag is still downstairs, isn't it?"

"Should be, if the cops didn't confiscate it as evidence."

In the front hall, he checked that the door was locked. "Why don't we just leave your stuff here for now. The kid only lives at the end of the road."

AN HOUR LATER, sitting on an unmade bed in a stuffy basement room as dark as a cave, Zach exchanged a triumphant high five with Aaron. "You see," the kid explained, "the files are different, and then there's the ones you couldn't access."

"It's all there, isn't it?" Zach said.

"What's all there?" Abby asked, confused by the jargon that had been shooting back and forth.

"Everything. Part of it is even a diary. Eleni was burning out, looks like, and had turned over more and more of her business to Lance. It looks like he was siphoning off as much as he could into accounts he'd set up, that were ostensibly part of the group of corporations."

He grinned broadly. "And the best thing of all, several of the diary entries are dated the day after Eleni supposedly disappeared. So she was alive then."

He stood up, clapping Aaron on the shoulder as he took the disks from him. "Thanks, Aaron. You'll keep all of this stuff to yourself, won't you?"

Aaron cast him a scornful look. "Me, talk to the cops? Not a chance. Anyway, I'm going to crash for the day. Close the door when you go out."

Outside, Zach locked his computer in the trunk of the car. "I think it's time we had a little talk with Lance."

Abby frowned. "Shouldn't you turn the disks over to the police?"

"Plenty of time for that," Zach said grimly, starting the car. "I've mailed extra copies to my office as insurance. want to know what he has to say first."

"If he killed Eleni—"

"We don't know that. But okay, we'll call the police and get them to meet us at Lance's place. Let's pick up your stuff."

He pulled up in front of the house, and handed Abby the keys. "Can you manage your bag? I want to check out something at the back. It'll only take a minute."

Abby unlocked the door and entered the house. Dust motes shimmered in the sunlight streaming into the front hall. The empty front hall.

"I thought I left my bag here," she muttered.

She glanced around. Yellow tape still draped the closed living room door. No sign that the police had been back. She shrugged. Maybe Zach had brought it upstairs after the police left.

She ran upstairs, into Zach's bedroom. Her bag lay on the floor, the contents scattered around the room. She froze, a chill enveloping her.

"Well, what a cozy little love nest you've got here. Too bad it's not going to last."

Abby spun around. "What are you doing here?"

"Waiting for you." Lance Stuart gestured with the snub nosed pistol in his hand, jingling the key dangling from one finger. "Nice of Zach to leave so many keys around. Where is he?"

A calm fatalism seized Abby. "Calling the police." She looked at her watch. "They should be here at any moment."

"Then I'd better make this quick. Where are those disks?"

"What disks?" She bluffed.

"The computer disks. I was sure Zach gave them to you to keep but I didn't find them when I tossed your place. So I assume you still have them."

"I don't," Abby said. "They're where you won't find them." She stealthily slid her feet to the right. He had moved farther into the room, until he could glance out the window, although he still remained between her and the door. If he took his eyes off her—

"Come over here," he ordered. "Call Zach."

She lifted her chin. "I don't have the disks. Neither does Zach. We dropped them into the mail this morning."

He laughed nastily. "Not a chance. I've been watching you. And you didn't call the police because the cell phone's right over there on the table."

He poked the gun into her ribs. She flinched, her breath catching in her throat. "Call Zach."

No choice, she decided. But she wasn't going to make it easy for him. She leaned out of the open window. "Zach." He was crossing the yard below her, carrying a ladder. He looked up. "Zach, call the po—"

The back of Lance's hand smacked into her face, cutting off the words in a gasp of pain. Lance poked his head out. "Do it, Zach, and I'll kill her. Bring those computer disks and we'll talk."

Abby touched her lip, feeling the blood trickling over her fingers. She could see Zach's face turn pale with fury, his fists clenching at his sides. "Did he hurt you, Abby?"

She swallowed hard, bringing moisture into her dry mouth.

"Not yet," Lance snarled. "But if you don't get up here with the disks, I'll do worse than hurt her."

"Zach, don't listen to him. Get out—" Pain jolted

through Abby as Lance grabbed her shoulder and slammed her into the wall.

"Shut up, or I'll kill you right now."

She licked her swollen lip. "Like you killed Eleni? And tried to frame Zach? How are you going to cover this up?"

"By burning the house down." Lance cast his gaze around the room. "Lots of solvent and paint downstairs. It'll be so tragic, two lovers dying in one another's arms. A fire is so final, isn't it? I rather enjoyed the last one."

"Hello, Lance," Zach said from the doorway. "Are you all right, Abby?"

She scowled at him. "Why didn't you stay downstairs?"

He held up his hand. "I brought the disks. Just out of curiosity, Lance, where was Eleni all this time?"

An evil grin spread over Lance's face. "At my place. Lucky we were out that day you came by. She was having a great time, messing with your mind." His expression hardened. "Enough chitchat. Hand over the disks."

Zach took a step forward. "They won't do you much good, Lance. I've made copies and they're on their way to the police."

"Doesn't matter," Lance said. "Toss them on the cot. And don't come any closer or I'll shoot."

Zach complied, eyeing the pistol dispassionately. "It's obvious this country needs stricter gun laws."

Lance glared at him. "Always ready with the wisecracks, aren't you Zach?" Without taking his eyes from them, he picked up the disks. "You might sing a different tune if I shoot Abby here in the kneecap."

Zach stepped in front of Abby, the movement almost casual.

Lance sneered. "How touching. But it won't do any good. Sit down on the cot." He pulled a length of cord from his pocket. "Abby, tie him up. And make it good."

Abby glared at him. "I won't. You'll have to shoot me."

"Abby—"

Lance's eyes narrowed. "That can be arranged." He stepped up to her and raised the gun.

"You rotten bastard," Zach yelled. Fueled by surging adrenaline, he leaped up, grabbing the belt that lay in the jumble of clothes on the cot. He doubled it on one motion and swung the buckle at Lance's face.

Lance recoiled. The heavy metal struck him a glancing blow on the cheek. He howled in rage, his gun hand jerking up.

"Abby, get out," Zach yelled, swinging the belt again.

Already in motion, Abby snatched up the phone and ran for the door. Lance managed to get off one shot. It buried itself harmlessly in the ceiling above the door.

Frantically, she glanced up and down the hall. She didn't know how long Zach could fight him off. If she ran down the stairs, there was no cover, should Lance follow. Better to take her chances up here.

Another shot rang out. Her body jerked in reaction. Gory images of gunshot victims ran through her head, this time with Zach as the central player. She ruthlessly cast them from her mind, battling down the nausea that rose in her stomach.

The closed door just down the hall promised temporary sanctuary. If she could hide in the front room, she might be able to gain enough time to make the call. Hearing muffled thuds from Zach's room, and afraid to speculate on whether that was good or bad, she turned the door handle and slipped inside. She closed it, her heart hammering loudly enough for someone to hear through the panels, she thought hysterically.

Leaning against the door, she punched in 911. How many times had she dialed that number in the past few days? Maybe Zach should program it into speed dial.

"I need the police," she whispered, her voice shaking only slightly.

"I'm sorry. I can't hear you."

Closing her eyes, she raised her voice to a murmur, hoping it wouldn't be heard in the hall. She moved across the room, reaching the line of masking tape marking off the rotten section of floor. "The police. I need them. There's a man with a gun." She rattled off the address. "Please come quickly."

"Are you in danger?"

"Yes." The silence outside wore ominously on. "Someone may be hurt. Send an ambulance as well."

The door crashed open. Lance, blood trickling from a shallow cut on his cheekbone, burst into the room.

"Zach," Abby cried. "What have you done to Zach?"

Lance laughed nastily. "He's not going to be bothering us for a while."

She gulped for breath. *A while?* Did that mean he hadn't killed Zach?

"Drop the phone," he snarled, gesturing with the gun.

She glared at him, clutching it closer to her chest. "You won't shoot me. You aren't that stupid. Even if we die in the fire, the bullets would be found in our bodies. And the police are on the way. You'll never get away."

"Sure I will. Once the house starts to burn, I'm gone." He patted his pocket. "I've got a plane ticket right here. I've already transferred what I could to an off-shore bank. By tonight I'll be lying on a tropical beach, laughing."

"Not if I can help it," Abby muttered.

A thin smile curled his lip. "It's too late. You should have stayed out of it. Now come over here, nice and quiet. You can't get out of this room. That balcony's too high to jump from."

"Don't tempt me, Lance. There's a big wisteria growing under it. I could make it." Edging backwards, she sidled around the weakened boards, then dashed for the French doors.

Lance launched himself across the floor. He made it two steps past the tape. A terrible shriek of breaking wood ripped through the room. His foot crashed through a rotten board. Another, next to it, tore loose. Lance flailing his arms, desperately tried to stop his momentum. The gun flew from his hands, spinning across the floor into the corner.

He slid down through the hole, hands scrabbling to hold the jagged edges of the broken wood. Abby watched in horror as his fingers clung for an instant, then slipped. As if in slow motion, he fell through, landing with a sodden thud on the quarry tiles in the entrance hall ten feet below.

A sound at the door drew her eyes up. Zach, one hand holding the side of his head, stood swaying in the doorway.

"Zach." Giving the hole in the floor a wide berth, Abby ran across the room and threw herself into Zach's arms.

"Oh, Zach, I thought he'd killed you." She held him tightly, running her hands up and down his body to reassure herself that he was all right.

"Guess my head's getting harder. It didn't hurt nearly as much as the other times."

Abby laughed in relief. "We'd better go check on him. We can't let him get away."

She cautiously moved to the corner and picked up the fallen gun, holding it gingerly by the trigger guard. "Here, maybe you should hold this."

Zach took it from her hand, his grip as awkward and wary as hers. They ran down the stairs. Lance lay on the floor, his leg twisted at an unnatural angle. He groaned as Abby ran her hands over him to assess his injuries.

"Broken leg, for sure. Possible broken arm," she pronounced. "Unless he has internal injuries, it's not life threatening."

"Too bad," Zach said dispassionately. "Or maybe not. At least he'll rot in prison for a few years."

"Let's hope so," Abby said somberly. "Here come the police," he added as sirens wailed in the distance.

NIGHT AGAIN. Moonlight silvered Abby's room, painting a path over the bed where she and Zach lay. Exhausted after spending most of the day repeating their story over and over at the police station, they held each other. They hadn't made love; that might come later. For now, they savored the feeling of being together, and safe.

The phone rang, making them both jump. Zach swore. "What do they want now?"

"Might be your grandmother," Abby said. "Better answer it."

Muttering, he snagged the receiver. "Yes?"

He listened for some time, muttering an occasional response, then said, "Thanks," and hung up. "That was the police. Apparently Lance has been singing like a canary. He must have given up when he realized that Eleni had taken out a little insurance by detailing most of the plan on the disks. And they've picked up Lance and Eleni's accomplice, some muscle-bound laborer who's worked at a couple of my construction sites. He confessed to driving the truck the other night, and to running the forklift into my car." He swore again. "He had a criminal record. Guess we'll be more careful about checking references even for casual labor."

"References aren't foolproof," Abby said. "Did Lance kill Eleni?"

Zach's eyes clouded. "Yeah, he did. Actually, he didn't mean to. He was in on the little scenario of her lying on the rug in the house, pretending I'd killed her. They were getting along fine then, planning to run away to some tropical paradise. But, apparently she discovered he'd been milking her companies dry. She went ballistic. According to Lance, she went after him with a kitchen knife. He's claiming self-defense.''

''Will he get away with that?''

''Maybe, with a smart lawyer,'' Zach said. ''But I hope not.''

''I wonder,'' Abby said thoughtfully. ''Was Eleni trying to kill you or frame you, or wasn't she quite sure what she wanted?''

''Any of those accidents could have been fatal.''

''Yes, but they weren't. If you really want to kill someone, you can hire a hit man.'' She sighed. ''Maybe it's better that we don't know.''

The phone rang again. ''Oh, hell,'' Zach said. ''Can't they leave us alone? Yeah?'' he barked into the receiver. ''Oh, hello, Dora. What's up?''

Abby could hear hysterical sounds coming from the phone. ''Don't worry, Dora,'' Zach cut in. ''I'll be sure somebody looks after it.'' He listened again. ''Yes, that's fine. I'll call David. He'll help you.'' He laughed as he hung up.

''What, has she been arrested?'' Abby said fatalistically.

''No, but they've taken Gretchen in for questioning. That was why she was upset. Now she's got no one to look after the day-to-day running of that big house. But the other thing she wanted was advice. She just got a letter from a lawyer.'' He laughed again. ''Eleni must have had some conscience or a diabolical sense of humor left. She really was planning on leaving and she signed over the house to Dora and Gretchen.''

Abby groaned. ''That ought to be fun. They can barely stand each other. Maybe that was the ultimate wickedness on Eleni's part, after all.''

''Well, they can sort it out. David's gonna love me when

I send Dora to him." He settled back down, snuggling Abby into his side. "Ah, Abby, I'm so glad it's over."

"So am I. So am I."

"I think I'll sell the house," Zach said quietly after a long silence. "So much has happened there, I don't think I'd ever be able to forget it." His arms tightened around her. "I nearly lost you."

"And I you," Abby whispered. Goose bumps popped out on her skin as she recalled the flight from Zach's room, the desperation to think of the best way of escape and yet not leave Zach to be killed. "I hated to leave you, but I figured you could beat him."

"I almost did but the gun went off, next to my head. While my ears were ringing, he slugged me with the barrel."

He shifted, tugging her closer. "Abby, will you let me live with you until I find another house?"

She smiled at the hesitation in his voice. "Depends."

"On what?"

"On whether you love me. Oh!" She clamped her mouth shut. "I didn't mean to say that."

"Why? It's easy, isn't it? I love you, Abby. I think I did from the first day when you stared Eleni down in the hospital."

Her heartbeat tripped, then went on at twice its usual speed. "Oh, really? I thought you were still hung up on her."

"No." Keeping her head pillowed on his shoulder, he rolled over onto his back, staring up at the ceiling. "No, I wasn't hung up on her. She was more like a ghost haunting me. But I'm finally free of her."

He paused and she knew he was thinking of how Eleni had died. "It shouldn't have happened like this," he muttered.

"No," Abby agreed. "No one should die violently."

"She made an error in judgment, something that she didn't do often," Zach said. "When Lance agreed to help her with the crazy scheme of hers, she should have suspected his devious character." He sighed deeply. "You never seemed to doubt me."

"Neither did Katie."

"No, but Katie's known me all her life. You'd just met me."

"There were plenty of times I couldn't figure you out." A little twinge of guilt stabbed her. "If you want to know the truth, there was one moment—"

"It was only a moment," he interrupted. "And at that point, I doubted myself. Obviously you know me better than I know myself. I'll have to watch that in future. I'll never be able to put anything over on you."

He turned his head and nuzzled her hair, then raised himself and kissed her gently. "Have you ever thought of marrying again?" he said against her mouth.

Her mouth tilted in a smile. "Not until lately. And I'd figured you'd be totally disillusioned with the institution."

"Well, I've given it some thought and I think you could change my mind."

"Could I?" she asked playfully, nipping at his lower lip.

He pulled her head down and covered her mouth in a passionate kiss. "Yeah, I think you could. Starting now."

"Oh, Zach, I do love you."

"'Bout time you said it. Marry me, Abby. Be my wife, my partner."

Abby looked into her lover's eyes before responding. And, once she'd seen all she needed to see, all the love and honesty in those eyes, she knew what her answer would be.

"Yes," she said simply.

"Don't miss this, it's a keeper!"
—**Muriel Jensen**

"Entertaining, exciting and
utterly enticing!"
—**Susan Mallery**

"Engaging, sexy…a fun-filled romp."
—**Vicki Lewis Thompson**

See what all your favorite authors
are talking about.

Coming October 1999 to a retail store near you.

HARLEQUIN®
Makes any time special ™

Silhouette®

HARLEQUIN®
Makes any time special ™

WIN A DREAM

In celebration of Harlequin®'s golden anniversary

Enter to win a *dream!* You could win:

- A luxurious trip for two to *The Renaissance Cottonwoods Resort* in Scottsdale, Arizona, or

- A bouquet of flowers once a week for a year from **FTD**, or

- A $500 shopping spree, or

- A fabulous bath & body gift basket, including **K-tel's** *Candlelight and Romance* 5-CD set.

Look for **WIN A DREAM** flash on specially marked Harlequin® titles by Penny Jordan, Dallas Schulze, Anne Stuart and Kristine Rolofson in October 1999*.

FTD

RENAISSANCE.
COTTONWOODS RESORT
SCOTTSDALE, ARIZONA

K·TEL

*No purchase necessary—for contest details send a self-addressed envelope to Harlequin Makes Any Time Special Contest, P.O. Box 9069, Buffalo, NY, 14269-9069 (include contest name on self-addressed envelope). Contest ends December 31, 1999. Open to U.S. and Canadian residents who are 18 or over. Void where prohibited.

PHMATS-GR

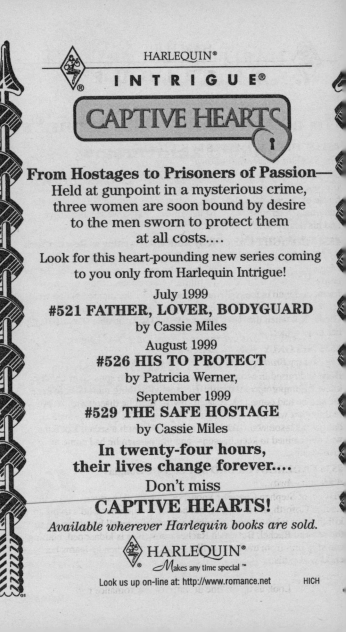

COMING NEXT MONTH

#533 STOLEN MOMENTS by B.J. Daniels
The McCord Family Countdown

Sexy cowboy Seth Gantry "kidnapped" Olivia McCord to save her
life, but his reluctant hostage refused to believe him—until their safe
house exploded. Now, in a race against time, Seth's the only man she
can trust. Determined to resist her allure, Seth vowed to keep her—
and his heart—safe at all costs....

#534 MIDNIGHT CALLER by Ruth Glick writing as Rebecca York
43 Light St.

Meg Faulkner is on a mission—one she can't remember. Inside the
confines of Glenn Bridgman's military-like estate, unsure of who is
friend and who is foe, she must fight to evoke the memories that will
set her free—and resist the temptation of the intensely desirable
Glenn. But when the memories come, will Meg be able to escape with
her heart intact?

#535 HIS ONLY SON by Kelsey Roberts
The Landry Brothers

Born and raised in Montana as the oldest of seven sons, Sam Landry
knew the importance of family. He wanted nothing more than to keep
the son he had come to love as his own—until he discovered the boy's
real mother was alive. Finding the alluring Callie Walters proved
dangerous—someone would kill to keep the truth a secret. But Sam
was determined to keep his son—and the woman he had come to
love—safe....

#536 UNDERCOVER DAD by Charlotte Douglas
A Memory Away...

FBI agent Stephen Chandler knows he and his ex-partner,
Rachel Goforth, are in danger, but he can't remember who's trying to
kill them or why—though Stephen can vividly recall his attraction to
the sensual Rachel. But when Rachel's daughter is kidnapped, nothing
can stop him from tracking a killer—especially when he learns her
child is also his....

Look us up on-line at: http://www.romance.net